CORRUPTED SOULS

CORRUPTED SOULS

A
JOE ERICKSON
MYSTERY

LYNN-STEVEN JOHANSON

LeVel
BEST BOOKS

First edition

ISBN: 978-1-68512-100-6

Cover art by Level Best Designs

This book was professionally typeset on Reedsy.
Find out more at reedsy.com

For Joyce, Aaron, Erikka, and Trevor

Praise for CORRUPTED SOULS

"Like Harry Bosch in LA and Vic Lenoski in Pittsburgh, Lynn-Steven Johanson's Joe Erickson is a detective struggling with his own inner demons as he takes on a case full of twists that requires all of his skill and intuition to solve. Johanson masterfully proves that sometimes a murder is just the tip of the iceberg." —Justin M. Kiska, author of Parker City Mysteries

"Chicago comes to life in Lynn-Steven Johanson's new page turner. Full of twists and turns, *Corrupted Souls* promises fans of police procedurals a favorite new detective to root for."—Jen Collins Moore, author of the Maggie White Mysteries

Chapter One

"Why the hell not?" asked Chicago detective Joe Erickson, angrily rising from his chair, his voice rising with him. "I was practically the lead investigator on those two murder cases in Iowa. I rescued Melissa Kincaid and terminated the offender after he killed the sheriff and a deputy. I'd say I was functioning pretty damned well. Now, I'd like to know why you think that doesn't demonstrate my 'psychological fitness' for returning to work?"

Dr. Bunsch, Joe's shrink, cleared his throat and calmly explained why he would not agree to sign off on Joe's request to return to work as an Area 3 homicide detective.

"Missing your counseling sessions and being out of touch over the period of time you were in Iowa leads me to believe additional psychiatric evaluation may be necessary before I can sign off on your release."

"But doctor, have—"

"You experienced traumatic events that brought about acute stress disorder that was directly related to your work—"

"I know that I—"

Dr. Bunsch interrupted, "You have to understand that from a clinical point of view, I have to be absolutely sure you are psychologically fit to function as a police detective. And because I haven't seen you for months, I cannot attest to that. I'd be guilty of malpractice if I simply deemed you fit for duty based on something I haven't observed."

Joe pulled a sheet of paper from his file folder and handed Dr. Bunsch a list of contacts who could attest to his performance. "I have references and contact information from Acting Buena Vista County Sheriff Jon Taylor, Deputy Will Tucker, and Agent Jeff Carey from the Iowa Department of Criminal Investigation. They worked with me on the murder case."

Dr. Bunsch looked over the references, then looked back at Joe.

"These people can vouch for my competence as a detective on the job," Joe said. "I suggest you contact them and save yourself any further psychiatric evaluations. Once you've talked to them, we should talk again." Joe ended his session with Dr. Bunsch by walking out of his office. Bunsch was not pleased.

Walking out on his shrink probably wasn't the smartest things Joe could have done. His girlfriend, Destiny Alexander, was right about Dr. Bunsch. He was a stickler for detail, and he was not going to budge. *Why the hell did I have to get such a dick for a shrink?* Joe wondered if Bunsch would even bother to make those calls, and he feared further evaluation and counseling could take months. He wanted to work, needed to work. His next step would be to get a second opinion.

Joe drove to the Area 3 headquarters and went straight to Lieutenant Vincenzo's office. His door was ajar, so Joe stuck his head inside.

"Got a minute?"

Vincenzo looked up, "Well, if it isn't the celebrity."

"More like an out-of-work detective."

"What's up?"

Joe laid out the problem he was having with Dr. Bunsch and asked if Vincenzo could refer him to one of the department's psychiatrists who could clear him to return to the force.

Vincenzo agreed to send through a referral, and two days later, Joe was in the office of Dr. Elizabeth Lemke, a fifty-something psychiatrist who had evaluated and treated a number of Chicago PD personnel. Joe didn't quite know what to make of her. She didn't reveal much about herself, but her manner was less antiseptic than Dr. Bunsch's.

He handed her another copy of the references from his Iowa contacts. He had added Destiny to the list since she worked as a criminal profiler on the case, and he knew she could give her professional opinion. Dr. Lemke agreed to make the calls. She also told him she would request a copy of his file from Dr. Bunsch's office. At the end of their session, she scheduled a second meeting with Joe in a week and told him to be prepared for a battery of tests. Joe already felt more comfortable with her than with Dr. Bunch. When he walked away from his appointment with Dr. Lemke, he felt upbeat and hopeful.

* * *

The next week during Joe's appointment with Dr. Lemke, Joe learned she had contacted the people on his list of references and obtained a copy of his file from Dr. Bunsch. She put him through tests, and he answered enough questions to last him a lifetime. It got to be stressful after a while, but if it put him back to work, some annoyance would be worth it.

The following week, Joe's session with Dr. Lemke yielded good news.

"I've decided to clear you to return to work, but there are two conditions. One, you continue taking your Lexapro prescription for depression, and two, you meet with me for counseling once a week until I determine it's no longer necessary."

"Once a week?" Joe responded.

"Once a week to begin with. And if things go well, it'll be tapered off and may eventually be discontinued. You're okay with that?"

Her implication was clear. "Yeah. I'm okay with that. Thank you. So, when can I start work?"

"This is Thursday...I'll send this through today, so you should be able to start on Monday."

She scheduled his first counseling session for the following week, then told Joe she was looking forward to seeing him. He thanked her, and as he turned to go, he saw her smile ever so slightly. As he walked out of her office, Joe was elated. *Thank god!* A huge weight had been lifted. Going back to work meant everything to him. He wasn't crazy about a counseling session each week, but if that's what it took to get him back on the force, it was a small price to pay.

Fortunately, he wasn't having any side effects from the Lexapro prescription he was taking other than some occasional drowsiness, and he dealt with that by drinking strong coffee and getting up and moving around. He was limiting himself to no more than one alcoholic drink per day, and that small amount did not seem to affect his depression. Maybe there would come a time when he would no longer need his medication, but for now, his "happy pills" were necessary for his continued well-being.

He texted Vincenzo informing him Dr. Lemke cleared him to go back to work, and he should expect him in on Monday. Then he texted his partner, Sam, letting him know that he would be back on the job Monday. After that, he decided to call Destiny and share his good news.

"Why don't you come over and we'll celebrate," she said.

"You're home?"

"My plane landed an hour ago. I'm on my way home as we speak. Give me half an hour, okay?"

"Do I have to?"

"Yes!"

Chapter Two

As usual, Joe showed up early to work on Monday, and his habit of bringing his lunch was not lost on Detective Cardona who he ran into at the refrigerator.

"Well, look who's back," she said as she eyed his sack lunch. "I see you're continuing to bring in your gourmet lunches."

"Healthy eating is all. Not really gourmet," replied Joe.

She smiled and told him she was glad he was back. That meant a lot. Cardona didn't smile much, and to get a verbal pat on the back from her was unusual to say the least.

"Thanks, Michelle."

Joe walked to his desk, glad it had been kept vacant for him, awaiting his return. He needed to speak with Vincenzo this morning to get his star back. That is, if Dr. Lemke's paperwork had gone through. He sat down and logged into his computer. Success! It looked like his reinstatement was official.

He walked to Vincenzo's office and stuck his head in the door. "Hey."

"I was expecting you. Sit down," said Vincenzo.

As Joe sat down, Vincenzo reached into his drawer and produced Joe's star, sliding it across his desk. Joe picked it up, and as he did, he slid his thumb across it, feeling its texture. It was the only thing he was missing in order to begin work.

"Will Sam be my partner again?" asked Joe.

"I don't see any reason to split up a good team," said Vincenzo. "You guys work well together, and you get results. So, yeah. You and Renaldo start working together today. Cardona's been working with him while you've been off. I'll put her with Murphy. She worked with him when she was in Vice."

"That's good. Sam and I are a good fit."

"I want you to take it easy. No more of that superman shit you pulled tracking down Burton, you know what I mean?"

"Yeah. I've burned my cape. I don't intend to do that to myself again."

"Tough lesson."

"It was."

"And if you think you need a little time, don't be afraid to ask."

"Got it."

They talked for a little longer, then Vincenzo said, "Okay, get outta here."

Joe left Vincenzo's office, and as he was walking back to his desk, he met Sam who was carrying two large cups of Starbucks coffee. He handed one to Joe.

"Welcome back."

"Thanks. Looks like we're back working together."

"Vincenzo…?"

"Yeah."

"Kinda figured."

Sam brought Joe up to speed on what he and Cardona had been working on. He didn't know which cases would be divided between him and Cardona now their partnership was being dissolved. That would be up to Vincenzo. They were on the verge of completing an investigation of a homicide that occurred in the 18th District. An arrest had been made, and now it was a matter of completing the paperwork. And there was the murder of a small-time drug dealer who was knifed in an alley in the 12th District. The victim had a long rap sheet for drug offenses. No witnesses, no evidence, and no one knows anything. Such homicides are not a high priority, sad to say, and the case would remain open but no longer investigated unless additional evidence surfaced.

Joe did not have the luxury of easing into the job this morning. He and Sam got called to an apparent drowning on the shore of Lake Michigan, only a short walk from the edge of the Loyola University campus. The body of a male victim had washed up onshore. Before Joe and Sam arrived, uniforms had blocked off the area and the Cook County Medical Examiner's van was already there. Joe and Sam showed their IDs to Officer Treadwell who was monitoring the scene. They stepped under the crime scene tape and walked to the edge of the lake where Joe saw a familiar individual dressed in hooded Tyvek coveralls, foot coverings, and Nitrile gloves. Kendra Solitsky, one of Cook County's Medical Examiners, was absorbed in examining the body of a shirtless young man clad in jeans, dripping wet from the cold Lake Michigan water.

"Good morning," said Joe.

"What's good about it?" she mumbled. Then she glanced up and saw it was Joe. "Well, you're back."

"Yeah. I'm back. What've you got?"

"Daniel Silverman, twenty-four. According to his ID, he's a graduate student at the University of Illinois at Chicago. His father is Jacob Silverman. Ring any bells?"

"The attorney?" asked Sam.

"Yup."

"Got a cause of death?" asked Joe.

"It's not a drowning. Have a look." Kendra rolled the body over onto its front to reveal a swastika cut into his back."

"Holy shit."

"Yeah, that's what I thought."

"The Silvermans are Jewish, aren't they?" asked Sam.

"I think so." Then Joe looked back at Kendra. "But this didn't kill him, did it?"

"No, a gunshot to the back of the head did." She pushed some hair aside. "See here."

"Oh, yeah. There an exit wound?"

"Doesn't appear to be. Hopefully, the round's still in there and in good enough shape for ballistics to get a read off it."

"Any idea how long he's been in the water?" asked Sam.

"Not that long. I'd say less than twenty-four hours. I can give you more details when I do the autopsy."

"You'll let me know when that's scheduled, right? I'll want to attend," Joe said as he put away his pen and notebook.

"I can do that." Looking at Sam, she said, "I assume you'll prefer to skip it."

"Yeah. Can I see his wallet? I need his address information."

Kendra handed Sam the plastic bag containing the victim's wallet. While Sam was getting that information, Joe walked over where a uniformed officer was standing with what appeared to be two college students. The two held backpacks and sat on a wooden bench placed near the shore. He showed his ID to the officer and identified himself.

The officer responded, "Montel Brown. These two spotted the body and called it in."

"I see," said Joe. And he turned his attention to the young man who looked barely old enough to shave. "And you are?"

"Lance Hanley," the young man stated, standing and offering his hand. Joe shook it, then looked at the curly blonde-haired girl. She stood and said, "I'm Linda Gustafson. I, uh, saw the body first."

They explained they were students at Loyola and were walking together to campus from their apartment complex. Linda happened to look toward the shore and spotted the body bobbing near the rocks at the shore.

"We went down there to see if it was someone in trouble but when we got there, we could tell he was dead," said Lance.

"It was gross," added Linda.

"You didn't see any boats or anything on the lake at the time? Something reasonably close or motoring away?"

"No. Nothing," said Lance.

Linda looked at Joe and shook her head.

"Would either of you happen to know someone named Daniel Silverman?"

Neither Lance nor Linda said they knew him or heard of him. When asked why, Joe simply responded, "He's a student. I was wondering if you might know him, that's all." That seemed to satisfy them.

After writing down their contact information, Joe handed each one of them his card and told them to call him if they remember anything else. He asked Officer Brown if he had their contact information, and he confirmed he did. At that point, Joe excused them both and told them not to discuss any of this with anyone.

They agreed, but Joe knew they wouldn't abide by it. They would blab to all their friends about the dead body they saw, how gross it was, and that they were interviewed by the police and blah, blah, blah. He was young once and knew what he would have done.

Joe walked back to Kendra and asked, "How long before the next of kin can come in for an ID?"

"I'm ready to wrap things up here. Give me a couple hours."

"Thanks, Kendra. I'm not looking forward to this one. Rich people. Lawyers."

"That's what they pay you the big bucks for, right?"

"Yeah." He stepped to Sam and asked, "You have the victim's address information?

"Uh-huh. He had "in case of accident" info in his wallet, too. Gold Coast address."

"You ready for the notification?"

"No, but let's get on with it."

Chapter Three

Joe and Sam drove to the Gold Coast's historic district on North Astor Street where the Jacob Silverman family lived, an area where homes sell in the multi-million-dollar range. Next to the Upper East Side of Manhattan, Chicago's Gold Coast is probably the next most affluent neighborhood in the country. They stopped in front of a stone, three-story Victorian. A black iron fence with a gate separated the home from the public sidewalk. Joe and Sam walked to the gate and pressed the intercom button. After a short wait, a male voice answered.

"Could you identify yourself, please?"

"Detectives Erickson and Renaldo, Chicago Police Department," said Joe.

"If this is about a client, please contact our office."

"This is not about a client. We need to speak with Mr. Silverman."

"About what?"

"A family member."

"Could you be more specific?"

"We need to speak with Mr. Silverman."

"Not unless you are more specific."

Joe was tired of beating around the bush. "A death."

Following a brief pause, the gate buzzed open, and Joe and Sam began approaching the house. As they reached the door, it opened revealing a tall young man in his late twenties. They held up their IDs, and before they could say anything, the young man spoke.

"You said someone died?"

"May we come in, please?" asked Sam.

At that moment, an attractive woman in her late forties appeared behind the young man and asked, "What's going on, Adam?"

"Police detectives."

"Police?"

"Go get Dad," he told her in a quiet, serious voice.

"But, he's in—"

"Please," he said, looking at her. She could tell by the look on his face and the emotion in his voice that it was serious. She disappeared into the house. Then he turned to Joe and Sam. "Follow me."

He led them from the foyer into a large room with a couch in front of a fireplace at one end and a dining table at the other.

"I'm Adam Silverman. I'm an attorney with my dad's law firm."

At that moment, a silver-haired man came down the staircase followed by the woman. Dressed in a black pinstriped suit, he looked ready for work, and his demeanor was strictly business.

"I'm Jacob Silverman. My wife tells me there's a problem."

"There is," answered Joe. "Mr. Silverman, I'm afraid I have some bad news. I regret to inform you that your son, Daniel, was found dead this morning."

Mrs. Silverman gasped, her hand going up to her mouth. Adam grabbed her in order to keep her standing and helped her to the couch where she sat, beginning to cry. Mr. Silverman, on the other hand, stood firm, his body quivering ever so slightly. He looked Joe in the eye.

"And you're sure it's him?"

"We'll need someone to make an identification. But his wallet contained his identification, and the photo on his driver's license appeared to be a match."

Looking at Sam, he asked, "What happened?"

"He was found on the shore of Lake Michigan near Loyola," replied Sam.

"I don't understand."

"From the evidence, I'm sorry to say, this is being treated as a homicide."

"He was murdered?" Adam blurted out.

"Omigod!" murmured Mrs. Silverman.

"Adam, please," his father admonished.

"What evidence suggests it was a homicide?"

"Mr. Silverman, this may be upsetting to—"

"I want to know. Tell me."

Sam looked at Joe. It was a cue for Joe to deliver the details despite the fact he was reluctant to do so. "He was found with a bullet wound to the back of the head…and a swastika cut into his back."

Silverman closed his eyes and muttered, "Good god!"

Mrs. Silverman fell forward, her elbows on her thighs, and she began sobbing. Adam put his arm around her, trying his best to console her.

Looking at Sam, Silverman asked, "Do they know when?"

"The Medical Examiner suspects within the last twenty-four hours."

"I see."

"I'm sorry. I know this comes as a terrible shock. Is there anyone we can call? Clergy? Relatives?" asked Joe.

"You can call Rabbi Kaplan…and Daniel's mother…my brother. I have the numbers here," said Silverman. He fumbled with his cellphone and gave Joe the phone numbers.

"I'm sorry—you said, 'Daniel's mother'?"

"My ex-wife. We've been divorced for many years."

"We'll need to ask you some questions, but we'll come back for that, Mr. Silverman. Please accept our condolences for your loss," said Joe. "I assume the funeral will be tomorrow?"

"Yes."

"Then, I'll contact you the day after. It's important for us to get information for our investigation as soon as possible."

Silverman nodded. He was very direct and to the point. Perhaps stifling his emotions was his way of dealing with adversity. "When and where can I make the identification, detective?"

Joe looked at his watch. "We should be able to go to the Medical Examiner's Office in an hour or so. We can take you—"

Silverman interrupted. "No. That won't be necessary. I'll go on my own."

"You're sure?"

Adam spoke up, "Dad. I can do it if—"

"No. I'll do it." Then he turned to Joe and Sam. "Now, if you'll excuse me, I was supposed to be in court this afternoon. I need to make some calls." He walked past them and climbed the stairs leaving his son to deal with his wife and the detectives.

Adam stood and stepped to Joe and Sam. "You'll have to excuse my dad. That's how he deals with bad news. He suppresses everything."

"I understand. Everyone has their own way," remarked Sam. "Is there a number we can reach you? We'll need some information about your brother the day after tomorrow."

Adam gave them his cell phone and his office numbers as well as contact numbers for his father. He told them he would be here at the house for the next few days.

"Is Daniel's mother, your mother as well?" asked Joe.

"She is."

"This number for your mother is an 847-area code. Where does she live?"

"Winnetka."

Winnetka, a northern suburb of Chicago, is about sixteen miles from the Loop. And that meant Joe and Sam needed to travel to make a face-to-face notification.

"Look, Adam. We're going to need to notify your mother in person. Do you know if she's home?"

"She's in Europe with her husband."

Joe noticed Adam didn't say "step-father" to describe his mother's husband, so he assumed they weren't close. It prompted another question.

"Are you close—you and your birth mother?"

"She and dad divorced when Daniel and I were in grade school, and she married an architect shortly thereafter. Dad got custody of Daniel and me, and he married Jennifer three years later. She's always been like a real mother to us."

"But I assume you still speak since you know she's in Europe, right?"

"We, Daniel and I, try to maintain a civil relationship. Yes."

"How do you think she would like to be notified? Normally, it's our job to notify family of a death. Would it be better coming from you?"

"No. You should do it. Make it official."

"Since the funeral will be tomorrow, I assume she'll want to make arrangements to return immediately."

"She won't." Joe gave him an incredulous look. Adam saw his reaction and responded, "Look, Detective, she gave birth to us. We acknowledge her for that, but she hasn't really been a part of our lives."

His cold, impassive reaction led Joe to believe there was some residual animosity over his parents' divorce and his mother's subsequent remarriage. He sensed there was more to it than what Adam stated.

Adam glanced toward Mrs. Silverman, then back to Joe and Sam. Joe detected Adam's discomfort, apparently torn between caring for his stepmother and dealing with the detectives.

To put him as ease, Joe said, "Your stepmother needs you. We can talk later. We'll make those phone calls now." Joe and Sam walked over to the table and sat down. Joe first called Sarah Conover, Daniel's birth mother, who was vacationing in Italy with her husband. She was upset by the news and put her husband, Leon, on the line to obtain the details about Daniel's death. Afterwards, he called to inform Mr. Silverman's brother-in-law, Solomon Silverman, in New York, who was quite distressed when he heard about his nephew's death. He wanted Joe to pass along word he and his wife would be flying into Chicago as soon as they could make arrangements. Sam made the call to Rabbi Benjamin Kaplan, who said he would be at the house shortly.

When Rabbi Kaplan got there, Adam let him in, and he began comforting Mrs. Silverman. Mr. Silverman came down the stairs, and when he greeted the rabbi, his fragile façade began crumbling away. Tears rolled down his face as he sat on the couch next to his wife. Joe and Sam felt it was an appropriate time for them to leave, so after a few consoling words, they showed themselves out.

Upon leaving the Silverman residence Joe and Sam drove to the Area 3 office to make phone calls. They needed to obtain phone numbers for Daniel Silverman's university, check his social media platforms, and wait for Kendra to confirm Jacob Silverman's identification of his son's body before making calls to set up interviews. Then Joe would attend the autopsy once it was scheduled later today.

Chapter Four

After Jacob Silverman appeared at the Medical Examiner's Office and made the identification, an autopsy was performed in accordance with Jewish beliefs. It was done immediately since according to Jewish custom, the funeral needed to take place twenty-four hours after death. Joe attended the procedure, which was conducted by Kendra, her assistant, Kenny Miller, and monitored by Dr. Benjamin Blum, a halachically knowledgeable physician. Such a physician who is knowledgeable in Jewish law or a rabbi must oversee the autopsy if one is permitted. In the case of homicide, one is required. Kendra had conducted autopsies on members of the Jewish faith in the past, and she was familiar with the special protocols associated with Jewish religious practice.

After opening the cranial vault and removing the brain, Kendra recovered a .38 caliber slug. Deformed but in good enough condition for comparison purposes, it would be sent to ballistics for forensic analysis. No water was found in the lungs, and there were no other contributing factors. The gunshot wound was determined to be the singular cause of death.

Kendra concluded mild post-mortem abrasions present on the head and face had been caused by the body bobbing against the large rocks on the lakeshore. And the swastika cut into Daniel's back was determined to have been inflicted post-mortem. All in all, prior to his death, Daniel Silverman was a healthy, twenty-four-year-old.

Joe usually left during the tissue dissection part of the autopsy, but since there wasn't any in this case, he traveled back to the Area 3 office when Kendra concluded her abbreviated work. He found that Sam had called

Daniel's university and was given the number of his department chair, Dr. Catherine Blumenthal. After delivering the bad news, he asked her about Daniel's program of study. She explained the focus of his master's degree and gave him the name and office phone of his supervising professor, Dr. Felix Huang. Sam tried calling his office, but his call rolled over to voicemail. He left a message urging Huang to return his call. If he had not heard of Daniel's death, it would not take long since his chair was now informed. Such news travels fast throughout a department.

Given the fact Daniel Silverman was Jewish and a swastika had been cut into his back, Illinois state statutes would regard his death as a potential hate crime. If convicted, those responsible for his death could receive even harsher sentences. In addition to the police investigating such crimes, the FBI often steps in since the Bureau is the primary federal agency responsible for investigating alleged violations of federal civil rights statutes. Hate crimes are the highest priority of the FBI's civil rights program.

The Chicago Police Department's Civil Rights Unit investigates hate crimes, and Joe met with Sergeant Annie Bloom from the unit to discuss the possibility that Daniel Silverman's death was a hate crime given he was Jewish, and a swastika was cut into his back. Sergeant Bloom, whom Joe had not worked with previously, was adamant about her office being part of the investigation and kept apprised of any progress on the case. Joe agreed to keep her current with periodic updates.

Joe began exploring hate groups online and found a website that tracked these groups in Illinois. The site listed nearly twenty hate groups operating out of Chicago alone: white nationalist, black nationalist, anti-Muslim, Neo-Nazi, racist skinhead, and general hate. *General hate. I guess they hate everybody.* As a detective, he had never ventured into this area during any of his previous investigations, thankfully.

While pouring himself another cup of coffee, a thought entered Joe's mind. He dealt with clever criminals before, most recently the killer, Barry Henderson, back in Iowa. What if the swastika was used as a ruse to throw off investigators? If Daniel's killer was ingenious and wanted to send the police investigation in the wrong direction, cutting a swastika in the back of a Jewish person would accomplish the deception. At least, temporarily. But then he reconsidered and thought maybe he was reading too much into it and the killer was simply a hater, someone who didn't care and just wanted to send a message. In any event, it would be a matter of Joe and Sam expending some shoe leather to discover the truth.

At the end of the day, Joe compared notes with Sam before they left work. He was not looking forward to interviewing grieving members of the Silverman family one day after the funeral, but it was a necessary part of their investigation. As he drove home, his mind was focused on the motive, and why a college student working on a business degree would have been murdered. Who or what could have motivated someone to kill him in such a manner?

As he opened the door to his apartment, he was greeted by a most wonderful aroma and a voice he'd grown to love.

"Hello there, detective," said Destiny, rising from the table.

"What's this?"

"Oh…since it's your first day back at work, I thought I would treat you to a home-cooked meal." She poured him a glass of Pinot Noir, his favorite wine, and gave him a kiss before handing it to him.

"Wow. What a nice surprise."

As she was pouring herself a glass, she asked, "So, how was your first day back?"

"Caught a murder right off the bat."

"Already?"

"Yeah. High profile one, too. You'll probably read about it in the paper tomorrow. Have you heard of the attorney, Jacob Silverman? His son."

"Oo. That'll make the news. What happened?"

"It looks like a hate crime or made to look like one. Not sure. Found him washed up on the shore of the lake with a swastika carved in his back."

"Oh, boy. The FBI is going to be interested in this one."

"I know, but I don't want them getting in our way. Or taking over the investigation."

"It doesn't work that way. They'll work with you if they do come in. You may be able to benefit from their resources."

"Mm. What's that wonderful smell."

"Me."

"Besides you. You always smell wonderful."

"If you're talking about what's in the oven—that's a surprise!"

"You're such a tease."

"You'll just have to wait."

"How long?"

She laughed. "Not that long. Why don't you sit down and tell me about the murder?"

They adjourned to the living room couch and Joe related what he discovered so far about Daniel Silverberg's homicide.

"Killed at short range?"

"Uh-huh. The lake water washed away any fouling that may have been present, but there was stippling visible around the entrance wound. Luckily, the slug remained inside the skull."

"Fifty-fifty chance of that with a .38. Probably a snub nose."

"Maybe ballistics can turn up something."

"It's possible he may have been killed by someone he knew. A bullet in the back of the head when he wasn't looking or when he was distracted. Someone he trusted could have approached him from behind and put a round in his head. Easy enough to do if he's sitting in a chair or in a car."

"The trajectory of the bullet indicated he was probably leaning over. The bullet entered the occipital area at the base of the skull and impacted the frontal bone of the upper forehead."

"Interesting. Maybe ballistics can match it to something already in the system."

"We'll see."

At that moment, the oven buzzer went off, and Destiny rose from her seat to check her culinary creation. When she opened the oven door, the wonderful aroma wafted throughout the apartment. Removing the dish from the oven, she placed it on a trivet to cool.

"Are you going to tell me what it is now? It smells terrific."

"Couscous with spinach and pine nuts. I made extra so you should have enough for your lunch tomorrow."

It was a delicious meal, and he was grateful for Destiny's thoughtfulness. Afterwards, they decided to take a walk to burn off some of the calories and enjoy their time together amidst the sounds and bustle of the city.

* * *

The next morning, Joe was up early and jogged two miles. When he returned, Destiny had showered, dressed, made coffee, and was reading the newspaper.

"The murder got some serious space in the Tribune," she said.

Filling his coffee cup, he remarked, "Oh, yeah?"

"It says police are continuing to investigate but have no suspects at this time."

"God! Give us a break. It's been one day." He took a couple of sips from his coffee and set it down. "I'm going to jump in the shower."

"What do you want for breakfast?"

"I can fix it."

"Tell me and I'll have it ready for you when you're dressed. Take advantage of me while I'm here."

That made Joe laugh. "I already did."

"Zheesh! I should let you fix it yourself."

"All right. Three eggs scrambled and two slices of wheat toast buttered with roasted red pepper hummus."

"Coming right up." As she started to rise, she knocked a spoon onto the floor. As she bent down to get it, Joe said, "Stop. Don't move." Then he moved behind her, used his finger and thumb as a gun, and pointed it at the back of her head.

"What are you doing?"

"Determining the angle of an entrance wound."

"Really? Can I get up now?"

"Yeah. I'm done."

She turned to him. "Well?"

20

"It's possible."

"I've been used for a lot of things, but this is the first time I've been a ballistics dummy."

"Sorry, it was a spur-of-the-moment thing."

"Speaking of spur-of-the-moment, I've been thinking about visiting my mom, so I called her yesterday. I'm going to leave today and should be back sometime later in the week."

"So, you're going to leave me to my own devices during my first week back on the job?"

"I'll call you. Now, get your butt in the shower!"

Chapter Five

Joe and Sam met with the Silvermans at their home the day after Daniel's funeral. They asked questions about Daniel's background, personality, pursuits, his social life, and what he may have been doing up until his death.

"I was hoping he would become an attorney and follow his brother into the firm," said Mr. Silverman, "but he was more interested in business than law. So, I went along with his vision for a career in the business world. He was extremely bright. He could've succeeded in anything he chose to do."

"He was really smart," said Adam. "A lot smarter than me, really."

"Oh, don't say that," admonished Mrs. Silverman. "You graduated at the top of your class."

"But he was more than smart, Mom. He was brilliant. He could see things…"

"What do you mean by that?" asked Joe.

"Little things that no one else would notice. So insightful. He could put two and two together with another two and two. And pretty soon, he'd have information no one else ever would have come up with. Always thinking several steps ahead. He could've made a great detective."

"We could use people like that," said Sam.

"You said his master's degree was focused in supply chain management. Do you know what that involved?" asked Joe.

"Management and leadership in logistics and distribution—for large companies," said Adam. "He explained it to me once, but you'll have to ask his professors about it. He was nearly done. He was completing a final internship when…"

"Did he have any enemies you know of?" asked Sam.

"No," answered Mr. Silverman. "Daniel was an affable kid. Always got along with people. I doubt he made any enemies."

"We always taught the children to handle things diplomatically," added Mrs. Silverman. "He was good with people."

"He was diplomatic, but he was no wimp," said Adam. "He didn't let people push him around. He could take care of himself if he needed to."

"What do you mean by that?" asked Sam.

"He means my boys were taught self-defense, detectives," said Mr. Silverman. "I made sure they were taught how to defend themselves if they ever found themselves in a situation. But they were only to use those techniques for self-defense. When you're Jewish, you can face things others never have to encounter."

"So, if a situation got tense, he would talk his way out of it first?"

"Definitely."

"Have you ever known him to use his defensive skills?"

"Not to my knowledge."

Joe looked at Adam. "No, detective. He's never been in a fight that I know of. And neither have I."

"You said he was on an internship. Do you know what he was doing? Where he was working?" asked Sam.

"No, I don't," said Mr. Silverman. "I know that sounds like I was out of touch with my son, but he's always been the independent one, and he didn't always keep me in the loop. That's the way he's always been."

"He told me it was for a big transportation firm, but that's all I know," added Adam.

"We'll find out," said Joe.

An hour of questioning generated a lot of information. Joe could see the Silvermans had grown fatigued, and he thought they had exhausted most of their questions. He glanced over at Sam.

"You have any more questions for the Silvermans?"

"No, I think we have what we need."

23

"Well, I have something for you, detectives," said Mr. Silverman. "I don't know if it's relevant or not. But in case it is, you may have some evidence to look over." He walked to the table and handed them a large file folder.

"What's this?" asked Joe.

"Anti-Semitic letters, emails, Facebook posts, and other disgusting material our office has received during the last two years. In other words, the hate we've received ranges from stupid to vicious. You can look it over and see if anything is useful."

Joe and Sam thanked them for their assistance and left. Once in the car, Sam said, "You know, for rich people, they weren't bad. At least they didn't have lawyers swarming all over the place."

"That because two of them are lawyers, Sam," laughed Joe.

"Smartass!"

Returning to the office, Joe copied his notes into his computer. Then he opened the file folder and began looking through the various hate mail sent to Silverman's office. After looking through about half of it, he stopped. It was sickening. Most people would be shocked and wonder how these people could have such hateful feelings? But Joe had seen hate acted upon over and over again. Envy, contempt, humiliation, and hate learned from others and passed on.

Afterwards, he made a call to Dr. Felix Huang, Daniel's program director at the university. This time, he picked up. Joe identified himself, and they set up an interview during his office hours tomorrow.

* * *

The next morning, Joe and Sam, drove to the campus of the University of Illinois at Chicago and met with Dr. Felix Huang. He was speaking with a female student who was standing in front of his desk when they appeared at his door. When he noticed Joe and Sam, he finished giving her instructions.

Dr. Huang rose from his seat and began walking toward the door. "You're from the police?"

"Yeah," said Joe, showing his ID. "Detective Joe Erickson."

24

"Detective Sam Renaldo," said Sam.

"Come in and take a seat." As he plopped down in his chair, Dr. Huang said, "What can I do to help you?"

"You know we're investigating the death of Daniel Silverman," said Joe.

"Yes. This is such a tragedy. It just makes me sick to think we lost such a wonderful person like Daniel."

"You were his supervising professor, correct?"

"Yes. He was finishing up his degree. The internship is a capstone project that serves as the final course necessary to fulfill the degree requirements."

"And do all of the students in this program participate in internships?"

"They do. The practical experience gained from the internship interfaces with the more theoretical knowledge gained through research and classroom interactions. In other words, it puts theory into practice in the real world."

"Where was Daniel's internship?" asked Sam.

"He was working with Fielding Enterprises. It's one of the country's largest interstate freight companies. You've probably seen their orange trucks with "Ficlding" on the side. They're all over the place."

"Yeah, I have. You know what he was doing there?"

"You'll have to ask them for specifics. But he was working in the main office for the Office of Logistics Management."

"Which is?"

"I suggest you ask them. But logistics management essentially plans, implements, and controls the forward and reverse flow and storage of goods between the point of origin and point of consumption, and does it as efficiently as possible to meet customer requirements."

"Okay. You got that Joe?" asked Sam.

"Of course," replied Joe. "Sounds like we need to get more specifics from the main office at Fielding. You have their address information, Dr. Huang?"

"I do."

Dr. Huang pulled up their contact information on his computer and sent it to the printer. A few seconds later, the printer whirred as it printed out the page.

"Who was his immediate supervisor at Fielding?" asked Sam.

"That would have been Robert Curtis."

"Robert Curtis. And he would be...?"

"The Head of the Office of Logistics Management."

"How do you acquire internship companies for your program, if you don't mind me asking?" asked Joe.

"Some of them advertise for graduate interns because they're willing to work with universities. We provide highly competent students, and they get free labor to perform basic tasks and work within the business. Sometimes it can lead to an entry-level position. Others have connections through our professors or alumni who like to give back to university departments that helped them succeed. And then, we approach some of the largest, most prestigious companies to ascertain if they're willing to take on our graduate students. We have a singular reputation for student excellence."

"And do you know what the situation might be with Fielding Enterprises?" asked Joe.

"Yes. The head of the company, Mr. Fielding, is one of our alums. He's been a very generous donor to this university."

"What can you tell us about Daniel Silverman as a student in your program."

"Oh...He was brilliant, if I may say so. One of the best, most creative thinkers I've ever encountered. Insightful, inventive, witty. He was destined to succeed in whatever endeavor he chose to pursue. That's why his death is so tragic, so painful."

"Did he have any disagreements with other students? Anyone who would wish him harm?" asked Sam.

"Oh, no. We have small classes, and our students are a cohesive group. Like an ensemble in music. There are always those who prefer their own space, of course. But we don't tolerate grad students who aren't team players in this program. I can tell you his classmates who I've spoken with are quite upset."

"Could we get a list of those who might be interested in speaking with us?"

"I can ask. They're all on internships at the moment. But I'll send them emails and forward their responses to you."

"That would be great," said Joe. "Thanks."

They spoke a little longer about the nature of the program and what his students do in the business world. Business has become more and more complex, and specializations in areas like logistics management and distribution have become the norm.

Joe and Sam got up to leave, and Dr. Huang pulled the page with Fielding Enterprises address information from the printer and handed it to Sam. They thanked him for his time and left.

"I think it's time we paid Fielding Enterprises a visit, don't you?" asked Joe.

Chapter Six

Fielding Enterprises' headquarters was located in the Loop in a tower on East Randolph Street. Joe and Sam took the elevator to the seventh floor where Fielding Enterprises occupied the entire floor. They stepped off the elevator and saw polished oak floors, a large Mac Hornecker sculpture, and original paintings hanging from the cream-colored walls. They walked to the receptionist's desk where a strikingly attractive young woman with Nordic features was seated. The desk's nameplate identified her as Astrid Nielson. She rose as they approached her desk.

"Good morning," she smiled. "How can I help you gentlemen today?"

Joe and Sam identified themselves and showed their IDs. "We'd like to speak with Robert Curtis," said Joe. "Is he in?"

Their presence didn't seem to faze her. She simply replied, "Let me check." Picking up her phone, she punched in some numbers. After a moment, she spoke into the phone, "Mr. Curtis. There are two detectives here asking to see you...Very well." She hung up the phone and looked up. "He can see you now. If you'll follow me, please."

She led them down a series of hallways to a suite. She opened the door to reveal a trim man about forty with a winning smile and a perfect tan.

"Thank you, Astrid," he said. "Come in, detectives." And he ushered Joe and Sam into his office. They showed their IDs and introduced themselves.

"I think I can guess why you're here. Why don't you have a seat?" he said, pointing to a table a few steps away from his desk.

Joe and Sam sat at the table and Curtis sat across from them. "So, why do you think we're here?" asked Sam.

"Well, we got word about our intern, Daniel Silverman. Just awful," he said, shaking his head. "I can't tell you how upsetting this whole matter is to us."

"We were told you were his supervisor, is that correct?" asked Joe.

"Yes, he was assigned to my department, that's correct. He was working on a special project headed by Rachel Granger. He was working directly for her. It was recently completed, as a matter of fact, and we're looking forward to implementing it. Daniel had a lot to do with its final development."

"How did Daniel fit into your department?" asked Sam.

"He fit like a glove. I would have hired him in a minute if I could have."

"So, there wasn't anyone who resented him or would have held a grudge about him being here?"

"Oh, hell no. The guy was a gem. I even took him to a party on the CEO's yacht to celebrate the completion of the project. Three days later, we heard… Uh! Terrible."

"What kind of project was he working on?" asked Joe.

"It's a way to link transportation assets with shipping clients in real-time. It would eliminate much of the lag time between purchases and requests for transport."

"So, it could save you a lot of time and money."

"Exactly."

"So, who was at this party?" asked Sam.

"Is this necessary?"

"It is," answered Joe.

Curtis sighed. "All right. There was Jay Fielding, the Vice-President of the company, and his wife; Riley O'Hara from Innovation Technologies; our company attorney, William DeForrest, and his wife; my assistant, Julia Vandevere; a couple of Jay's friends, I don't remember their names, and Daniel, of course."

"What kind of party was it?"

"Just a little celebratory get-together. Drinks, hors d'oeuvres, that sort of thing."

"Rachel Granger wasn't there? I thought she headed up the project."

"She had a sick kid. Otherwise, she would have been there, too."

"What time did it break up?"

"About eleven."

"And Daniel rode back with you?"

"No, he left earlier. Around ten. Mrs. Fielding was leaving, and she said she'd give him a lift back to his apartment."

A red flag went up. "Nice of her," remarked Sam.

Curtis picked up on Sam's intimation. "She's a considerate person. I wouldn't read anything more into it."

"Did you notice anything out of the ordinary that evening regarding Daniel's behavior?" asked Joe.

"No, not really. I introduced him around. He was mixing, talking with people. But I got the feeling he got bored after a while. Too many older folks, maybe he was feeling a little out of place. But I thought it'd be good for him to get to know influential people, let them know what he did for the project, you know? He wound up spending most of his time talking to Julia and Cindy."

"Cindy?"

"Cindy Fielding. Jay's wife. She and Julia are closer to his age, so I suppose they had more in common. Probably felt more comfortable talking to them."

"We'll need to speak with some of the people in attendance," said Sam.

"Is that really necessary? These people are very busy, and I can assure you—"

"This is a murder investigation, Mr. Curtis. It's our job to investigate."

"Great." It was apparent Curtis was not pleased about getting so-called influential people involved in a police investigation.

Joe looked at his notes. "It looks like we'll need contact information for Jay Fielding, his wife, and your assistant to start with. Is Rachel Granger here today."

"She's taken a few days off. Her father passed away and she flew to Mesa, Arizona, for the services yesterday."

"Then we'll need her contact information. We'll need to interview her when she gets back."

"All right. I guess I can provide you with that." He rose from his chair.

"Can I email it to you?"

"Sure." Joe stood, reached into his blazer pocket, and handed Curtis his card. "My email address is right there. I'll expect that information from you later today." He looked into Curtis' eyes to reinforce his expectation. Curtis returned his look, and Joe could see in his eyes he resented his arm-twisting. But a split second later, Curtis flashed his winning smile.

"Of course, Detective Erickson. My assistant will have it for you shortly."

"We appreciate your cooperation."

"Thank you for your time," said Sam.

Outside on the sidewalk, Joe said, "I don't like him. He's fake. Behind that smile lies a scumbag."

"What do you expect?" said Sam. "He's a suit."

"Just goes to prove not all suits are cut from good cloth."

Chapter Seven

When Joe and Sam met the next morning, they spoke about the interviews they needed to do, and both agreed they could cover more ground if they split them up and conducted them separately. But before they could finish their discussion, Joe received a call from someone identifying himself as Anthony Freiberger who said he was a friend of Daniel Silverman. He told Joe he had some information that may be pertinent to Daniel's murder but didn't wish to discuss it on the phone. He was a graduate student at the Art Institute and suggested Joe meet him there during his lunch hour.

Joe wasn't about to pass up an opportunity to go to the Art Institute, so he agreed to meet him in the Impressionist room near Georges Seurat's painting, "A Sunday Afternoon on the Island of La Grande Jatte." He was familiar with that area of the Art Institute and had been in that room many times. He let Sam know about his meeting with Freiburger, and Sam urged him to go on his own since he had a dental appointment was at 11:30. They agreed to begin their interviews that afternoon.

Joe entered the Art Institute and made his way to the Impressionist section. Glancing at his watch, he saw that he was right on time as he stepped into the room that housed Seurat's painting. Standing in front of the painting looking at his phone was a bearded man in his mid-twenties, his long, dark hair pulled into a ponytail. As Joe took a step toward him, he gave Joe a wary look.

"Detective Erickson?" he asked tentatively.

"Yes. I assume you're Anthony?"

"Call me Tony." They shook hands and sat on one of the benches facing the Seurat painting.

"You said you may have something that could be important regarding Daniel's death?" asked Joe, getting straight to the point.

"I guess I'll let you be the judge of that. But a couple of weeks ago, Danny and I met in a bar on Friday after classes to have a beer and catch up. We were sitting in a booth talking, and a couple of guys in the booth behind us were talking kinda loud, and one of them started making anti-Semitic comments. He went on for a while—I swear he must have been a neo-Nazi or something, you know. That began to piss Danny off. Well, they ran their mouths for a few more minutes, and finally, Danny couldn't take anymore, he just lost it. He got up and confronted the guys. One of them stood up and got right in Danny's face, calling him a "Hymie-bastard" and other shit like that. This guy was good-sized, a lot bigger than Danny. But Danny called him out and said, "Have at it, fat boy." And the guy swung, and Danny put him down. Hard. I mean, he was laying there gurgling on the floor in seconds."

"What happened then?" asked Joe.

"The bartender saw the whole thing and stopped the other guy from getting involved, and he called the cops. They came and interviewed each one of us and ended up arresting the guy who swung at Danny—for assault. They didn't do anything to Danny because he was just defending himself."

"You find out the name of this piece of work Daniel put down?"

"No, sorry."

"That's all right. The police will have it since they arrested him. What was the name of the bar?"

"The Lion's Share on North Milwaukee."

"Got it."

"You think he could have done it?"

Joe looked up from his notepad. "It's hard to tell. But we're going to look into it. Can you describe the guy he was with?"

"Shaved head, goatee, earring, tattoos. Kinda like the other guy."

"Skinheads."

"Maybe. I don't know anything about those kinda people."

"I would steer clear of them, if I were you. And avoid that bar in the future in case it's a hangout for their kind. You wouldn't want to run into them a second time."

"Scary guys."

"Yeah. They are."

Joe passed Tony his card and told him to call him if he remembered anything else or if he could be of assistance to him in the future. He could see Tony was still uncomfortable talking about it. To calm his nerves, Joe changed the subject and asked him what he was studying, Tony told him he was getting his MFA degree in Photography and had another year to go before he would graduate. Once he began discussing his work, his manner changed, and he relaxed. It was enough to jog his memory.

"I just remembered something. I think the guy overheard Danny giving his address to the police officer."

"Which guy?"

"The one he put down."

Great, Joe thought. *If he knew where Daniel lived, he could have stalked him.* This information would have made him vulnerable for payback at the hands of a Jew-hater. He would need to follow up, but he wasn't looking forward to questioning a skinhead, if indeed that's what he was. But the evidence Tony just provided was pointing in that direction.

Joe thanked him and they parted company. He drove to North Milwaukee and parked near the Lion's Share Bar. It was shortly after 1:00 pm, and the establishment just opened. Stepping inside was like entering an English pub. The bartender, a stout man in his fifties, greeted him with an Irish accent. "Har ya."

"Fine, thanks," Joe replied.

"What can I get for ya?"

"Information."

"Ah. On duty, are we?"

"You made me," Joe chuckled and showed him his ID. "Joe Erickson."

"Hugh O'Morrison. It's always a copper that comes in and orders a shot of information."

"Like you said, I'm on duty. Did you happen to be working two weeks ago when a fight broke out in here? It was over some anti-Semitic comments being made."

"Oh, indeed I was. Had to call the constabulary."

"Rather ugly, was it?"

"I was getting ready to boot their arses out when it got heated. Ugly talk doesn't go well in here, I'm tellin' ya. Before I could make my way 'round the bar, it was over. I never seen a fella defend himself like that. Except on the telly, o' course. Can't say that maggot didn't have it comin'."

"What about his buddy?"

"I made sure he stayed where he was."

"So, from your point of view, this was self-defense?"

"For sure. The big, ugly guy took a swing and the little guy ended it. Damnedest thing! I explained that all to police at the time. I don't understand why you—"

Joe interrupted, "The little guy who ended it was found murdered. We're investigating his death."

"Oh, Jesus, Mary, and Joseph. And he seemed like such a nice young fella."

"He was. Have you seen either of the other men since?"

"Naw, they're barred from this establishment. I told those bloody maggots if they came in here again, I'd call the police."

"You happen to remember this maggot's name?"

"As I recall, it was uh…Evan or somethin' of the sort. Didn't hear his surname. Sorry."

Joe thanked him for his time and left. Once he got back to his office, his priority was finding the identity of the man who was involved in the altercation with Daniel as well the guy sharing the booth with him.

Joe checked the address of the Lion's Share and confirmed it was in the 12th District. He made a call to 12th District headquarters and spoke to a Sergeant Owens. He provided her with the information on the assault and explained he needed a copy of the police report and the address information on the man taken into custody. She told him she would look it up and get back with him shortly.

Sam returned from the dentist looking pale and told Joe he was feeling lousy and taking the rest of the afternoon off.

"My nerve was infected, and the Novocain wouldn't deaden it. He gassed me and still…I've never experienced pain like that in my life."

"Cried like a little girl, did ya?" razzed Joe.

"Go ahead and laugh! Just wait 'til you have to have a root canal!"

"You look like crap. Go home and take it easy. You'll feel better tomorrow."

Sam left, and Joe returned to his screen. After making notes on his meeting with bartender O'Morrison, he ate a late lunch and began mapping out where they needed to take the investigation.

His phone rang. Sergeant Owens was returning his call. The person charged with assault as a result of the altercation at the Lion's Share was Devon Michael Schmidt. She told Joe she was faxing over a copy of the arrest report as they spoke. He thanked her, and when the call ended, he walked over to the fax machine to await her transmission. Shortly thereafter, the machine spit out the police report.

Back at his desk, he read the report, then ran Devon Michael Schmidt through the system. Schmidt had a rap sheet for minor offenses: trespassing, assault, and resisting arrest, all pled down to misdemeanors. His friend was William John Higgins. Joe ran him as well and found he also had an arrest record for similar misdemeanor offenses. Surprise, surprise. A couple of real jewels. The more he investigated Schmidt, the less he liked. He found his Facebook page and discovered links to extremist websites and racist posts. Further research showed he traveled to Charlottesville, Virginia, in August 2017, and marched in the Unite the Right Rally with other White Supremacists and neo-Nazis. Joe had guessed correctly. Schmidt frequented skinhead and neo-Nazi websites, but Joe couldn't tell if he was an actual member of any of these groups. Knowing his racist beliefs, one thing was for sure: he would not take a beating lightly, especially by someone Jewish.

Joe had his first suspect. He made a call and found Schmidt made bail. Tomorrow when Sam returned to work, they would pay Mr. Schmidt a visit.

Chapter Eight

Having bounced back from his root canal procedure, Sam and Joe drove to Devon Schmidt's West Monroe Street address in Greektown. When Sam rang the apartment, a woman answered. "Yes?"

"Chicago PD. We need to speak with Devon Schmidt."

"What about?"

"An altercation at the Lion's Share Bar."

After a moment, the door buzzed to let them in. Schmidt's address was apartment number 24 on the second floor, so Joe and Sam took the stairs and found the apartment door. Sam used the brass knocker on the door. Moments later, the door was opened by a woman in her thirties dressed in blue jeans and a black t-shirt with an American flag on the front. Both arms were sleeved with tattoos.

Showing their IDs, Joe and Sam introduced themselves and asked to see Devon Schmidt.

"All right. Come on in." She held the door open revealing the small apartment. "Devon can't work because of the injuries he received."

"Where's he work?" asked Sam.

"In a terminal for Fielding Enterprises. He unloads trucks."

Joe made the association immediately. *Fielding. That is an interesting connection.*

Devon Schmidt was sitting in a recliner. The skin of his nose and both eyes still showed purple from the beating. "Excuse me if I don't get up," he said in a gravelly whisper." He looked like Hugh O'Morrison described him:

husky, shaved head, goatee, and well tattooed with a stud earring in one ear. A permanent scowl seemed to be his natural expression.

"I'm Shari Moroso," said the woman. "I'm Devon's sister. Have a seat."

Joe and Sam sat down on the couch. "Are you going to arrest the guy that beat up Devon?" she asked.

"We can't," answered Joe.

"Oh, and why's that?" she asked, her tone turning belligerent.

"Because he's dead. He was found murdered five days ago, a bullet wound to the back of the head."

Shari went silent. Then she looked at Devon and said, "Karma."

"Yeah, well...I'm sure as hell not gonna cry over one less of his kind in the world. Whoever did it deserves a medal. Get me a beer, would ya? This calls for a drink," said Schmidt.

Shari moved to the kitchen, got a bottle of beer from the refrigerator, and handed it to Schmidt. He unscrewed the cap and took a long drink.

"So, where were you the evening of June 14th?" asked Joe.

"You think I did it?" laughed Schmidt. "Yeah, right."

"You had motive. He kicked your ass."

"Let me tell you something. He sucker-punched me with a hit to the throat. And when I couldn't breathe, he broke my nose and fucked up my knee. I still can't talk right, and I may need an operation on my knee."

"From all accounts, you threw the first punch."

"Bullshit! They're lying."

Joe decided to push him farther. "Hey, you were the one charged with assault."

Hearing that, Schmidt flew into a rage. "You know what? I wish I woulda killed the hymie bastard. Nobody does this to me and gets away with it, especially scum like him. It's too bad somebody got to him first."

"Like one of your buddies. You have one of them do it for you?"

"And take away the pleasure of getting payback myself. I don't think so."

"You still didn't answer his question," said Sam. "Where were you on the night of June 14th?"

"If you have to know—here. I was here. Now, I'm not answering any more of your questions without my lawyer present. So, fuck off!" Schmidt tipped up his beer and killed half the bottle.

"All right," said Joe. "If that's the way you want it." He rose, removed handcuffs, and stepped to Schmidt. "Put down your beer and stand up."

"What are you doing?" protested Shari.

"Taking him in for questioning," replied Sam. "Maybe he'll be more cooperative at the station."

"This is bullshit!" cried Schmidt.

"Yes, it is," agreed Shari.

"He's refusing to cooperate, so we'll have to finish our questioning at the police station," said Joe.

In desperation, Shari yelled, "Tell them what they want to know, you dumb shit!"

"Shut up, Shari!" snarled Schmidt.

Sam stepped between Shari and Joe. "Calm down. You don't want to be charged with obstructing."

"All right, god dammit," said Schmidt.

"All right what?" asked Joe.

"All right, I'll answer your questions—as long as you don't charge me or Shari with any related crimes based on my answers."

"Drugs we don't care about," said Sam.

"Okay. I'll level with you."

Joe and Sam sat back down on the couch while Shari sat on the arm of Schmidt's chair, one hand on his shoulder.

"One of my buddies and his girlfriend…they came over here…and we hung out, drank some beer, smoked a little weed, and watched a DVD."

Joe looked at Shari. "Is that what happened?"

"Yeah. His knee was hurtin' him, and he was havin' a lotta trouble walkin'. Couldn't go anywhere. So, we just sat around all night and got high."

"And who was this buddy? Wouldn't happen to be William Higgins, would it?"

"Willie? Yeah, it was him."

"You know we'll need to speak with him and confirm it, don't you?" said

Sam.

"Yeah, yeah."

"He's gonna love you for that," said Shari.

"He'll get over it."

After a few more questions, Joe got Higgins' contact information, then he and Sam left. Out on the street, Joe was feeling suspicious about Schmidt's alibi. "I'll bet he's on the horn to Higgins right now letting him know all about this meeting and telling him what to say to us."

"No doubt," said Sam. "I wonder if the knee injury is as bad as he's making out."

"If Daniel knew how to incapacitate someone, his knee would be a logical target. He sure did a number on his throat and nose."

"Say, not to change the subject or anything, but did you catch the fact he works for Fielding Enterprises?"

"I did," noted Joe. "Interesting, huh?"

"Very."

"I think that little coincidence is worthy of some further investigation."

Joe pulled out his phone and dialed Willie Higgins number. Joe was surprised that Higgins answered at all, much less on the first ring.

"Yeah?"

"This is Detective Joe Erickson, Chicago Police Department. We have some questions to ask you about Devon Schmidt. Where can we reach you?"

"I'm working on a job right now, but...I suppose I can talk to you on my lunch break," said Higgins, obviously not enthusiastic. But at least he was agreeable to meeting.

"That works for us."

Higgins gave him the address and said he took his break at noon. Joe confirmed the address of his work site and said they would meet him there right at twelve. The address Higgins gave was in a residential neighborhood in Wrigleyville.

Joe and Sam got there about ten minutes prior to the scheduled time. The address was a two-story house. A large dumpster in front filled with old building debris sat in the front yard. On the street, a flatbed truck was parked, loaded with stacks of sheetrock. Two pickup trucks were parked next to the truck with "Rogers Plaster & Drywall Services" painted on the doors. As Joe and Sam watched, pairs of men dressed in t-shirts and painter whites lifted sheets of sheetrock off the truck and carried them into the house. The sounds of power drills emanated from inside.

Sam glanced at his watch and said, "Should be any time now."

Moments later, eight men walked out of the house. Some went to the pickups and grabbed lunch buckets while others piled into the two pickups and drove away. One in particular eyed Joe and Sam. A burly man in his thirties, he had a shaved head and arms sported lots of tattoos. Carrying his lunch bucket, he began walking toward Joe and Sam, stopping about six feet in front of them.

"You the cops that wanted to talk to me?" he said, looking back and forth from Joe to Sam.

"You William Higgins?"

"Yeah."

"I called you," replied Joe, showing his ID. "Detective Joe Erickson. My partner, Detective Sam Renaldo."

Higgins didn't seem impressed. "So, what do want?"

"To ask you a few questions."

"Shoot."

"What were you doing on the night of June 14th?"

Higgins sighed, reached into his back pocket, and removed a daily planner. "Let's see. The fourteenth." He made a show of thumbing through the pages. "My girlfriend and I were with some friends all evening."

"And those friends would be...?"

He sighed again. "Devon Schmidt and his sister, Shari Moroso."

"And where were all of you?"

"His place."

"What time did you leave?"

"I dunno know. One maybe."

"And what's your girlfriend's name?"

"Lisa."

"Last name?"

"Veroni.

"We'll need her phone number and address."

"Is this really necessary?"

"It is."

With another sigh, he gave Joe and Sam Lisa Veroni's contact information. He was getting fed up and asked, "What the hell is this about?"

"You were in the Lion's Share Bar with Devon Schmidt when he was injured in a scuffle not long ago, right?" asked Sam.

"Uh-huh."

"You remember the man who laid out your friend?"

"Yeah. The fuckin' irate Jew-boy. I remember him."

"He was found murdered five days ago."

Joe and Sam watched for a reaction. There wasn't one. He wasn't surprised or affected by the news in the least. After a few moments, he raised his eyebrows.

"Isn't that a shame," was Higgin's sarcastic response. "Guess he punched out the wrong guy this time, huh?" he chuckled.

"You think it's funny?" asked Sam.

"Yeah, as a matter of fact, I do. You think I care if there's one less matza-gobbler in the world? In my opinion, he got what he deserved given what he did to Devon."

"You sure you didn't deal out a little payback for your injured buddy?"

"I have an alibi. Check with Devon and Shari. Lisa, too."

"Yeah. You do. We already checked." Joe paused. "You own a firearm?"

"What's it to you?"

"We may need ballistics to test it. To eliminate it as the murder weapon."

That was the last straw for Higgins. He sneered, "Get a fuckin' warrant." Then he turned and walked away, wiping beads of sweat from his head with his bandana. Joe and Sam watched as Higgins sat down under a tree and began eating his lunch.

Sam looked at Joe in astonishment. "What a piece of work, huh?"

"Hate. And to think there were hundreds like him who gathered in

Charlottesville. And there are thousands of white supremacists out there who feel the same way. Kinda makes you nauseated."

"Kinda? You gonna apply for a warrant to get his gun?"

"I don't even know what kind of gun he owns. I haven't checked. If he owns a .38, yeah, I'll definitely get one."

"You want to go interview his girlfriend? After we eat lunch, I mean."

Joe looked at him with a grin. "So, you're not really nauseated after all?"

"Figuratively speaking."

After they grabbed lunch, Joe and Sam caught up with Lisa Veroni where she worked as a massage therapist at a spa in Wicker Park. She was a small, petite woman, and looked considerably more sophisticated than her boyfriend, Willie Higgins. Her schedule was booked solid with clients, and she politely asked if they could meet her after work. Sam agreed to interview her at 4:30 pm, and he would share his findings with Joe the next morning.

"She'll probably confirm everything we've found out so far," said Joe.

"No doubt. But she might give us something. We'll see."

"I think you're just bucking for a free massage."

"I already have a massage therapist, thank you very much."

"Really. Let me guess. Her name is Hilda, she's blonde and has magic hands."

"No, his name is John, he's got dark hair, a wife, two kids, and yeah—he has magic hands!"

Chapter Nine

S am got nothing but a further confirmation of alibis from Lisa Veroni when he interviewed her the day before. Like her boyfriend, Willie Higgins, she also held white supremacist views and wasn't afraid to express them. Standing next to Joe's desk, he gave him a rundown of his interview.

"She lectured me on how 'white people' built America and, I won't repeat the ethnic slurs she used, but she said 'people of color' are destroying it. I was shocked to hear those words flow so easily from her mouth. It was..." He shook his head, his disgust palpable since her indictment included him, and she had no qualms about saying it to his face.

"Surprising how seemingly 'normal people' can have those views and you'd never know it. They do a good job hiding it. I'll bet none of her co-workers or supervisors at the spa know she's a white supremacist," said Joe.

"It makes you wonder if she has to give massages to non-whites, you know?"

"If she has seniority, she may have approval from management regarding who she's willing to take on as clients."

"Could be. Where to from here, Boss?"

"I think we'd better check on the Firearm Owners Identification database and see if Schmidt and Higgins are registered. Better look up the sister and the girlfriend, too."

"Okay, I'll get started on that. What are you going to do?"

"I'm going to call and see if Rachel Granger is back in town. If she is, I'll set up an interview."

Joe made the call to Rachel Granger's phone and a female voice answered, "Rachel Granger."

Joe introduced himself and told her he was investigating Daniel Silverman's death. Her voice immediately changed, and it became obvious she was affected by his loss. She agreed to meet with him during her lunch hour at a cafe not far from the Fielding Office on East Randolph. She told him he could recognize her by her purple dress.

Joe informed Sam of his meeting with Rachel at noon. In return, Sam reported that all four individuals were in the FOID database. "That only tells us if they are registered as gun owners. It doesn't tell us anything else."

Joe knew a former colleague who worked in the Chicago Bureau of Alcohol, Tobacco, Firearms, and Explosives, and it was time to give him a call. "Let me call Cliff Stewart, my contact over at ATF, and see if he can look up serial numbers on weapons they have registered. That way, we can tell if they have something worth pursuing," said Joe

"It's a start," said Sam.

"You can fire a .38 cartridge in a .357. Could be a way of disguising the weapon it was fired from, so I'd be interested to know if any of them own one of them, too."

Joe made a call to Cliff Stewart and asked if he would check on the gun ownership for Devon Schmidt, Shari Moroso, William Higgins, and Lisa Veroni. He explained the situation and told him he was specifically looking for ownership of .38 and .357 caliber weapons. Stewart agreed to the favor and said he would get back to Joe sometime that afternoon.

"If they got their guns at gun shows, they won't show up in the Federal E-Trace database," said Sam.

"I know," said Joe. "You want to bet on any guns showing up on the check?"

"No. I'm not taking any bets on this one."

Before going downtown to meet with Rachel Granger, Joe called Annie Bloom in the Civil Rights Division to give her an update on the investigation. He told her about their investigation of Schmidt and Higgins and the neo-Nazi connection they were pursuing.

"You think one of them was getting payback for what Daniel did?" she asked.

"We're following that path at the moment, but with Schmidt's knee injury, I doubt he was the offender. But his buddy could have done the job for him," said Joe. "I'm going to get a warrant for any weapons matching the caliber. That's the next step."

"Good. Well, thanks for keeping me in the loop, Joe."

Following his phone call, Joe went to meet with Rachel Granger. Traffic was moving so he got there a little early. He waited inside the door looking for a woman dressed in purple, hoping only one woman had chosen to wear that color today. Ten minutes later, a woman about forty stepped through the door wearing a purple business suit. She stood all of five feet tall with light brown hair pulled into a French roll. She gave Joe a look.

"Rachel?" Joe asked.

"Detective Erickson, I presume," she said, tongue planted firmly in cheek.

"Yes," replied Joe. They simultaneously reached out hands. Her handshake was firm and confident. "Thank you for seeing me."

"Of course."

Joe stepped to the head waitress. "For two, please."

"If you'll follow me," she replied and escorted them to a booth laying down menus in front of them. "Your server will be with you shortly."

Following a little chit-chat, they studied the menu, and after a few moments, Rachel put hers down. "I come here at least once a week, so I know the menu. The food's excellent."

Joe put his menu down. "I haven't been here before, but I noticed they have vegetarian, so I may have to bring my girlfriend here sometime. I usually cook my own dinners and bring in leftovers to work. But when I have to catch a bite somewhere, my partner insists on fast-food. We usually don't frequent these places."

"So, you cook?" she asked, seemingly wanting to know more. But Joe sensed it was because she didn't want to talk about a painful subject like Daniel Silverman. Before he could answer, the waitress showed up to take their orders: a wild berry salad for her and a wild mushroom omelet for him. *Apparently, we're both going wild today*, Joe thought. It brought a quirk of a smile to his face.

Then his thoughts reverted to the task at hand. "I suppose I should get down to business since that's why I asked for this meeting," said Joe. "As I mentioned, I'm working the Daniel Silverman case, and anything you could give me might help with the investigation. Was there anything at work that could be viewed as suspicious? Any conflicts with others? Anything out of the ordinary regarding work on your project?"

She sighed, "To tell you the truth, I've been wracking my brain ever since you called. I can't think of a single thing that may have led to his death. Everyone liked him."

"What was the nature of his work? Was it all in the office in front of a computer or what?"

"That's precisely what it was. The modeling was done by computer. The interfacing was outsourced to a company—we've used them for years. Daniel was very insightful, and he pointed out some potential flaws in the program and suggested some fixes. We wound up implementing them. I've never had an intern of his caliber. He was brilliant."

"Everyone I've talked to has said the same thing." Joe sighed and admitted, "I seem to be at an impasse. I don't know who else to contact."

"Well, you could try speaking with Cindy Fielding."

This revelation took Joe by surprise. "Cindy Fielding? You mean Jay Fielding's wife?"

"Yeah. They worked at a food bank together. You know, boxing up food for the poor."

"Interesting. How did you know about that?" Joe asked.

"He mentioned it in passing once or twice."

"Do you happen to know which food bank it was?"

"No, sorry. I don't. Like I said, he just mentioned it in passing. I didn't think anything about it until now. Maybe I shouldn't have said anything. I don't want to get into trouble."

Joe didn't want to give the impression that it might be important, so he shrugged it off. "It's probably nothing. I wouldn't worry about it. Besides, I don't reveal my sources."

"Oh, well that's good. The company's pretty particular about information on employees getting out. They're tight-lipped about everything. Mr. Curtis can be a real a-hole sometimes, pardon my French."

Joe laughed. "Pardon accepted. I got the impression he was more of a scumbag, myself. But then, I don't work for him."

Rachel giggled. "He's that, too. I could tell you a few stories, but that would take several glasses of wine. Just kidding. No, I just put my head down and do my work. And I get paid handsomely for it, I don't mind saying. It makes a little stink more tolerable."

Joe smiled, "I understand."

Their conversation continued as they ate their lunch. Rachel was right in her assessment of the food here. Joe picked up the check, and on their way out, he thanked Rachel for her time and the information she provided. Then he asked her if he could call if he had any follow-up questions. She agreed and they parted ways.

On his drive back to the office, he began thinking about Daniel working with Cindy Fielding at the food bank. He remembered what Robert Curtis said about Daniel the night on the boat. "He wound up spending most of his time talking to Julia and Cindy." Was something going on between Daniel and Cindy? An affair, maybe? Could that have been a motive for his murder? He would need to start digging. But first, he needed to attend his scheduled session with the department shrink, Dr. Elizabeth Lemke.

He had not been meeting with Dr. Lemke long, but he had no reason not to trust her. He convinced himself to play it straight with her knowing that she may be able to help him. With her counseling, maybe his nightmares would completely cease, the reoccurring images of Jamie Chambers's lifeless body would stop haunting him, and the guilt he felt at not saving her from the knife of serial killer David Eugene Burton would go away forever.

Did he like Dr. Lemke? Well, so far. He liked her a lot better than Dr. Bunsch. For some reason, he felt more comfortable talking to Dr. Lemke than Dr. Bunsch about personal things. Odd, because he always found it easier talking to his father about personal stuff than his mother. But he tried not to over-think it. *No need trying to psychoanalyze yourself, Joe. You already have one shrink. You don't need an amateur inside your head, too.*

After his half-hour session concluded, he felt good about what they had discussed and hoped he would continue to feel positive about his sessions.

Back in the office, he touched base with Sam about the lead he got from Rachel.

"So, you think the husband might have offed him out of jealousy?" asked Sam.

"It's a possibility. I don't think we can eliminate him or anyone else at this point."

"What about the swastika cut into his back?"

At that moment Joe's phone rang. It was Cliff Stewart from ATF.

"I have what you wanted," said Cliff.

"Great," replied Joe.

"Devon Schmidt owns a Smith & Wesson 686 which is a .357 revolver, and William Higgins owns a Colt .357 Magnum Python."

"Something for his bedside table," said Joe with a hint of sarcasm.

"It would deter most anyone, no doubt about it. Those are the only two .357's. None of the four had any .38's registered. The two women in question each own a nine-millimeter."

"Thanks, Cliff."

"These guys own a lot of weapons in addition to the ones I mentioned. Take care, Joe."

Neither one of these is a snub nose. A round fired from either of these models would not have stayed in the skull. Maybe they have pieces they bought at gun shows. Joe walked over to Sam and asked, "We need to get warrants for Schmidt and Higgins guns?"

"Applications are ready to go. I've already drawn them up."

"Devon Schmidt and Willie Higgins both own .357's. None of them own .38's according to the ATF database. Looks like we have two."

"I can finish up the applications and run them down to Judge Warner's office. I checked. He's in this afternoon."

"Nice work, partner. I'm pretty sure he'll sign them."

"He should."

"You need me to come as backup?" teased Joe.

"I think I can handle it," replied Sam. Joe returned to his desk and looked up Cindy Fielding's contact information. Then, he changed his mind and called Daniel's brother, Adam, who said Daniel volunteered at the Logan Square Food Bank. Joe looked up the address and drove to the location. The building was an old storefront with a large black and white hand-painted sign above the door.

Shelves lined the walls and other standing shelf units formed rows. The majority of the items were made up of cans or boxes. Looking around, Joe spotted a middle-aged Hispanic woman wearing an apron and looking like she worked there.

"Are you one of the managers here?" he asked.

"Yes. How can I help you?" she asked politely.

He showed his ID and introduced himself. Her reaction showed the slightest bit of attitude when she answered, "Okay."

"I'm investigating the death of Daniel Silverman. He volunteered here. Did you know him?"

Her attitude changed and became sympathetic. "Yes. We all knew Daniel. Maybe we should talk in the back." Joe followed her into a back room where a card table and a few chairs were set up along with a coffee pot and a refrigerator.

"Why don't we sit down?" she suggested.

They sat at the card table, and the woman said, "I'm Renata Rodriguez. I'm one of several people who organized this food bank several years ago, so I know all the volunteers who work with us."

"What can you tell me about Daniel?"

"Everybody liked working with him—he was so much fun to be around. Funny. Nice to the customers, too. Went out of his way to help everybody. It was such a shock when we heard about what happened."

"Did he have any friends here? Someone he worked with more than others?"

"Oh, that'd be Cindy. They were pals."

"Cindy…? Got a last name?"

"Fielding. They volunteered the same days most of the time. Not always, but most of the time."

"Could they have been more than just pals, do you think?"

"I didn't see any touching or kissy-kissy stuff going on between them. But Gwen—Gwen Stoltz—she's one of the other managers—she said she saw Daniel pick up Cindy one evening, and when she got in the car, they leaned over and kissed each other."

"Is Gwen here?" asked Joe.

"Yeah. You want me to get her?"

"If you don't mind," said Joe.

Renata got up and left the room. A minute later, Renata returned with a middle-aged woman dressed in black jeans and a designer blouse over a lacy undergarment. Joe rose from his seat to greet the tall brunette.

"Gwen this is Detective Erickson. He's investigating Daniel's death."

"Oh," she said as she extended her professionally manicured hand. "Nice to meet you."

"My pleasure." They all sat at the table and Joe began asking questions.

"Renata tells me you saw Cindy Fielding getting into a car driven by Daniel Silverman and witnessed them kissing. Is that correct?"

"I did."

"When was that?"

"Ohhhhh…six weeks ago, maybe."

"And what were you doing that you were able to see them?"

"I was outside smoking a cigarette, and I was standing between this building and the next one. Kinda by myself and out of the light, you know. Anyway, this black car pulls up. Beemer, I think. And Cindy comes out and gets in, and before she closes the door, they lean over and give each other a kiss."

"And you're sure it was Daniel?"

"It looked like him to me. I'd seen him drive that car before."

"I see," said Joe. "Did you ever see Daniel and Cindy making any romantic moves or gestures toward one another while they worked in here?"

Gwen thought for a moment. "Well, I can't say that I did. But I don't keep watch on our volunteers that closely. I'm not like a bus monitor." She pulled a package of long cigarettes from her apron and asked, "Mind if I smoke?"

"Yeah, I do," said Joe.

Gwen sighed and returned the pack to her apron. She gave Renata a glance. Joe noticed.

"You can go if you like," he said. "Thank you for your time."

Gwen stood and walked out, removing her cigarettes on the way. Renata looked at Joe and said, "Cindy hasn't volunteered since Daniel was killed. I don't know if that means anything or not."

"That's helpful, thanks."

"I hope she's not going to get into any kind of trouble. She's a nice person and a good volunteer. I hope she comes back."

Joe saw the look of concern on her face and sought to put her at ease. "She's probably grieving for her friend. Give her some time." She nodded, seemingly accepting his explanation. "What days does she usually show up?" he asked.

"Tuesday and Thursday afternoons."

Joe wrote it down in his notebook. Looking at Renata, he said, "I think I have enough information. Thank you. If I need to contact you, what's the best way?"

She gave him her phone number and her work schedule. Joe left and drove back to the office. He met Sam at his desk.

Seeing Joe, Sam stood and waved the warrants. "Got em."

"Good deal."

"And you?"

"I need to interview Cindy Fielding. I might have a lead on some hanky-panky between her and Daniel."

"Progress." Sam looked at his watch, then at Joe. "And now, it's Miller time!"

Chapter Ten

That evening when Joe got home, Destiny was waiting for him with a bottle of Pinot Noir breathing in a carafe and two wine glasses sitting on the counter. Joe saw she had been entertaining herself reading an Anne Perry novel.

"Working on crime all day and then you read about it for entertainment, too?" he smiled teasingly as he put his arms around her. "Don't you need some variety?"

"You never know. I might learn something from those Victorians," she said and kissed him. "I missed you."

"I missed you more. How was your mom?"

"Fine. She sends you her best. Are you up for a glass of wine?"

"Oh, yeah."

She poured them both a glass from the carafe and they retired to the couch in the living room.

"You make any progress on your case this week?"

"Some, maybe. Too early to tell. At least we have some leads to follow up on."

"Not bad this early on. How's Sam doing?"

"Other than a root canal, the same. He was glad to get me back as a partner."

"Who wouldn't be?"

Joe laughed. "I could name a couple." He took a drink of his wine, savoring its flavor. "Mm. Very nice."

"It is, isn't it. A new vineyard I read about."

Joe paused, gathering his thoughts. Then, he looked at Destiny and asked,

"Have you ever heard that Yogi Berra expression, "When you come to a fork in the road, take it?""

"Yeah, I've heard that," she chuckled.

"Well, right now, I've come to that fork in the road, and I wish I could take it. I don't know whether to pursue the straighter left path, which is a revenge-hate killing, or the twisting right path which is a killing someone may have disguised to look like a hate killing."

"So, you want to take both paths, is that it?"

"Yeah," he chuckled.

"If only you could."

"Until I have evidence that more clearly points me in the right direction, I'm not sure which path is the correct one. I'm looking at the left path at the moment, but…"

"If you were a neo-Nazi, and you were bent on revenge, would you sign your homicide or prefer to leave no evidence?"

"Depends. If the guy simply wanted to get even, he'd choose to leave no evidence behind. But if he was arrogant enough, savage enough, he'd want to sign his work to send a message."

"Are your two suspects arrogant enough to carve a swastika into your victim's back? And smart enough to evade police by dumping the gun afterwards?"

"Possibly. They have alibis for the time of death—the girlfriend and sister. Flimsy but they are what they are. But neither one of those guys strikes me as an Einstein."

"What's your next move?"

"Tomorrow morning, we're serving warrants for their .357's and anything else that could fire a .38 cartridge. ATF told us both Schmidt and Higgins own .357's. The sister and girlfriend own nine mils, at least that's what they have registered.

"Given the gun show loophole, who knows what they may have in their possession," said Destiny. "If ballistics doesn't check out, then what do you do?"

Joe took another sip. "Well, then it looks like it's going to take expending

54

some shoe leather. And that means exploring that twisting right-hand path to see where it takes me. I have a lead in that direction, but it's hard to follow two paths at once."

"You're good at exploring twisting paths. You couldn't get much more twisted than the Iowa murders. You solved that case and put Barry Henderson away."

Joe took a drink from his glass and put it down on the coffee table. "Yeah. Things had a way of working out in that one. I was lucky."

"No. You weren't lucky, you were good."

Joe leaned over and placed a long, kiss on her. When they came up for air, Destiny said, "Slow down, mister. You need to save this for later because we have reservations at a Himalayan restaurant down in the Loop.

"For us?"

"Well of course, for us."

"Oh. Well, I didn't want to assume."

She laughed. "You are..."

"A twerp? That's what my mother used to call me."

"And well deserved, I'm sure. I thought we could take an Uber down there and back, so you don't have to drive."

"Himalayan, huh?" asked Joe.

"You like Indian cuisine, right?"

"Yeah."

"Himalayan is a lot the same. Just a few twists. You'll like it."

"If you say so. How much time do we have?"

"An hour. We should leave in thirty minutes given the traffic. Enough time for another glass of wine." You don't mind, do you?

"Go ahead. I wish I could."

Destiny rose, went into the kitchen, and came back with the carafe.

She poured herself a half-portion and sat down next to him.

She raised her glass. "Here's to your first case. May your amazing intuition and detection skills solve this case and show your colleagues you're back on top."

"I'll do my best," Joe replied, picking up his glass and clinking hers.

* * *

The next morning was a Saturday, and Joe and Sam met in the office early to go over the procedure for serving the warrants on Devon Schmidt and William Higgins. They determined it would be best to serve them simultaneously so Schmidt and Higgins would not have time to warn each other. They flipped a coin, and it was decided that Joe would serve the warrant on Schmidt while Sam would take Higgins.

Joe called for assistance since Schmidt was armed and considered dangerous. He met two officers at Schmidt's address a few minutes after 8:00 am. He explained the situation to Officers Zavodny and Proskovec, and they walked the half block to Schmidt's apartment building. Joe pressed the super's button, and when he answered, Joe identified himself and asked for admittance. The super came to the door, verified Joe's identity, then let them in.

They took the stairs to the second floor and walked down the hallway to Schmidt's residence, Apartment 24. Joe listened at the door and could faintly hear the television. Rapping loudly with the knocker, he announced himself, "Chicago PD. Open up." Then he stood away from the door, not knowing if Schmidt would respond by unlocking of the door or blowing it open with a shotgun.

Proskovec chomped on his gum while they gloved up. Joe rapped again and repeated his announcement. Shortly thereafter, they heard the chain on the door slide off and the deadbolt turn. The door opened revealing Devon Schmidt on aluminum crutches standing in front of them.

"What the fuck you want now?" he asked in a surly half-whisper.

Joe pushed the warrant in his face as he and the two officers pushed past him into his apartment.

"We have a warrant," Joe stated.

"Warrant for what?"

"Warrant for any .38 or .357 caliber weapon you have on the premises," replied Joe.

Schmidt was clearly pissed. "You have no right to barge in here and take my guns."

"That warrant says I have every right. I know you have at least one registered to you—a Smith & Wesson 686 revolver. We need it and any others you may have."

"And if I don't choose to hand it over to you assholes?"

"Then we'll toss your apartment and charge you with obstruction. You can make this easy or difficult. Your choice, Devon. Makes no difference to me one way or the other."

Schmidt cursed under his breath and started to move toward his chair.

"Just stay where you are."

"I was going to get the 686 for you."

"You tell us where it is, and we'll get it."

"Don't trust me, do ya? Okay, see that table by my chair over there? Look in the drawer."

Joe looked at Zavodny. "You want to check?"

Zavodny walked over and opened the drawer. Reaching inside, he removed the stainless steel revolver. Holding it by its black handle, he examined it and said, "It's loaded."

"Of course, it's loaded, ya dumb ass. What good's a gun if it ain't loaded?" crowed Schmidt.

Joe pulled an evidence bag from his pocket. "Better unload it. Zavodny pushed open the cylinder tipped it up and turned the cylinder, so the cartridges fell out into his hand. Then he dropped the gun along with the cartridges into the evidence bag.

"May I be so bold as to ask why you need this particular gun?" asked Schmidt.

"Ballistics test. You have any other .357's or .38's?"

"Hell, no."

"Where are the rest of your weapons?"

"Why?"

"I want to see them. Just to make sure you're not bullshitting me. And you better not be. You've got one more chance to come clean. If I find you've got another .357 or .38 somewhere, I'll charge you with obstruction. Now, do you have another one somewhere or not?"

"Hell no!"

"All right. Let's see the rest of them. Where are they?"

"Assholes," he muttered under his breath. "Bedroom. In the closet. And my sock drawer."

"Zavodny, you watch him. Proskovec and I will check out his bedroom." Joe and Officer Proskovec walked into Schmidt's bedroom. Proskovec found a Smith & Wesson AR-15, several loaded clips, and boxes of ammunition in the closet. Joe found the sock drawer and discovered a Smith & Wesson Shield, a small easily concealed nine-millimeter, and several boxes of ammunition for both the nine-millimeter and the .357."

They looked through the rest of the closet and other drawers but found nothing else. Returning to the living room, they found Schmidt sitting in his chair with his TV remote in hand.

"He was complaining about his knee hurting, so I let him sit down," said Zavodny.

"I'm in a lot of pain because of that son-of-a—"

"We know, we know. We know all about you getting your ass kicked," interrupted Joe. "You don't need to go into it again."

Schmidt bristled at the comment but decided not to pursue it.

"It's Smith & Wesson all the way with you, isn't it? Something to be said about brand loyalty."

Schmidt just sneered. "Yeah. So, when can I get my gun back?"

"After ballistics runs its test. I imagine a couple of weeks if it checks out clean."

"Of course, it will. It's new. I haven't even fired it yet."

"Then you have nothing to worry about, do you?" Joe looked at the two officers. "We're done here." At the door, Joe turned back to Schmidt. "Thank you for your cooperation, Devon."

"Fuck you!"

As they walked toward the stairs, Zavodny said, "A real upstanding citizen, isn't he?"

"Just your average neo-Nazi white supremacist that might be tied to a murder."

"Hopefully, he won't open his window and target us with that AR-15 as we walk to our vehicles."

"He can't," smirked Proskovec. "I disabled it just in case. They don't work well with chewing gum in the magazine."

"I didn't hear that," said Joe.

Once outside, Joe thanked them for their assistance and drove back to the office. He wasn't in his chair more than five minutes when Sam walked in carrying an evidence bag containing a .357 Colt Python and six rounds of ammunition.

"So, I see you got Willie's .357," said Joe.

"Yeah, and let me tell you, he made a hell of a lot of noise about it. "That's a fifteen-hundred-dollar gun blah-blah-blah. You'd think we were kidnapping his first-born child."

Schmidt wasn't much better. Claimed his gun was brand new and never been fired."

"Yeah, right."

"Did he have an arsenal in his bedroom like Schmidt did?"

"Oh, yeah. He was ready to go to war, man. AR-15, two nine-millimeters, a shotgun, and enough ammunition to make a Latin American dictator drool."

"These people are freakin' dangerous. And to think how many guys like this are out there."

"Yeah. Come on, we better get these things locked up so they can go to ballistics Monday morning."

Chapter Eleven

After Joe finished his jog Monday morning, he was ready to step into the shower when his phone rang. He assumed it was Destiny, but when he looked at the number, he saw it was a call from work. The duty sergeant was calling to inform him about a homicide related to his case. When he heard the name and address, he felt a sudden twinge in the pit of his stomach. The victim was Devon Schmidt.

Joe showered and dressed quickly. He grabbed a hard-boiled egg and a hunk of cheese from the refrigerator and filled his travel mug with fresh coffee. Twenty minutes later, he arrived at Devon Schmidt's apartment.

Two police cruisers were on the scene with their lights flashing. Officers had already set up a yellow tape perimeter. He badged his way past the officer and through the building's entrance.

"Detective Joe Erickson," he said, showing his ID to the officer manning the door to Apartment 24.

"Officer Mike Murphy," replied the dark-haired officer.

"What do you have?" asked Joe as he pulled on a pair of gloves.

"Apparent suicide. The guy's sister found him earlier this morning and called it in. She's pretty upset."

"She in there?"

"Yeah. My partner, he's with her. In the kitchen."

"Medical Examiner's Office been notified?"

"Yeah."

Joe gloved up and stepped through the door. Devon Schmidt was in a seated position, his head at an unnatural angle against the back of the recliner. He didn't venture too close to the body but couldn't help but notice the hole in his right temple and blood and brain matter sprayed against the wall. Schmidt's injured leg was still stretched out on the recliner but the other had fallen to the floor. What especially caught Joe's eye was the short-barrel revolver next to Schmidt's hand. When he heard sniffing and voices coming from his left, he followed them.

Entering the kitchen, Joe saw Schmidt's sister, Shari Moroso, seated at a table along with an officer, who rose when Joe entered. Joe held up his ID.

"Detective Joe Erickson."

"Jack Sparks," replied the tall, curly-haired officer. "This is Shari Moroso, the deceased's sister. She found the body."

"We've met," said Joe. "Has anyone touched anything?

"Not me," replied Sparks, showing his gloved hands.

Joe looked at Shari. "Nothing other than the door, and this chair and table," she said. "I used my cellphone to make the call."

"Good." Joe pulled out the chair and sat down. Removing his notebook and pen, he said, "I know this is hard right now, but I need to ask you some questions, okay?"

"I told the officer everything I know."

"I know, but now you need to tell me."

Joe looked at Sparks and said, "Why don't you go down and wait for the Medical Examiner. Take him up here when he arrives."

"Sure thing," said Sparks, and he left.

"What time did you get here?"

She dabbed at her eyes with a paper towel. "About 5:30 or so."

"And do you usually stop and see your brother so early in the morning?"

"Since the injury to his knee, he has trouble getting around, so I sometimes stop in before work to see if he needs anything."

"Where do you work?"

"Home Depot. The one on Halstead." She sniffed and said, "I guess I better call in and tell 'em I won't be in today, huh?"

"I think you have a pretty good excuse for skipping work."

"I know what it looks like, but Devon didn't kill himself. No way. This is murder."

"Why do you say that?" asked Joe, a little taken aback by how adamant she was.

"He's not that way. He would never kill himself. He wasn't depressed. He didn't have any kind of mental issues. He's my brother. I would have known about those kinds of things."

"Sometimes people hide their pain from those closest to them."

"Bullshit! He was a happy, normal guy and looking forward to getting back to work after his knee healed up," she insisted.

"Did you see him yesterday?"

"No."

"When's the last time you did see him?"

"Friday after work. I brought over some beer, and Willie stopped over for a while. You can ask Willie. He was fine."

"By Willie, you mean William Higgins?"

"Yeah, Willie Higgins."

"We will."

"Did he have company Saturday or Sunday night? There are two empty wine glasses and a wine bottle in the living room."

"I don't know. He could have."

"Does he have a girlfriend?"

"No, not at the present time."

Joe thought for a moment, then remembered something. "Since his injury, does he go out? I noticed the other day that he uses crutches."

"No, no. He'd fall down and hurt himself. He could barely get to the bathroom using those things."

At that moment, Sam came through the door and said, "The ME's here. It's Kendra."

"Glad you could make it," said Joe.

"Yeah, yeah," Sam replied.

"You remember Devon's sister, Shari Moroso? She found him this morning."

"My condolences," replied Sam.

A barely audible "thank you" escaped Shari's lips, and she got up and pulled another section of paper towel from the roll on the wall.

After blowing her nose, she asked, "Can I call work now?"

"Sure, go ahead," assured Joe. "I think I have what I need for the time being. We'll need you to move out of the apartment now the Medical Examiner's here."

Joe stood up, then he and Sam escorted her out into the hall. Sam verified Shari's contact information while Joe spoke with Kendra who was putting on her Tyvek coveralls.

"What do we have here, detective?" asked Kendra.

"It looks like a suicide, but his sister swears up and down he never would have offed himself," replied Joe.

"Well, it wouldn't be the first time somebody did it to the surprise of everyone else. We'll see," she said. And she pulled on her booties and mask, picked up her kit, and moved into the living room to begin her work.

Half an hour later, the Evidence Techs showed up in the persons of Art Casey and Jerry Bristow. Art had gone out of his way to help Joe with evidence from the David Eugene Burton serial killer case when Joe had little more than a few cat hairs to go on.

"Art, Jerry," said Joe, greeting them when they got close to the door.

"Good morning, Detective," said Art. "You couldn't have waited until I'd eaten breakfast?"

"You know what they say about the early bird, right?"

"Yeah, he died of hunger because all the worms were still sleeping."

"Kendra's inside," said Joe.

As Art and Jerry suited up, Kendra came to the door and motioned Joe inside. She removed her mask and said, "It looks like death occurred sometime between eleven and twelve last night. The gun next to the body is a Colt Cobra, two-inch barrel, firing a .38 caliber cartridge. The bullet entered the temple on the right side, exited through the temporal area on the left side, and looks to be lodged in the wall. Powder burns and damage at the entrance site suggest it was held against the head and fired."

"So, it looks like suicide," said Joe, seeking confirmation.

"Well, there's this. I found it in the printer." She handed Joe a sheet of paper inside a plastic sleeve. On it was written, "I'm not going to prison for some Jew-boy."

"Hold that, would you please?" And Joe snapped a photo with his phone.

"Probably sent from his computer. He has a laptop, and it's sitting open on the coffee table. It'll have to be checked to see if it originated from there and if there's anything else incriminating on it." Kendra picked up on Joe's expression. "Why, are you thinking otherwise?"

"We recently obtained a warrant for all his weapons that could fire a .38 round, and on Saturday, we seized a .357 Smith & Wesson that we planned to drop off to ballistics this morning. We conducted a search for all his weapons, and we never found that one. Everything he owned was Smith & Wesson. He even made a remark about 'only owning the best.' What bothers me is why would he off himself with a Colt?"

"Good question, Joe. They don't pay me for those kinds of answers."

"I think I need to speak with his sister, again. Thanks, Kendra. You conducting the autopsy today?"

"Probably. I assume you want to be there?"

"Yeah. Text me when you have the time scheduled."

"Will do."

Joe turned and went into the hall looking for Shari. He spotted her talking with Officer Sparks and Sam a few doors down. Joe approached her and as he drew close, she gave him a strange look and addressed him."

"These officers say I can't go until you clear it."

"That's correct. Since I'm lead detective, that's my call. Before I release you, I have one question about your brother. All of his guns were Smith & Wesson. Why would he shoot himself with a Colt?"

"What?" she said incredulously.

"The suspected weapon used in his death was a .38 Colt Cobra."

"He didn't own any such gun. He wouldn't own one of those things. He was strictly a Smith & Wesson man. I told you he was murdered. That was not his gun!" She began tearing up and whimpered, "Some son-of-a-bitch killed him!"

"We'll be looking into that," comforted Sam. "It's important you provided us with that information. It's important to our investigation."

"Thank you, Shari. You can go. Do you need a lift anywhere?" asked Joe.

"No. I have my own car."

She walked down the hall and pressed the button on the elevator. It opened right away and she stepped inside.

"Kendra said time of death was sometime between eleven and twelve last night. Let's start knocking on doors and see if anyone heard anything," said Joe.

"Got it," replied Sam.

They questioned the surrounding neighbors as well as neighbors on the first and third floors. Of those they found at home, none of them heard anything like a gunshot or loud noise the previous night. In addition, no one saw anyone they didn't know in the hallway or elevator that night, either. The apartment complex was old, and it had no surveillance cameras. If this was not a suicide, then it looks as though the offender had easy access to Schmidt's apartment. He almost certainly would have been known to Schmidt or he would not have been let in. They need to check Schmidt's phone to see if he may have ordered take out from somewhere, and the offender got in that way.

"I would like to know who drank wine there over the weekend," wondered Joe aloud.

"He seemed to drink beer, not wine," added Sam. "Looks like he had a guest or two."

"Yeah. Hopefully, their prints show up in the system."

Chapter Twelve

By noon, Art Casey and Jerry Bristow had finished their work inside Devon Schmidt's apartment, and Kendra had removed his body and taken it to the morgue. The apartment was sealed, and the yellow crime tape had been removed from the outside entrances.

As they left the building, Sam looked over at Joe, "I think we need to talk to his buddy."

"Yeah. Let's go. Maybe he hasn't heard the news."

"Lunch first."

"Okay, but let's make it quick."

While getting a quick bite at McDonald's, Joe got a text from Kendra. "Autopsy 3:00." He texted her back, "CU there." After wolfing down a salad, Joe and Sam drove separate cars to the West Grace Street address of William Higgins and his girlfriend, Lisa Veroni.

Identifying themselves, they got buzzed in. The apartment was on the ground floor, and Lisa opened the door for them as they approached. It was clear she already heard about Devon's death as her eyes and nose were red from crying, and she was holding a wad of tissues.

"Come in," she said.

They entered the studio apartment that was decorated with a lot of red, white, and blue paraphernalia. Upon first glance, it might pass as patriotic, but upon closer inspection, it depicted a sinister aspect.

"I figured you'd show up today."

Joe said, "Then, I take it you've heard about Devon."

"Shari called. It's terrible."

At that moment, they heard a distant flushing of a toilet, and a few seconds later, William Higgins entered from the hall. Upon seeing the two detectives, he muttered, "Don't waste any time, do ya?" He reeked of alcohol as he passed by. He continued to the couch and plopped himself down. Picking up one of several beer bottles sitting on the coffee table, he tipped it up and took a couple gulps.

"We're investigating your friend's death," said Sam. "Anything you can tell us would be helpful."

"Well, I can tell you he didn't kill himself, that's for damned sure," stated Lisa in no uncertain terms.

"What do you think?" asked Sam, looking at Higgins.

"Well, he was..." Higgins trailed off.

"Not suicidal!" said Lisa, finishing his sentence.

"What were you going to say?" asked Sam.

"Well...It..." stumbled Higgins. "It was a fuckin' Mossad hit," Higgins finally got out in slightly slurred speech. "That's what it was. Payback for who his family thinks killed their kid."

"I'll bet that's what happened," added Lisa.

"His family's rich and they've got connections high up in Israel."

"They're wicked—those agents. They can sweep in and murder somebody, then stage it, make all the evidence look like suicide. And it's like they're never ever there."

"They killed the wrong guy. He didn't do it!" roared Higgin, slamming his fist into his thigh. "He didn't kill that guy!"

Joe removed his phone and pulled up his photo file. "This was found in Devon's printer," he said, showing a photo of the message Kendra found earlier.

"That's bullshit!" said Lisa. "Look at this, Willie."

She showed Higgins the photograph, and he scoffed. "Fake."

"How do you know that?" asked Sam.

"Because he'd rather shoot it out with you guys than go to prison. He'd go down fightin', not take the coward's way out. That wasn't his nature," said Lisa.

Retrieving his phone, Joe asked, "When's the last time you saw him?"

"Friday," replied Higgins, taking another swig of beer.

"And what was his state of mind?"

"Usual. His usual self."

"And his sister was there?"

"Yeah, I brought over a twelve-pack, and we downed a few."

"Where were you?" Joe asked Lisa.

"I wasn't feeling well so I stayed home," she replied. "Migraine."

"She did," confirmed Higgins.

"Look," said Lisa, looking from Joe to Sam. "Are you going to treat this as a suicide or a murder?"

"Depends where the facts take us," replied Sam.

"You're just going to let this go, aren't ya? The rich Jews get away with murder."

"Let me tell you something," interrupted Joe. "If I find anything that leads to the Silverman's being involved in Devon's death, I'm going to pursue it. I don't care if killers are rich or poor. And I don't care what their religion might be. I'll arrest them if there's evidence pointing to their guilt."

"Yeah, sure."

"I have another question for you. The gun that killed Devon—it was a .38 caliber Colt Cobra. I thought he only owned Smith & Wesson models."

"No way!" said Lisa. "A Colt?"

"He wouldn't own a Colt," insisted Higgins, turning in his seat. "He wouldn't even have one in the house. He hated anything Colt. I don't know why. Nothin' wrong with 'em. Some kinda weird prejudice he had."

Joe glanced at Sam, then back at Higgins. "How many people knew that?"

"It's not somethin' he advertised. Nobody would've known about it unless you knew him really good."

"That would not be a mistake Mossad would make, I can tell you that," said Joe. "If someone killed him and made it look like a suicide, they did a pretty good job. Except...they appeared to make this one little mistake. If that's the way it actually went down."

There was no reaction from Higgins.

"You own Colt weapons. Where were you Sunday evening?" asked Sam.

"You're accusing Willie?" protested Lisa.

"Simply asking."

"You've got a lot of nerve!"

"I was at a meeting, and 'no,' I'm not telling you the name of the group, who was there, or where it was held," answered Higgins.

"I suppose they all looked like you," said Sam.

"More or less. They sure as hell didn't look like you."

Joe could see Sam bristle after hearing that comment. "What about you?" Sam asked, glaring at Lisa.

She shot him a mean glance and held it. "I was there, too."

Joe intervened. "I'm attending the autopsy this afternoon. We may have more answers then. I think we've got what we need, huh Sam?"

"Yeah. More than enough." He gave Lisa a parting glance. "We'll see ourselves out."

Before leaving the apartment, Joe handed Lisa his card. "In case you think of anything helpful." She begrudgingly took it.

As soon as they stepped into the hallway, they heard the door close and the deadbolt turn. "Nice couple, don't you think?" asked Joe with a quirk of a smile.

"Yeah. Real sweet," Sam replied. "Real sweet."

* * *

The autopsy began on time, right at 3:00 pm. Joe was in attendance along with Art Casey. Kendra and her assistant, Kenny Miller, performed the procedure.

Devon Schmidt was a thirty-eight-year-old male who was overweight, technically obese but not considered morbidly so. His injured knee was examined, and it was as serious as Schmidt led on. It was badly bruised, and the ligaments and cartilage had sustained damage. His heart showed early stages of arteriosclerosis, but the rest of his body showed no signs of disease or serious conditions.

The bullet was fired at point-blank range and passed from the right temple through the frontal part of the brain and out the left temporal area. Once the cranial vault was open, Kendra observed and made note of the damage done by the bullet as it passed through. Death would have been instantaneous. The brain was removed and weighed.

While examining his lower pelvic region, Kendra found traces of a red substance just above the pubic hair and on the inside of each thigh. She swabbed each area, and the samples would be sent to the lab for analysis. She swabbed his penis and had Kenny prepare a slide. After looking into her microscope, she looked over at Joe and said, "He appears to have ejaculated sometime during the night of his death." Kenny took additional swabs to discover if there was DNA from a partner present.

Blood samples were taken for a tox screen. The stomach was emptied of its contents and would be analyzed later. Individual organs were weighed, and samples taken. Once Kendra began preparing samples for microscopic examination, Joe left. He would call her tomorrow and follow up.

Back at the office, Joe made notes before he went home. He shared what he found out with Sam, and they looked forward to getting the results of fingerprints from the wine glasses the next day. DNA results, the lab analysis, and tox screens would take longer.

Chapter Thirteen

As Joe jogged the next morning, he thought about something he saw in Devon Schmidt's apartment. He recalled the two wine glasses on the coffee table, and he could swear he saw a subtle smear of red on the rim of one of them. Lipstick. Not wanting to contaminate the crime scene, he had not ventured into the room to closely examine the glasses. But the subtle red smear stuck in his mind. One of Schmidt's visitors was a woman.

When Kendra found a trace of red substance on Schmidt's thighs and pubic area, Joe wondered if the substance was the same as the substance on the glass. If the substances matched, then maybe Schmidt did have a woman visiting him that night. People he interviewed reported Schmidt did not have a girlfriend. So, who could she have been? And could she have been his killer? Did she share a bottle of wine with him, have sex, then put a bullet through his head? That didn't make sense...unless she was an assassin. Actually, a woman would be a perfect choice if it was a hit. *Come on, Joe. Stop thinking like Willie Higgins!*

Joe continued to run various scenarios through his mind until he came to the end of his three miles and had cooled down. Entering his apartment, he poured himself a cup of coffee, drank a few sips, and headed for the shower. While rinsing off, it came to him. *A friend with benefits!* Maybe there was someone Schmidt would see occasionally for sex. No strings attached. That could explain the wine—it was for her.

When Joe got to the office, he logged into his computer. There was a message he had been hoping for. The fingerprints on the wine glasses belonged to Devon Michael Schmidt and Roselyn Gabrielle Bertrand. Thankfully, she was in the system. Joe pulled up Bertrand's information. She was thirty, born in Chicago, arrested for assault when she was twenty, but the charges were eventually dropped. No other arrests or citations since. After some searching, he found she lived on Kimball Avenue in Albany Park and worked as a teacher's aide at Summers Elementary School. *Doesn't seem like an assassin.*

He checked the FOID system, and her name was listed. She was a registered gun owner in Illinois. *One thing's for sure, she knows her way around firearms.*

When Sam walked in, Joe motioned him over. "Got a hit on the fingerprints on the wine glasses," said Joe. "One was Schmidt's and the other belonged to one Roselyn Gabrielle Bertrand. She works at an elementary school in Albany Park."

"You want to have uniforms pick her up?" asked Sam.

"If she's innocent and they walk her out of her school, it could create all sorts of problems for her and the administration," said Joe. "I think I want to test the waters and call her first."

"You checked for priors?"

"Her prints are in the system because of a prior arrest for assault, but charges were dropped. Ten years ago, when she was twenty. Nothing since. But she's got a FOID card."

"Girlfriend?"

"I'm thinking…Friend with benefits kind of thing, maybe?"

"Well, make the call, I guess. We'll go from there."

Joe waited until 9:00 am and called the general number at Summers School. He asked the woman who answered the phone if Roselyn Bertrand worked there.

"Who's calling, please?" was the response.

He was hoping she wouldn't ask, but since she did, he was forced to identify himself. "This is Detective Joe Erickson of the Chicago Police Department."

"Oh!" she replied, voicing concern. "Why, yes. She does."

"Is she there today? If so, I'd like to speak with her."

"Is something wrong?"

"No, it's nothing she's done wrong. It has to do with one of our investigations. I can't go into detail. We'd simply like to ask her a couple of questions, that's all."

"Well, I don't know if I should—"

"Maybe you would prefer I come down there personally and show my badge around? What did you say your name was?"

"That won't be necessary. Let me get her for you." She put Joe on hold. About two minutes later, the phone clicked.

"This is Roselyn," said the young woman.

Joe identified himself and told her he was investigating the death of Devon Schmidt. She was silent for a few moments, then agreed to speak with him. They settled on meeting at the 17th Police District office on North Pulaski Road at 3:30 that afternoon.

Just before lunch, the prints came back on the gun. They were Devon Schmidt's. No other prints were found. No prints on any of the cartridges. Now, that was odd. Apparently, they got wiped clean or inserted into the cylinder by a person wearing gloves. That threw up a red flag. Normally, one would assume Schmidt's prints would be on the cartridges if he had loaded the gun.

Early that afternoon, Joe called Kendra to see if there was any additional information that would be included in the autopsy report.

"I tested his hands for gunshot residue," she said. "There was GSR present on his right hand, none on his left."

"I suspected that," said Joe.

"Are you still thinking this wasn't a suicide?" asked Kendra.

"Yeah. I'm thinking it was staged but I can't prove it. Not yet."

"I see."

"That red substance you found on his thighs and lower abdomen. Do you think that could be lipstick?"

"It's possible. The lab will make that determination."

"Did you notice lipstick on one of the wine glasses? I thought I saw a smear, but I didn't get close enough to be sure."

"As a matter of fact, there was. You think a woman could be involved in his death?"

"I haven't ruled it out, but I think he may have had a female visitor prior to his death. She may have had sex with him before she left. Whether she set him up or killed him, that remains to be seen."

"So, you're thinking the lipstick on the wineglass will match the red substance on his body."

"It's a logical assumption."

"One additional thing I can tell you is his stomach contents were mostly beer, crackers, and cheese, if that helps you."

"Beer? This is getting more and more interesting. Let me know as soon as the tox report and the lab work come back, okay?"

"Will do."

Joe had no more than hung up when Sam stepped to his desk. He was holding a report from ballistics.

"Ballistics matched the slug the Evidence Techs dug out of the wall to the Colt Cobra found at the scene. Seventy percent match. It was the gun that fired the round that killed Devon Schmidt," said Sam.

"Not surprised," noted Joe.

"And…the round was also a match to the round that killed Daniel Silverman."

Joe paused and looked at Sam. "You're kidding."

Sam handed Joe the report. "It's all right here in black and white."

"Wow. I hope ATF can trace its ownership."

"Bet you a beer it's a purchase from a gun show."

"I say it's stolen."

"I'm not sayin' it's not stolen. I'm sayin' it originated from a gun show."

"Okay. I'll take that bet," said Joe.

When 2:30 rolled around, Joe and Sam drove to the 17th Police District to await Roselyn Bertrand. They spoke to the duty sergeant about their investigation and their need to use a secure interview room. He obliged and they waited for Roselyn to arrive.

A few minutes after 3:30, there was a knock on the door, and an officer told them Roselyn Bertrand had arrived. Joe told him to show her in. Roselyn

Bertrand was a wispy, ash-blonde about five-seven. She appeared self-confident as she entered the room. The one thing Joe noticed immediately was she wore lipstick. A shade of red lipstick.

"Thank you for coming in," said Joe. "I'm Detective Joe Erickson and this is my partner, Detective Sam Renaldo."

"Pleased to meet you," she replied, and she followed up by shaking their hands.

"Please have a seat."

"Is this being recorded?"

"No, and there's no one else watching or listening. This is a secure room."

"Good. Then I can speak freely?"

"You may," replied Sam.

Joe got straight to the point. "While we were investigating the death of Devon Schmidt, your fingerprints turned up on a wineglass in his apartment. When did you last see him?"

"Early Sunday evening. I left about eight-thirty."

"And what's your relationship with Devon Schmidt?"

"We have an arrangement."

"An arrangement?" asked Sam.

"Yes. An arrangement."

"Would you care to explain?" asked Joe.

Without so much as a blink, she said, "I have sex with him twice a month."

"So...are you his girlfriend?" asked Sam.

"No. He pays me to have sex with him twice a month. It's an arrangement. He's nice to me, always has my favorite wine there, and we have a drink before and after. We talk a little and have a few laughs and I leave. That's the way he wants it. That's the way I like it."

"And did you have sex with him the night he was killed?"

"I did. Because of his injured knee, he wanted me to perform oral sex, so that's what I did. Two hundred dollars for about two minutes. Good money, what can I say? And yes, a condom was used. Does that answer your question?" she asked in a most matter-of-fact way.

"And do you do this with other clients?" asked Sam.

"One. He's a disabled Iraqi War vet. Got his legs blown off by an IED. He says I'm all he's got to look forward to. Nice guy, and he appreciates me very much." She looked to Sam, then Joe. "Call me a whore if you want, but I don't do married men and I'm not into kinky stuff. The money pays the tuition for my online bachelor's degree program. You don't make much being a teacher's aide."

"I'm not judging you," said Joe.

"I'd lose my job if this ever got out," she said.

"This is confidential," Sam assured her. "This information is for our investigation, not for the media."

"So, you wouldn't mind emailing me a copy of your grades from your online university, right?" asked Joe.

"You don't believe me?"

"You ever heard the phrase 'trust but verify'?" asked Joe.

"Yeah. Okay, I can do that."

"What was Devon's state of mind that night?" asked Joe.

"No different than it usually was. Look, I knew what he was, and I don't approve, but he was always nice to me and treated me with kindness. That's all that mattered."

"So, he didn't appear suicidal to you?"

"Are you crazy? Him? No way. You think he committed suicide? He made another appointment with me in two weeks."

"That's what it's looking like," said Sam.

"I don't believe it. Why would he make another appointment with me if he was going to commit suicide? That makes no sense."

"Do you own a gun?" asked Joe.

"Why? Is that how he died?"

"Gunshot wound."

"I can't believe it."

"You haven't answered the question. Do you own a gun?"

"Yes. For protection."

"What is it?"

"A Ruger LCP II."

"You have a conceal-carry permit?"

"No, I don't carry it. It's for protection in my apartment. Why do you need to know?"

"This is a murder investigation. We have to ask questions of people who were connected with the deceased," explained Joe. "And you are one of them."

"We have to get to the bottom of this. If it wasn't suicide, then we have to determine what happened and who was responsible," explained Sam."

"Okay. I get it."

"Did he say anything about someone coming to see him later that evening?" asked Joe.

"No."

"How long did you stay?"

"About an hour or so. Like I said, I left around eight-thirty."

"Did you eat anything while you were there?"

"He had some cheese and crackers on a plate. He always had that for me along with the wine. Smoked gouda," she said with a sad smile."

"And he drank wine with you?"

"A little. He always said he was a beer man, but he'd drink a glass of wine with me." She paused. "I think he really liked me you know. To look at him, you wouldn't think he'd be a tender sort, but he was with me."

"Since Schmidt had a mobility problem and used crutches, did he leave his door unlocked for you?" asked Joe.

"Yeah, he did."

"And did you lock up when you left?"

"No."

"Did he follow you to the door and lock it when you left?" asked Sam.

"No, he didn't get up. He could have later, I suppose."

Joe looked at Sam as if to ask if he had any more questions. Sam shook his head and then Joe said, "If we have additional questions, what's the best way to contact you?" She provided them with her contact information and asked if they would avoid calling her school since their calls would raise eyebrows.

With her slender figure and ash blonde hair, Roselyn reminded Joe of seventeen-year-old Jamie Chambers, and what she could have looked like if she'd lived until her thirtieth birthday. Unfortunately, she was the last of serial killer David Eugene Burton's victims, and the girl Joe was unable to save. His mind flashed back to that evening when he entered the dark alley to capture Burton and rescue Jamie only to see Burton hunched over her body with a knife. He recalled the look on Burton's face as he—

"Joe!" said Sam, jolting him out of his flashback.

"Yeah," Joe reacted, snapping back to the present.

"You okay?"

"Yeah," he smiled, tossing it off. "Just thinking."

As they left the secure interview room and stepped into the hall, Joe said to Roselyn, "If you try to pick up another client, be careful. There's a lot of crazies out there, and I'd hate to see you get hurt...or worse." He gave her his card. "You can call me if you need to."

"I appreciate your concern," she replied. Then she leaned into him and said, "You can call me if you need to."

Joe looked at her not knowing if she was serious or kidding. "No need," he said. She gave a shrug and walked out the door. *Now that takes balls*, he thought.

Joe and Sam left the police station and drove back to Area 3 headquarters. Joe was waiting for a red light to change when Sam looked over and asked, "What were you thinking back there? You were in la-la land."

Joe didn't want Sam to know the truth, so he lied. "I was...thinking how I'm going to write up this interview in my notes."

"Yeah? So, how are you?"

"No sense revealing anything that could come back to haunt her in the future. She visited Devon Schmidt, they had sex, and she went home. End of story. Whatever else she admitted to is irrelevant to the case." He looked over at Sam.

Sam nodded. "I'm good with that. So, you ruling her out as the killer?"

"For the time being."

Chapter Fourteen

When Joe met with Dr. Lemke, he described how seeing Roselyn Bertrand triggered a flashback to the alley with serial killer, David Eugene Burton, and his victim, Jamie Chambers. He was sleeping much better lately, and his nightmares less frequent and less frightening. Dr. Lemke asked if the flashback caused a nightmare the following evening, and Joe said it did not.

"That's good. That means the imagery rehearsal therapy you received with Dr. Bunsch proved to be an effective treatment for you."

She went on to explain that certain things including sights can trigger such a flashback. And since Roselyn closely resembled Jamie, that alone could have been enough to bring forth that memory.

"How long did the flashback last?" asked Dr. Lemke.

"Only a few seconds. I snapped out of it when my partner said something to me," replied Joe.

"Have you had any more of these recently?"

"None. Just this one time."

"Have you been under more stress recently?"

"No more than usual."

"I think this may simply be an isolated incident. But if these flashbacks continue or your nightmares reoccur, you need to let me know."

After work, Joe called Destiny. He hoped she was home, but his call went to voice mail, so he left a message for her to call him.

Removing his Glock, he placed it in its drawer, removed his sport coat, and got a wine glass from the cupboard. Filling it with what was left from a bottle of Pinot Noir, Joe moved to the living room and sat down in his recliner, a ritual he performed nearly every evening after arriving home from work and before preparing dinner. But tonight, he didn't feel like cooking. His mind was still preoccupied with work and the flashback he had earlier. He hoped Destiny could help him let go of it.

He had just taken his first sip of wine when Destiny returned his call.

"Hi."

"Hi. Sorry, I couldn't pick up. I was talking to Mom."

"She okay?"

"Yeah. She had a little skin cancer lesion removed from her forehead today. Basal cell carcinoma. Not a melanoma, thankfully. Too much sun worshipping when she was young."

"How's she doing?"

"Fine, she's annoyed she may have a scar. At sixty-two, she's still vain about her appearance."

"The next time you call her, tell her I think women with scars are sexy."

"I don't think she'd appreciate that."

"Then, give her my best."

"I will."

"I called to see if you wanted to go out for dinner, but maybe tonight's not a good night, huh?"

"No, maybe some other time. But you could come over and we could get something delivered."

"Sounds good," Joe said. "When?"

"Anytime. I've got a bottle of that new wine you liked."

"Great. See you in a few." Joe put his unfinished glass of wine aside knowing Destiny would have a glass ready for him when he got there.

Sure enough, Destiny had wine ready for him when he came in. She asked how the investigation was going. He ran all the details past her, and she said, "It sounds like your original investigation into Daniel Silverman's death is stalled."

"It is," Joe said. "And I have to get back to that. Devon Schmidt's death has become an obstacle."

"You remember the fork in the road? You've taken the twisting path because, despite its obstacles and distractions, it will ultimately lead you in the right direction. Sounds like it's led you to yet another fork in the road."

"Yeah." He paused and took a sip of his wine. "Not to change the subject or anything, but I had a strange experience today as we were winding down an interview with Schmidt's friend with benefits."

"Strange in what way?"

"As she was preparing to leave, I looked at her, and she reminded me of an older version of Jamie Chambers, and I had a flashback to that night in the alley. Sam made mention of the fact I was in 'la-la land' for a few seconds. I haven't had that recurrence for months. It's weird that a passing resemblance could trigger that."

"That is weird. Maybe you should mention it to Dr. Lemke the next time you have a session."

"I already did when I saw her today. She asked if I was under a lot of stress, and I told her I wasn't. After discussing it, she thought it might be an isolated incident. But if it happens again, she wants to know about it."

"Those distractions could be dangerous in certain situations."

"I know. It concerns me. What if it causes me to freeze up at a critical moment with an offender?"

"I wouldn't worry about it unless it continues to happen. Besides, when your adrenaline is flowing, I think it would repress any flashbacks."

"Something I need to ask Dr. Lemke."

"I haven't noticed that nightmares have been waking you up."

"Only once in a while. I'm sleeping a lot better now."

"That's good. Hopefully, it's an isolated incident, like she said."

"Yeah." Joe took another sip of wine as he contemplated his vulnerability. Destiny knew she needed to get his mind off of it, so she changed the subject.

"What sounds good for dinner?"

* * *

Early the next morning, Joe left Destiny's apartment and drove to his place where he changed clothes and continued on to work. He met Cardona in the parking lot as he was walking in.

"How's your case going?" she asked.

"It's going," said Joe.

"Have you read the Trib?

"No. Why?"

"You victim's father is making some noise."

"Wonderful."

Joe logged into his computer and discovered a message regarding his case. The Colt Cobra used to kill Devon Schmidt had been stolen during a burglary from an Indiana gun dealer three years ago and was used in a homicide two years ago. It was a gang-related shooting on the Southside, and the mook charged with the murder, a habitual offender, was convicted and is spending twenty to life in the Pontiac Correctional Center. The gun went missing from a police evidence locker last year.

Great, thought Joe. *There's no way to tie it to anyone. No way to say Schmidt didn't buy it off someone on the street and use it on himself.*

With the Schmidt case at a standstill until the tox screen and lab reports come back, he needed to refocus on Daniel Silverman's murder. Looking through his notes, he felt his next step was to interview Cindy Fielding and follow up on Gwen Stolz's report about seeing her kissing Daniel Silverman inside a car outside the food bank. He looked up her contact information, and at 9:00 am, gave Cindy a call. Thankfully, she didn't lawyer up but agreed to come in for a meeting at Area 3 Headquarters the next day at 10:00 am.

In the meantime, he met with Sam and they both agreed that something didn't feel right about Daniel's attendance at a party aboard Fieldings' yacht and his murder two days afterwards.

"My gut's telling me there's a connection between Daniel's murder and Fielding Enterprises," said Joe.

"It's a big corporation. They could have their fingers in all sorts of stuff and hide it in their databases," agreed Sam. "You think Daniel might have accidentally stumbled on to something?"

"Maybe. Or if he was having an affair with Jay Fielding's wife, that could be a powerful motive for murder."

"You think Gwen Stoltz was telling the truth?" asked Sam.

"She seemed credible. I don't know what reason she'd have to lie about it. But the thing is, neither Gwen nor Renata said they noticed any of those non-verbals typically expressed by lovers while they're working together. That's odd."

"Maybe they just agreed to cool it while they worked here."

"Maybe, but I'd think that would be hard." Joe paused. "The eye contact, smiles, nudges. Oh, it's possible, I suppose. Maybe we'll find out tomorrow when she comes in for an interview."

"We need to interview Jay Fielding and Robert Curtis. And I think we should get hold of their staff, too. One on one. See if there's someone working in their offices who might be willing to spill some information."

"Good idea. Let's start with Fielding."

Joe said, "Before we do, let me do a workup on him and see if anything interesting turns up."

"Okay. While you're doing Fielding, I'll research Curtis," said Sam.

Both got busy. Jay Fielding was thirty-eight years old, born in Chicago to Thomas Lanier Fielding and Anne Georgina Smythe Fielding, deceased. He graduated from one of Chicago's top Catholic high schools, Saints Peter and Paul Academy in—*Wait a minute. That school rings a bell,* Joe thought. He began wracking his brain, then it hit him. *Omigod! Devon Schmidt graduated from that same high school.* He pulled up Devon Schmidt's records and found that both Schmidt and Fielding graduated the same year. Not only that, Schmidt worked in Fielding Enterprise's Chicago terminal.

Moving on, Joe found that Jay Fielding graduated from Loyola University majoring in business administration. Next, he searched for high school yearbooks on Ancestry.com, and found Saints Peter and Paul Academy yearbooks were listed. He entered a search for Jay Fielding, and after narrowing the search parameters, several photographs appeared. One of them showed the track team his senior year. Not only was Jay Fielding pictured, but so was Devon Schmidt. Even though it was twenty years ago, he could tell it was Schmidt. They weren't standing together, but they had to have known each other given they were on the same forty-member team. He printed the photograph.

Joe pulled the photo from the printer and walked to Sam's desk. Handing the sheet to Sam, Joe said, "Take a look at this. From Saints Peter and Paul Academy twenty years ago."

Sam looked over it, and when he saw Devon Schmidt's name, he said, "Wow!"

"Not only that," added Joe, "He was working for them in their warehouse terminal." You suppose Jay Fielding knew his old high school classmate was one of his employees?"

"Interesting. I wonder what he'll have to say about that."

"Anything on Robert Curtis?"

"Nothing of interest yet."

Joe returned to his desk and continued his research. Jay Fielding's mother, Anne Fielding, died of ALS six years ago. He was married to Jeanne Marie Mason for four years but that ended in divorce when he was twenty-nine. He married his present wife, Cynthia Mae Cooper, ten years his junior, five years ago. Prior to his nine-year stint as Vice-President of Fielding Enterprises, he held various managerial positions within the company. His address places him in one of the condos in the Gold Coast area overlooking Lake Michigan.

He owns a Mercedes, an Audi, and a Range Rover. He has no arrests but has accrued two citations for speeding in the last three years. He holds a passport and has traveled extensively to countries in Europe, Central America, and Africa.

Joe checked his name in the FOID system, and it appeared. Nothing really stood out about Fielding except his connection to Devon Schmidt, and that could be coincidence. But like most cops, Joe didn't believe in coincidences.

By noon, both Joe and Sam completed their research and felt ready to tackle their first interview—Jay Fielding. They drove to the Fielding Headquarters and walked to the receptionist's desk where they recognized Astrid Nielson from their previous visit. She rose as they approached her desk.

"Ah, detectives," she smiled. "You're back. What can I do for you today?"

"We'd like to see Jay Fielding, please," said Joe.

CHAPTER FOURTEEN

"Do you have an appointment?"

"No," Joe smiled back. "The police don't make appointments."

"Oh, I see. Well, let me check if he's available." She pressed buttons on her phone and a moment later she said, "Two detectives are asking to see you, Mr. Fielding." She listened to him for a few moments, then hung up.

"He can spare a couple minutes. He's getting ready to fly out of town, so his time is limited. If you'll follow me, please."

She took them down a series of hallways to an office with a double door. She knocked and a voice from inside said, "Come in."

She opened the door to an opulent office space decorated with antiques. Joe and Sam held up their IDs and introduced themselves. Jay Fielding, who rounded his desk, shook their hands, his confident manner matching his good looks.

"I'm sorry, I'm in a bit of a rush today. I have to catch a plane this afternoon, and I don't have a lot of time. But, please, have seat."

Joe and Sam took the two wingback leather chairs in front of his large antique partners desk.

"What can I help you with, detectives?" he asked as he sat in his chair.

"We're investigating the death of one of your interns, Daniel Silverman," said Joe.

"I heard about that," replied Fielding. "Tragic. From what I was told, he was a talented and likable young man. I had met him just a couple of days before he was killed."

"We're also investigating Devon Schmidt as a person of interest in the case. Do you know Devon Schmidt?"

"Not that I know of."

"Maybe this will jog your memory," said Joe, pulling out the picture of the high school track team with Fielding's and Schmidt's names highlighted below the picture. He handed it to Fielding who looked at it.

"Oh, my god..." he said slowly. "Devon the demon," he smiled. "Yeah. I remember him now. Not the sharpest knife in the drawer but one hell of a discus thrower." He handed the picture back to Joe. "He's a person of interest?"

85

"He was," said Sam. "It appears he committed suicide a couple of days ago."

"You don't say," responded Fielding, looking up at Sam. "Well...so, what does a twenty-year-old picture have to do with me?"

"He also worked for you. In your Chicago terminal," said Joe. "Are you aware of that?"

"No, as a matter of fact, I'm not. We employ thousands of people all over the country. I don't have any direct connection with human resources so I wouldn't have any knowledge of our lower-level personnel."

"I see. So, he's never contacted you?" asked Joe.

"No."

"And you've never contacted him?"

"Of course not."

Fielding looked at his Rolex and said, "Look gentlemen, I really do have a plane to catch." He stood, picked up his briefcase, and began walking around his desk. Joe and Sam stood as well. "If you have any more questions, you can contact my attorney. He knows me as well as I know myself. My secretary next door can give you his phone number. Now, if you'll excuse me."

All three left the office, and Fielding pointed to the door down the hall. "My secretary is right through that door." Then he turned and walked briskly down the hall.

Joe and Sam entered the office of his secretary. Several people worked away at desks in the room, and they had to ask where to find "Mr. Fielding's secretary." They were directed to the door on the left with the nameplate "Lenore Pritchard." Sam knocked and the door swung open revealing a severe-looking woman who Joe thought had a passing resemblance to Cloris Leachman in *Young Frankenstein*. After introductions and an explanation, her cold reception warmed, and she provided them with contact information for Fielding's attorney. Jay Fielding was represented by Wendell DeForrest, of DeForrest, Brown, and Whittier.

Joe thanked her for her time and gave her a hint of a smile. He thought he detected a little sparkle in her eyes when she said, "You're welcome."

Once in the hall, Sam confided, "One of the most powerful law firms in the city."

"Yeah, and represented by its senior partner no less," added Joe.

Joe made the call to the law office and spoke to the receptionist who forwarded his call to DeForrest's secretary. After explaining Jay Fielding's referral, she checked her boss's schedule and said he could spare fifteen minutes in half an hour. Joe agreed to the time slot since the law office was also in the Loop. Joe and Sam decided to walk from East Randolph since it wasn't that far, and it was a nice day.

The office of DeForrest, Brown, and Whittier was on the thirty-fourth floor of a fifty-story building on North Wabash that overlooked the Chicago River. As they got off the elevator, they entered Suite 3400 and were greeted by an attractive, middle-aged receptionist. The name plaque on her desk read "Audrey Taylor." Joe told her they had an appointment with Mr. DeForrest, and she made a short call. Afterwards, she asked them to have a seat.

No more than a minute later, a woman dressed in a gray business suit approached them and asked, "Detectives Erickson and Renaldo?"

Standing, Joe and Sam answered, "Yes."

"I'm Fiona, Mr. DeForrest's assistant. He'll see you now." She turned and they followed her past several offices to a large suite. She gave a knock on the door, opened it, and said, "Two detectives to see you, Mr. DeForrest."

"Send them in," replied a deep baritone voice.

DeForrest was standing in the middle of the room. He was a thickset man in his mid-sixties and greeted them in a folksy manner.

"Come in, come in," he said.

Joe and Sam went for their IDs, and he said, "You don't need to show me your badges. I know who you are, Detective Erickson, Detective Renaldo."

"You do?" asked Joe.

"I remember you from the serial killer case a year or so ago. Your name and face were splashed all over the news. So, I figured your partner here must be Detective Renaldo."

"That's very astute of you," said Sam.

He strode up to them and shook their hands. "So, my client lawyered up, did he?" asked DeForrest.

"I guess he did," said Sam. "He had to catch a plane and referred us to you.

Said you know him as well as he knows himself."

"I don't know about that," he chuckled. "Sit down, fellas."

They sat in sumptuous leather chairs in front of his desk and went through what they asked Fielding and the answers he gave.

"When we were talking with him, he seemed a little frazzled. Under pressure. What's his job at Fielding Enterprises?"

"Well, he's spread pretty thin so it's understandable that he may come across that way. His father is the President and CEO of the company." DeForrest leaned forward. "Now, this is not for public consumption mind you, but Thomas Fielding is at an age where he wants to step back from the responsibilities of running the company. He suffered a mild stroke about a year ago. Since then, he's been grooming Jay to assume his position. He'll eventually take his father's place as President and CEO. This will allow Thomas to devote more time to his wife and his family's charitable interests."

"I thought Mr. Fielding's wife was deceased."

"His first wife, Anne. Yes. But after being a widower for a number of years, he met someone and got married again. Jacqueline. Lovely person."

"I see," said Joe. "So, Jay's traveling and overseeing the operations?"

"Fielding Enterprises is a multi-billion-dollar company. Its trucks run all over North America, and there are centers in the United States, Mexico, and Canada. It's a huge operation, and Jay's previous job was to troubleshoot for all its centers. Now, in addition to that, running the entire company is falling on his shoulders," explained DeForrest. "He'll soon find out he needs to delegate more."

"I understand. Thank you for the explanation," said Sam.

"We're investigating the death of Daniel Silverman, and he was interning at FieldingEnterprises when he was killed," said Joe. "Devon Schmidt was a person of interest."

"Daniel Silverman. I know about that," noted DeForrest. "The legal community in this city's not that large. I've had some dealings with his father's firm over the years. Quite respectable. I have kids of my own...I can't imagine what they must be going through. A father's worst nightmare." He looked at his watch. "Is there anything else I can help you with, detectives?"

"Do we deal with you from now on if we have questions? I mean, was this an official 'see my lawyer from now on' request?" asked Sam.

"Sounds like it," said DeForrest. "It's not because he's done anything wrong, you understand. It's because he has so much on his plate right now."

"Thank you for your time, Mr. DeForrest.

"Call me, Wendell. And if you need to contact me, I don't see clients after three."

"So, you just squeezed us in today, so to speak?" asked Joe.

"Before my nap," he chuckled.

"All right. If you're Wendell, then I'm Joe and he's Sam."

"I want you to know I like the police. I have no problem with law and order because I don't represent criminals."

As they rode down the elevator, Sam said, "I never expected a senior partner to be like him."

"Don't kid yourself. Behind that folksy exterior is a brilliant mind. He wants people to take him for granted."

"A crafty old fox."

"You better believe it."

Chapter Fifteen

Cindy Fielding arrived at Area 3 Headquarters ten minutes before her ten o'clock appointment. Joe and Sam met the petite strawberry blonde at the door and introductions were made. Her handshake was firm, and her green eyes and facial features gave her a pleasant countenance. Joe couldn't help but notice the more extensive makeup on her left cheekbone. She followed them to an interview room Joe arranged for their meeting.

"Have a seat," said Joe.

"Sure. I assume you have questions about Daniel Silverman, right?" Cindy replied as she pulled out her chair and sat down.

"That's correct," said Joe. "We're interviewing everyone who knew and worked with Daniel."

"I see."

"You volunteered at a food bank with him. How long had you been doing that?" asked Joe.

"About a year."

"And how did you first become involved with the food bank?"

"It was through the university," explained Cindy. "We're both graduate students in the business department, although we have different majors. Mine's finance, his was supply chain management, so we never actually had classes together. We met at a university function. He was already volunteering at the food bank, and he told me I should donate some of my time and help out. He said they always needed volunteers, so...I volunteered."

"Was your husband all right with that?" asked Sam.

"He's not against assisting the needy, Detective. He donates money, I donate time. A few hours a week isn't going to make any difference to him given how little time he spends at home. His work schedule is very demanding."

"Do you always work the same hours, the same days?" asked Joe.

"Usually. I take classes at the university, so I have to schedule around them and my time at the library," she said.

"Did you always work the same hours as Daniel?" asked Sam.

"Not always. But our hours often coincided since his classes ended for the day about the same time mine did. It was fun working with him. He had a wonderful sense of humor, and it made the time go fast."

Did you and Daniel ever go out after you finished at the food bank? Out for a drink or anything like that?" asked Joe.

"No, we never went out. Not with classes the next day. We said goodbye and went our separate ways."

Joe's next question needed to bring up Gwen Stoltz's observation, and he was interested to see how Cindy would respond to it.

"There was a report that one time after work, Daniel picked you up in a black car. And when you got in, you and Daniel leaned over and kissed each other before driving away," stated Joe. "Any truth to that?"

Cindy quickly shifted from surprised to indignant. "None. My husband drives a black car, and whoever reported that probably saw me get picked up by my husband. It was not Daniel!"

"So, you categorically deny you and Daniel were having an affair," stated Joe.

"Absolutely. God! We were just friends. And I'll take a lie detector test to prove it." She paused. "I'd sure like to know who said that," she said, her face flushing red with anger.

"How do you normally get to the food bank?" Sam asked.

"What?"

"How do you normally get to the food bank?" Sam repeated.

"Sorry. That last question—ugh…To answer your question, sometimes I drive my own car —"

"Which is?" asked Sam.

"An Audi. And sometimes I'd ride with Daniel if we worked the same hours. Or sometimes I'd get an Uber. Usually, I drove."

"If your husband picks you up, what car does he drive?" asked Joe.

"Sometimes he drives his Mercedes, sometimes my Audi, sometimes his Land Rover. It just depends on his mood."

"And what color are they?" asked Sam.

"They're all black. His favorite color. When we bought the Audi, he told me I could pick out any color I wanted as long as it was black. But he did manage to let me choose the interior color."

"Very generous," quipped Joe.

"You have no idea."

"Did you know Daniel prior to attending graduate school?" asked Sam.

"No."

"You attended different high schools?"

"Different schools in different cities. Our families didn't know one another until we got married. My father doesn't like the Fieldings much."

"Why's that?"

"The Fieldings come from a long line of ultra-conservatives. Not fond of anyone who "isn't like them," if you know what I mean. You've heard of trickle-down economics? The Fieldings have trickle-down values."

"I take it you don't share their values," probed Joe.

"I don't. I was raised to be tolerant of others. But I just grin and bear it, so to speak. Something I have to overlook to be part of the family."

"How easy is that?"

"Sometimes it can be infuriating, but…Look, Detective. I signed a prenup. If there's a divorce, I get nothing. So…."

"Is that the reason you're in graduate school?"

"Partly. In the back of my mind, if it's ever necessary for me to bail, I won't be left destitute with no career options. But that's not the only reason. I like business and I want to work outside the home. Being stay-at-home arm candy is bullshit."

Joe paused to take it all in. Then Sam cleared his throat and said, "I'd like to pursue another line of questioning, if you don't mind. Where were you on the night of June 14th?"

"Uh...let me see." She pulled out her phone and checked her calendar. "On June 14th, I was having dinner with my parents in Elgin."

"We'll need their names and a phone number."

Cindy sighed and provided Sam with their contact information. "I suppose you're going to call them?"

"What about June 21st?" asked Joe. He wanted to know if she had an alibi for the night of Devon Schmidt's death.

Again, she consulted her phone. "Sorry, I...let's see...that was a week ago, Monday. I was at the library late because I had a paper due for a class the next day."

"Can anyone verify that?"

"I don't know. I was in a study carrel most of the evening. I'm sure the library has video surveillance you could get showing me coming and going."

"Sorry for the inconvenience," said Joe. "But we have to turn over every stone if we're going to find out who killed Daniel. Do you know where your husband was either of those nights?"

"No idea. You'll have to ask him."

"Just one more question."

"Yes?"

"What happened to your cheek?"

Cindy was not expecting that question, but she seemed clearly prepared to answer it. "Oh, that," she chuckled. "I was playing racquetball at the gym and took one in the face. You should have seen it three days ago."

"You have time for racquetball with everything else you have going on?" asked Joe.

"One has to stay in shape, Detective. What do you do to stay in shape?"

"As a matter of fact, I jog every morning."

She looked at Sam who replied, "I lift 12 ounces several times a day."

"Well, we all have our methods, don't we?" she smiled.

Joe and Sam asked a few more questions, then ended the interview, thanking her for her time and leading her to the door. Before stepping into the bright sun of the parking lot, she turned and said, "Daniel was a wonderful friend, and I'll miss him. If there's anything else I can do to help find his killer, please let me know."

"We may take you up on that," replied Joe. "We appreciate you coming in."

After she left, Sam turned to Joe and asked, "What do you think?"

"I'd say she's lying about that racquetball smacking her in the face."

"Yeah. More like someone's hand."

When Sam got back to his desk, he called the number Cindy Fielding provided for her parents. Her mother answered the phone, and after an explanation for the call, she confirmed her daughter came to Elgin the afternoon of June 14th, and they had dinner that evening at a steak house in town. Cindy stayed overnight and drove back to Chicago the next morning.

Sam informed Joe about his conversation with Cindy Fielding's mother and how she confirmed her alibi. As they were talking, Joe's phone rang. It was Gayle Crain calling from ballistics.

"I got some information for you on the gun recovered from your crime scene," she said.

"You found something else?" asked Joe.

"I assume you got the report on the seventy percent match on the round extracted from the wall at the crime scene, right?"

"Right. We got that."

"Well, I examined the gun. The barrel's been threaded for a silencer. When I put it under a microscope, I found faint striations on the end of the barrel. These striations are recent and consistent with screwing on a silencer. Now, I can't say the silencer was present on the gun when it fired the fatal round. It could have been used previously at some point. All I can tell you is the markings are present and recent."

"That could explain a lot, Gayle. Thank you. Could you send that over in a report?"

"Already on its way, Joe."

Sam was still standing by Joe's desk, knowing that a call from ballistics would probably provide important information. As Joe hung up the phone, he looked up at Sam and told him about the striations Gayle found.

"No wonder nobody heard a gunshot from Schmidt's apartment," said Sam. He held out his hand and finger like a gun and said, "Thup. Bullet to the head. Little noise."

"Neat and clean."

"But why didn't Schmidt notice and put up some kind of a fight? Not easy to conceal a gun with a silencer."

"Good question."

"Think he was drunk and passed out?"

"He didn't seem the type to drink that much. Maybe the tox report will tell us something."

"You think Roselyn Bertrand could have slipped him something?"

"So, he'd be unconscious for the shooter?"

"Yeah."

"It's possible, but she didn't strike me as someone who'd set him up. Besides, she'd lose one of her sources of income."

"Unless she got paid to do it."

"My gut tells me she's not part of it. I think Schmidt let someone in that he knew. And whoever that person was, took him out for whatever reason."

"Because he killed Daniel?"

"Yeah. Or he knew who did."

Chapter Sixteen

Two days later, Joe stopped at Destiny's apartment after work. He rang and she buzzed him in. When she opened the door, she said, "This is a nice surprise," and she gave him a kiss. "Come on in. My mom's here."

Oh, shit! he thought. In all the time Joe had known Destiny, he never once met her mother. Was she keeping her secret or something? Destiny mentioned several times she had gone to visit her, but she never offered take him to Winnetka and introduce him. Well, now he would have to face her for the first time. *Oh, God, please don't let her be Faye Dunaway in Mommy Dearest*, Joe thought.

"Mom, Joe's here," she called.

No more than a few seconds later a woman stepped out of the kitchen. She smiled as she saw Joe, who marveled at her. She could have been Destiny's older sister if weren't for the gray in her hair.

Joe stepped to her and said, "We finally get to meet. I don't know why she's been hiding you from me."

"Because she was afraid I'd steal you from her," she laughed. "You never told me he was this good-looking." Joe could feel warmth rush through his face, and he hoped he didn't give off a blush. She hugged him and said, "It's good to meet you, finally. I've heard so much about you."

"All good, I hope."

"Mostly," she quipped. "Of course, all good."

"Would you like a glass of wine?" asked Destiny.

"Love one," replied Joe. *Thank you, God.*

"Mom?"

"Yes, please."

"Are you a wine drinker, Mrs. Alexander?"

"Before we go any further…If we're going to be on good terms, you'll have to call me Vivien. None of this Mrs. Alexander stuff."

"All right. Vivien," replied Joe. He caught a glimpse of a small band-aid on her forehead which she carefully camouflaged with a comb-over. *Must be the little skin surgery she had.*

"Yes, I allow myself one glass a day. Red only, because of the tannins. Good for your heart. My blood sugar is high normal. And I'll be damned if I'm going to be a type two diabetic like my parents. So, I watch my diet."

"Your daughter and I are health-conscious, too."

"So, I hear. I also hear you're a good cook."

"I work at it."

Destiny returned with two glasses of wine and handed them off to Joe and her mom. Then she returned carrying one for herself. "What shall we toast?" she asked.

"To meeting your beau, of course," said Vivien.

Destiny looked at Joe with a twinkle. "To your meeting my beau," she repeated. And they clinked glasses and took a drink. Joe felt a little uncomfortable with the toast but played along. *I guess I am her beau*, he thought. *Just never thought of it with that term.*

"Normally, I would have called. Had I known your mom was here, I wouldn't have bothered you. I don't like to intrude."

"I'm glad you decided to pop in," said Vivien.

"What was on your mind?" asked Destiny.

"It was something for work, and I thought maybe you'd like to take a stroll on the docks at Burnham Harbor and look at some of the yachts down there."

"Sounds like fun," said Vivien. "Why don't you two go ahead?"

"I was wondering if you knew anyone who happened to have a yacht parked down there. I didn't want to appear to be snooping on the one I'm interested in."

"The term is 'moored' and yes, I do," said Vivien.

"Mom…" said Destiny as if she was cautioning her not to get involved.

"Well, I do know a couple of people who have yachts docked on Lake Michigan, you know."

"You do?" asked Joe.

"I do," Vivien replied.

Joe was amazed at Vivien's knowledge. He looked at Destiny and she gave her head a shake and mouthed, "Later."

"Both the Dykstras and the Affannatos have yachts down there," she said. "It's been a while since I've visited either one, but I could make calls and find out the dock numbers and the slips where they're moored."

"I don't want to put you out," said Joe.

"Put me out? Get out of here. It's nothing." Vivien walked to her purse, got her cell phone, and entered the hallway leading to the bedrooms.

"How does she know this stuff?" Joe asked Destiny.

"I didn't tell you, because I didn't want you to judge me," she said.

"What do you mean, 'judge you'?"

Destiny hesitated and knew she would have to tell him. "My mother's rich. Her father was President of the Chicago and North Western Railway."

"Oh."

Destiny was surprised at Joe's ordinary, low-key response. "That's all you have to say is 'Oh'?"

"Okay, she's rich. That doesn't change you, does it?"

"I hope not."

"Well then. She is what she is," said Joe.

"You said you didn't like rich people."

Joe needed to clarify that comment as she had misinterpreted something he had said. No wonder she was leery about him meeting her mother. "I said I don't like investigating rich people for the simple fact they too often refer me to their attorneys. Too many of them think it's beneath them to speak to the police. Especially the ones who have something to hide. I don't mind being around rich people as long as they don't flaunt it and look down on those of us who aren't rich like they are."

"She's not like that. She's always worked despite not needing to. She retired early and now she does a lot of charity work."

"I wouldn't have guessed if she hadn't gotten involved. She seems pretty down to earth."

"She is."

As they stood in the kitchen finishing their wine, Vivien entered carrying her phone and a folded piece of notepaper. She handed the paper to Joe.

"That's the locations of the harbors and slips where the Dykema's and Affannatos' yachts are located. Hopefully, the one you're interested in isn't too far away."

"Much appreciated," said Joe as he glanced at the note, then placed it in his inside jacket pocket. The Dykema's yacht was docked in Belmont Harbor. That was no help. Fortunately, the Affannatos' yacht was docked in the same place as Fieldings'—Burnham Harbor. That was located on the Near South Side across from Soldier Field. As luck would have it, both were docked in the North Basin, the Affannatos' in Dock D and the Fieldings' in Dock C. According to the slip numbers, they were not that far apart.

Joe knew the traffic on Lake Shore Drive was going to be atrocious this time of day and suggested they wait until early evening to make their trip to Burnham Harbor to reconnoiter Fieldings' yacht.

"If that's the case, why don't we reserve a table and have an early bite to eat? What do you say, Mom?"

"You two go ahead," said Vivien.

"Oh, come on. Come with us," encouraged Joe. "Destiny picks out great restaurants."

"If you're sure I wouldn't be a third wheel."

"You won't."

Destiny made a reservation for a neighborhood bistro, and they decided to walk the three blocks to its location. After a delicious meal of a New York strip steak in a brandy peppercorn cream sauce, Joe was glad he could walk it off during their journey back to Destiny's apartment. They saw Vivien in then left for Burnham Harbor via Joe's Camaro.

The traffic was heavy, but it was moving without any delays, so they reached Burnham Harbor in a timely manner. After finding a parking place in the McCormick Place parking lot near the C and D docks, Joe and Destiny first found the Affannatos' yacht where Vivien said it would be. *The Water Nymph* was painted on the bow. The sixty-foot vessel had a main deck with a flybridge, something only the very wealthy could afford. As they were admiring the craft from the security gate, a woman walked out onto the bow and saw them. "Hi, there," she waved.

"Hi," Destiny replied.

"Are you Vivien's daughter?"

Joe thought, *Oh, God. Here we go. Vivien must have said something.*

"Yes, I am."

"You look just like her. I'm Loretta Affannato. Why don't you come aboard for a few minutes?" And she walked down the dock to the security gate to let them through.

Destiny looked at Joe and saw he wasn't too pleased. "It'll only be for a few minutes. Promise."

"Okay, I'll play along."

She punched her code into the pad that opened the security gate and they followed her down to their slip and boarded *The Water Nymph*. Loretta led them onto the main deck and inside the salon. Joe had never been on a yacht before, and the amenities were overwhelming. Leather seating around the sides, large windows providing panoramic views, nicely appointed galley, and glass doors to seal out the weather. A person could live in luxury all year round.

"Let me show you around," said Loretta, and she gave them a tour of the yacht that included a look at the bedrooms and bathrooms. Even those had all the creature comforts.

Joe was curious about something, so he asked, "You don't happen to be related to a Bobby Affannato, do you?"

"He's my nephew. Why?"

"Just someone I ran into a couple of years ago. That's all." Joe didn't want to tell her he interviewed him after Bobby discovered his friend's body after he committed suicide.

"Why don't you go check out the flybridge," Loretta said to Joe.

Joe sensed she was getting rid of him to speak with Destiny privately, so he agreed and climbed up to the flybridge. It was complete with the same comfortable leather seating and tables, but what got his attention was the helm station. A person could pilot the boat from the flybridge as well as from the helm in the salon. Joe had to check it out. He sat down in the captain's chair. In front of him was a steering wheel much like a car along with an array of gauges on a dashboard. Placing his hands on the wheel, he felt its firmness and imagined the horsepower the engine must have.

Looking forward, he became aware of the great vantage point the pilot would have since he was positioned so high above the water. Scanning the slips before him, his eyes locked onto Fieldings' yacht two docks over. He could make out Jay Fielding as well as Robert Curtis. Curtis was lounging on the flybridge with a young woman dressed in a string bikini. They were having drinks and appeared to be enjoying themselves. Jay Fielding and a blonde woman, who was also clad in a bikini, disappeared into the main deck salon. Joe watched for a while but couldn't tell if any other people were on board.

"Joe?" called Destiny from below. "Are you ready to go?"

"Yeah." Once back on the main deck, Joe asked Loretta, "Do you ever take her out onto the lake?"

"Occasionally," said Loretta. "My husband likes to chill here more than sail in it. But we do take it out once in a while to enjoy the lake and to keep it seaworthy."

"That's a huge yacht a couple of slips over," remarked Joe, pointing.

"Oh, that eighty-footer? Yes, that belongs to the Fieldings."

"Wow. Does it go out much?"

"Oh yeah, they take it out at least once a week. Sometimes late in the evening when they're having parties."

"Parties, huh?"

"Well...it's none of my business what people do. Live and let live, I say."

"Of course," said Destiny. "Well, thank you so much for the tour."

"Yes. And thank you for letting me check things out. Very impressive," added Joe.

"You're most welcome. And you tell your mother to stop being a stranger!" Loretta chided with a chuckle.

"I'll do that."

"Nice meeting you, Loretta," said Joe.

"The pleasure was all mine. Now, you two enjoy your evening."

Joe and Destiny left the slip where *The Water Nymph* was docked and walked toward the dock where Fieldings' eighty-foot yacht was located. It was similar to the Affannatos' yacht, but twenty feet longer, and much more massive. Joe could make out *Field of Dreams* painted on the bow. *Hm*, he thought. *I guess that's appropriate.*

"Some party boat," said Joe, looking at Destiny.

"A six or seven-million-dollar party boat," she replied.

Joe turned to her. "You're kidding. Seven mil for something like that?"

"Uh-huh. And it wouldn't surprise me if they wrote at least part of it off as a company business expense."

"Yeah," replied Joe in disgust. "Must be nice."

"You need to get a closer look?"

"I doubt Fielding would open the security gate and let us through since he lawyered up."

"We could stand at the gate and act nonchalant. Watch the pelicans or something."

"No. When I was on the flybridge, I was able to get a good look at the Fieldings' yacht and the four people aboard. It's probably better they don't know I was here."

"Now what?"

"You have something in mind?"

"Let's go home and then we'll decide."

"Your place or mine?"

"Did you have to ask?"

Chapter Seventeen

As Joe jogged early the next morning, he thought about what he saw aboard Fieldings' yacht the evening before. The girl sitting next to Curtis bothered him, and he wondered why someone Curtis' age would be entertaining someone that young. She didn't look any older than twenty, if that. An attractive young girl aboard a seven-million-dollar yacht with a drink in her hand, and she was with a guy old enough to be her father. Curtis must have a penchant for young girls. There are plenty of gold diggers in this town willing to hang out with an older man rolling in money. And who was the blonde with Jay Fielding? She wasn't his wife, that's for sure. Maybe husband and wife were both having affairs.

Joe rolled into work, and as he was making notes, he questioned the dates Fieldings' yacht would have left the harbor. Shortly after 8:00, he called the Burnham Harbor office since he wasn't familiar with harbor rules and regulations. He asked if boats had to contact the harbor authorities if they were leaving or entering the harbor or if they were required to keep a log. The answer was "No." Boats are free to navigate in and out of the harbor at will. *Hm. No way to trace the dates and times the Fielding yacht left and how much time it spent away from the harbor.* But he understood. Keeping track of the movements of over 1100 boats docked in Burnham Harbor would be a daunting task.

Joe needed to know more about Jay Fielding. He thought about Fielding's clever excuse for not answering questions and deferring him to his attorney. Then it dawned on him. Who knows more about someone than his secretary? He thought about his encounter with "Frau Blücher," Fielding's secretary.

What the hell was her name? He looked in his notes and found it. "Lenore Pritchard." He wondered if she would volunteer any information or tell him to pound sand. It was worth a try. Instead of calling her, he decided to approach her in person when she got off work. He remembered the subtle sparkle in her eye when she looked at him before he left their initial meeting. Maybe there was a chance.

Joe guessed she worked regular hours, so shortly before quitting time, he placed himself outside the main door of the tower housing Fielding Enterprises on East Randolph and began watching for Lenore Pritchard. He didn't have to wait long. Ten minutes past five, Lenore Pritchard pushed through the doors. She was alone which made his attempt to contact her less awkward.

Joe began following her, hurrying to catch up. She was walking briskly, and when he was within a few feet, he said, "Ms. Pritchard?"

Lenore turned her head, made eye contact, then a brief moment later, Joe could see in her face she remembered him.

"Detective Joe Erickson," he said. "I wonder if I could have a few words."

She stopped and turned to him. "I'd rather we didn't talk here."

"Is there a place we can go?" asked Joe.

"I was going to a bar for a drink, actually. You drink, Detective?"

The subtext of her question was almost like a challenge, and Joe was a little surprised by her response. "Actually, I wouldn't mind a drink about now."

"Good. I know a place two blocks from here. Follow me." And she turned and began walking, apparently assuming Joe would follow.

She must have been thirsty because she walked at a good clip to a bar called, "GWilliquors." Joe didn't have time to strike up any casual chit-chat as they walked. He was doing his best to keep up with her. As they went inside, Lenore was greeted by the middle-aged bartender wearing a Greek fisherman's cap.

"Afternoon, Lenore," he said, a pleasant look washing across his face.

"Donnie," she replied. She looked at Joe and nodded toward a booth. They had no more than taken their seats when a waitress walked up.

"Hi, Lenore. Your usual?" she asked.

"A double Jim Beam Black on the rocks."

Jeez-Louise, thought Joe. *This woman is a serious drinker!*

"And for you, sir?"

"Guinness draft."

"Coming right up."

Joe's eyes met Lenore's. "Rough day?" he asked.

"Not really. Actually, it wasn't a bad day at all since the boss was out of town."

That brought a smile to Joe's face. "How long have you been Mr. Fielding's secretary?"

"Well, if you're referring to Thomas Fielding, twenty-one years. But in his absence, I've continued on as executive secretary to his son, Jay."

"I heard about Thomas Fielding's stroke from the company attorney. Have you seen him since he was taken ill?"

"No, unfortunately. No one has been allowed to see him. I asked if I could, but I was told he wasn't accepting visitors. Disappointing...but I guess he has his reasons."

"What kind of a boss was Thomas Fielding?"

"He was wonderful. Very respectful of his employees. I mean, right down to the custodians. Oh, he could be firm, and he demanded the best out of his staff. He didn't put up with loafing or incompetence. But he was the kind of man you wanted to please."

"Sounds like he was a great boss," said Joe. He was getting ready to ask her another question when the waitress brought their drinks.

"Thank you, Jerri," said Lenore, after she set the drink in front of her. She took a sip of her bourbon, and let it roll in her mouth before she swallowed. The look in her eyes was pure satisfaction. Then she looked at Joe and said, "You don't mind, do you?" as she reached back, unpinned her bun, and shook her hair loose.

"Ah, that's better," she breathed.

Joe smiled ever so slightly as he raised his pint of Guinness to his lips and took a drink. As he looked at her transformed appearance, Frau Blücher disappeared.

"I maintain a professional image at work, but I have to loosen up a bit when I get out of there. I let my hair down—literally."

"Understandable," said Joe. "We all feel a little that way." He paused and then asked, "So…what's Jay Fielding like to work for?"

"This is all off the record, right? I mean, I wouldn't want to get into hot water over this. Him being my boss and all."

"This is all between you and me," said Joe. "I'll keep it out of my notes."

"Okay." Lenore took a substantial sip of her whiskey as if it was liquid courage. Then she put down her glass and began. "He's the antithesis of his father. Self-absorbed, rude to his employees, disrespects me and other office staff, and I can't prove it, but I think he may have a gambling problem."

"Oh? What makes you say that?"

"He travels a lot for the company since he's the one who oversees all the regional centers. He flies via the company jet, but I see his expense account and there's a lot of hotel stays in Vegas. At least once a month. We have no regional office or center in Vegas."

"Could he be embezzling company money to pay his gambling debts?"

"No, I don't think he would do that. The auditors would catch any shortfalls and he'd be found out."

"Maybe he wins or wins enough to break even."

"Maybe he does. But he sure comes back in a foul mood sometimes."

Lenore polished off her double and raised her hand to attract the waitress to get her a refill. She caught Jerri's eye who nodded and looked at Joe. He shook his head. His pint was still half full.

"Do you know anything about Robert Curtis?" asked Joe.

"Head of Logistics Management. I don't deal with him directly. Sleazy from what I've heard. They say he and Jay are thick as thieves."

"Interesting you put it that way. How's the rumor mill at Fielding Enterprises?"

"About average, I suppose. You hear things."

"You ever been on the yacht?"

"Not recently. A few years ago, when Mr. Fielding was active, he would occasionally take employees out for a cruise on Lake Michigan. As a way of saying thanks to people for a job well done. But since his wife died, he stopped doing that. She was a wonderful hostess."

"He got remarried some time ago, didn't he?"

"He did."

"What's his new wife like?"

"I've never met her. Quite attractive, though." Joe looked at her, not quite understanding her contradiction. She noticed and clarified. "He kept her picture on his desk."

Jerri brought her another double and took away her empty. Lenore raised her glass, breathed in the bourbon's essence. After a sip, she looked at Joe and said, "I really miss Mr. Fielding."

Joe worked away on his pint as he probed Lenore for answers to questions about Jay Fielding. She didn't know much about his personal life, his relationship with his wife, or his past divorce. Since she worked for his father, she was more familiar with him and his late wife.

After Lenore downed her second double, she said, "Time for me to move on home, Detective. I only allow myself two."

"Actually, it's four since they were doubles," Joe kidded.

"You call it four, I call it two. To-mato, to-mahto. In any case, I hope I haven't wasted your time."

"On the contrary. Thank you for being so candid. I thought maybe you'd tell me to talk to Mr. DeForrest like everyone else."

"No. If this involved his father, I would've told you that. But Junior hasn't earned my silence. You care to know anything else, you can usually find me here de-stressing after work."

They both got up and Joe paid the tab. He hailed a cab for her, then Lenore was on her way home. As it turned out, she was nothing like Frau Blücher at all.

Chapter Eighteen

The next day was a Friday, July 2nd, the beginning of the Independence Day weekend. Things were about to get crazy. They always did on holidays. At mid-morning, Joe received a text from Kendra. "Tox report back. Call me." He had been anxious for the report, so he called her right away.

"So, what did the tox screen reveal?" asked Joe.

"Well…Devon Schmidt had three times the normal amount of diphenhydramine in his blood."

"Diphenhy-what?" asked Joe.

"Diphenhydramine. Better known as Benadryl," clarified Kendra. "With that much in his system, there's no way he would have been conscious when he was killed."

"So, would you say it's possible someone sedated him and then shot him."

"That could be a possible scenario."

"Exactly how could that much Benadryl be given to him without him noticing?" asked Joe.

"Benadryl comes in three forms: liquid, caplets, and liquid-gels. Now the liquid is bubblegum flavored, so he would notice if it was put in something unless it was sweet like birthday cake or pie. We didn't find anything like that in his stomach contents. But the caplets could be ground into a powder, and gels could be squeezed into something. It would take less to knock him out, especially since he'd been drinking."

"How much alcohol was in his system?"

"His blood alcohol content was .07, so he wasn't legally intoxicated. But alcohol combined with the diphenhydramine would have intensified the effect of the drug."

"How many Benadryl caplets or gels would it have taken to knock him out?"

"Oh…six maybe. The recommended adult dose is one to two caplets."

"If he was given that kind of dose, how long would he be unconscious?"

"A minimum of three hours."

"Would either of the pills have a noticeable taste?"

"Negligible if it was put in a beer."

"Wine?"

"Given the smaller amount of liquid in a glass, it might be noticeable."

"Interesting. You said his stomach contents included beer, right."

"That's right."

"But there were no empty beer bottles or cans found on his tables. Yet, we found a wine bottle and two empty wine glasses."

"I can't comment on that. But I can confirm the last thing he drank was beer."

"That's odd. Any other things crop up in the lab reports?"

"The red smears on his inner thighs and lower abdomen were definitely from lipstick. The lab was able to get DNA from the swabs if you want to try matching it to someone."

"We've identified a person who admitted to having sex with the deceased on the night of his death, so unless she becomes a suspect in his death, I think we can assume the DNA belongs to her. Anything else?"

"That's pretty much it. I'll send over the report."

"Thanks, Kendra."

Joe walked to Sam's desk and let him know about Schmidt's drugging. The revelation took Sam by surprise, and his suspicions immediately focused on Roselyn Bertrand as the person who could have slipped Schmidt the Benadryl cocktail.

"I don't think so," said Joe. "If she was going to kill him, why'd she leave her fingerprints and DNA behind to incriminate herself? If she administered the Benadryl and left by eight, there would've been wine in Schmidt's stomach contents. But there was beer. Time of death was around eleven."

"What if she stayed longer. They drank all the wine, and she goes and gets him a beer from the refrigerator. Before she gives it to him, she opens it, drops in the Benadryl, and an hour later, he's zonked out."

"And she shoots him and makes it look like a suicide, takes the beer bottle with her when she leaves?" asked Joe.

"Yeah. She was thinking it would be ruled a suicide and not murder."

"I suppose that's one scenario. But why did she leave her fingerprints on the wine glass?"

"What if she simply set him up and someone else came in and popped him?"

Joe thought about that scenario for a few moments. "I don't know," he said. "I think we should pick her up and get a search warrant for her apartment and see if she bought Benadryl or a generic version recently."

"Good idea. I think we need to lean on her to see if somebody made it worth her while to do that. Check her bank account for any large deposits recently. See if she stashed money somewhere."

"All right," said Joe. "Let's get that rolling. But let's conduct the searches first. She works as a teacher's assistant. No sense jeopardizing her job by picking her up for questioning at her school. Especially if she's not involved."

"Got it."

Sam secured search warrants for Roselyn Bertrand's apartment, bank accounts, and credit card information. Because she worked as a teacher's aide, they waited until 4:00 to drive to her apartment on Kimball Avenue in Albany Park. They knocked on her door, identified themselves, and presented her with a copy of the search warrant. She was both surprised and upset by the warrant and angry she had to remain outside in the hall while they conducted their search. However, she complied. Once inside, Joe and Sam gloved up and began searching. Joe took the bathroom and Sam took the kitchen.

Opening the medicine cabinet, Joe began looking through the medications present. Typical items for a woman of Bertrand's age: birth control pills, aspirin, Tylenol, toothbrush, toothpaste, and an empty antibiotic prescription bottle. Nothing containing Benadryl.

He checked under the sink and found only a wastebasket, a large bottle of mouthwash, and a makeup mirror. The drawers contained personal grooming items and makeup. He moved on to her bedside table which contained a notepad, pen, sleep aid and several condoms. Her dresser drawers showed neatly folded clothes which Joe looked through. Lifting her mattress, he found nothing stashed beneath it. So far, her apartment was clean.

Walking into the kitchen, he met Sam who was finishing up searching through her cupboards.

"You find anything?" he asked Joe.

"Nothing."

"You?"

"Only this." And Sam removed a small handgun from a drawer and laid it on the counter. "Ruger LCP II. Just like she said. Nice little conceal-carry weapon."

"They don't pack a lot of punch, but good enough for self-defense, I guess," said Joe. "Is it loaded?"

Sam popped out the clip and looked. "She sure is." Popping the clip back in, he returned it to the drawer. "She has a FOID card, so it's legal."

"While you searched her cupboards, did you run across a mortar and pestle?"

"No, didn't see one. Why?"

"It's what I would have used to crush caplets into a powder."

"Let's check the living room."

"Okay. I'll take the closet," said Joe.

Following a thorough search of the living room and coat closet, Joe and Sam both came up empty. No evidence Roselyn Bertrand has any Benadryl in her apartment.

"Of course, if she was smart, she would have flushed any remaining pills," said Sam.

Opening the door, they found Bertrand sitting in the hall, working her phone. She stood and said, "I hope you're satisfied, whatever it was you were looking for."

"We can't comment on that," said Sam.

"Did you leave a mess?"

"No, as a matter of fact. We didn't," Joe assured her. "We tried to be respectful."

"Can I go back in now?"

"We're finished," Sam replied, pulling off one of his gloves.

She walked past them into her apartment and slammed the door.

They returned their car to the Area 3 lot and checked out. Since it was late and the holiday weekend had begun, they would begin the process of obtaining her credit card and bank records next week.

* * *

On Tuesday, Sam and Joe met to decide who would research what. Sam agreed to deal with Rachel Bertrand's credit card companies while Joe would get her bank records. Joe began a search and found Roselyn Bertrand banked at Lakeview Bank & Trust. Their main branch headquarters was located in the Loop, and Joe was familiar with its location since he and Sam previously interviewed an employee linked to one of serial killer David Eugene Burton's victims.

Joe drove the twenty minutes to Wacker Drive where the Lakeview Bank & Trust building was located.

The legal department was on the tenth floor. Stepping out of the elevator, Joe was greeted by a man in his late twenties sitting behind a large desk.

"Good morning. Do you have an appointment?" he asked.

Joe showed his ID and identified himself. "I have a search warrant and need to speak with someone about acquiring the specified information."

"Certainly. Let me get someone for you." He punched in some numbers on his desk phone.

"Sorry to bother you, but there's a police detective here with a search warrant. Can you handle this?... Thank you." Then he looked up at Joe and said, "She'll be with you in a moment."

Joe eyed several chairs against the wall and was about to sit when he saw a woman in her fifties walking toward him. Her gait looked confident and determined, and Joe assumed she was the person who would deal with the warrant. When she approached him, he showed his ID, and she slipped on the reading glasses hanging from her neck in order to read it.

Looking at him, she said, "You could use a new photo, Detective Erickson."

"You're probably right," Joe said suppressing a grin.

"I'm Teresa Dailey. Gary said you have a warrant?"

Joe produced the warrant and handed it to her. She looked it over quickly and said, "Why don't we go down to my office?" She removed her glasses, turned, and walked down the hall. He followed her into a richly appointed office decorated in light earth tones with a wide floor-to-ceiling bookcase behind her desk.

"Sit down, Detective. I'm one of the senior attorneys for the bank, and this isn't the first time I've seen one of these. Bear with me a few moments."

She slipped on the reading glasses again, swiveled her chair to the computer at the side of her desk, and typed into it. Joe assumed she was pulling up Roselyn Bertrand's banking records. She looked over the screen, clicked a few keys, then turned to Joe.

"The warrant states you request Roselyn Bertrand's banking records for the past three months."

"That's correct."

"She only has one account, a checking account. So, we can do that for you. Once I print them out, I'm going to need you to sign for them. I hope that won't be a problem."

"No, no problem."

"All right then." She turned to her computer and began clicking away on keys. A minute later, she clicked one final key and the printer woke up and began sliding out sheets of paper. Dailey reached inside her desk and removed a fresh manilla folder. Once the printer stopped kicking out printed pages, she removed them, stapled them together, and slipped it into the file folder.

She handed Joe an agreement of confidentiality to sign for obtaining the records per the search warrant.

"That was easier than I thought it would be," said Joe, handing it back to her.

"Thought I was going to give you a hard time, huh?"

"I didn't know what to think. One more question, does she have a safety deposit box?"

"Let me check." After a moment of clicking her computer, she turned back to Joe and said, "No, she doesn't."

"I guess that does it. Thanks," said Joe, rising from his chair.

"You're welcome," she replied, rising. "And get a new picture. That one doesn't do you justice."

Joe grinned. "I'll consider it."

Back at Area 3 Headquarters, Joe began looking over Roselyn Bertrand's bank records. Her checking account didn't show anything out of the ordinary. Her deposits were automatic deposits from her school, and she made additional deposits in amounts of two hundred dollars, three or four times a month, consistent with her extra-curricular activities. Other than that, there was no suspicious activity regarding her deposits.

Stepping to Sam's desk, he asked, "How are you coming with her credit card information?"

"Working on it," he said. "You might know I'd have to get a credit card company that's slow on the uptake. I finally got through to their legal department, someone who's a native English speaker. Sounds like he's willing to help me with this."

"I got her bank records," said Joe, holding up the file folder. "Nothing suspicious. And no safety deposit box to hide cash."

"Even if nothing shows up, we still need to question her."

"Agreed. I'll call her and set up another interview for Thursday after the holiday. That should give us time to get all of her credit card records and let her cool down a little."

Joe walked back to his desk leaving Sam stewing on hold with the credit card's legal representative. He phoned Roselyn Bertrand saying they had a few more questions and requested another face-to-face meeting. Still angry about the warrant and their search of her apartment, she was not agreeable to another meeting. But when Joe threatened to interrupt summer school and take her in for questioning, she consented to meet again at the 17th District station at 3:30 on Thursday. Joe called the 17th and reserved a conference room for that time.

Joe was frustrated. The Fourth of July weekend was inhibiting his investigation. He was forced to put off Roselyn Bertrand's interview until Thursday. And on top of that, his gut was telling him she had nothing to do with Schmidt's death. The path they were following would lead to a dead end.

He looked at his watch and sighed. Time for his meeting with Dr. Lemke.

Chapter Nineteen

Joe got home and found Destiny waiting for him. He was grateful she stopped over because it had been a busy day, and he needed to unwind.

"Glad you're here," he said as he saw her rising from her chair at the table.

She walked to him, put her arms around his neck, and said, "So am I." They kissed, and she said, "You look tired."

"Busy day." He pulled his Glock, placed it in its drawer, and locked it. "I don't like serving search warrants, and I don't especially like searching through people's stuff. It's such an invasion of privacy."

"Did you find anything?"

"No. It was futile. Necessary to eliminate her as a suspect, I think. If she's involved, then she's a lot more conniving and mercenary than I give her credit for. She doesn't feel right for this."

"Where's your investigation without her?"

"Stalled."

"You want a glass of wine."

"I do."

Destiny poured two glasses of Pinot Noir and handed one to Joe. They clinked glasses and Joe asked, "Your mom glad to be home?"

"Oh, yeah. She wanted nothing to do with the holiday in the city."

As they walked into his living room Joe said, "I thought maybe she'd want to stick around and watch the fireworks over Lake Michigan."

"Oh, she's seen those fireworks many times. I think I may have tired her out going so many places during the week. She said she was going to be glad to get home and to have me stay with her for a couple days."

"You're a good daughter."

"You made a good impression," she said as she sat on his couch.

"Oh, yeah?" said Joe, as he sat beside her.

"Mm-hm. She approves of you," Destiny said chuckling.

"What's so funny?" Joe asked, not understanding her reaction.

"You're lucky. She's hated most of my boyfriends."

Joe grinned. "Just how many have you had?"

"Not many, if you must know. And I wouldn't probe any further if you know what's good for you."

"Understood."

"Let's change the subject. You said your case is stalled?"

"I think so."

"Then you need to back up and look at motives. Who would want Devon Schmidt dead and why?

"Well, for one, someone wanting payback for killing Daniel Silverman, possibly."

"Or…it could be the classic 'kill the assassin' scenario."

"I've considered that," said Joe. "But with his bum knee, his mobility would have prevented him from killing Daniel. He had to use crutches to get around. I don't see it."

"So, you think he was used as a patsy?"

"I do."

"Question is then, by whom?"

Joe took a drink, then said, "Someone set up Schmidt to take the fall for Daniel's death. I believe the swastika cut into Daniel's back was a ruse to get us thinking it was a hate crime committed by a neo-Nazi skinhead. Actually, that was very clever. But whoever it was didn't know about Schmidt's knee injury and his dislike of Colt weapons. Schmidt was adamant about owning only Smith and Wesson firearms. If he was going to off himself, he wouldn't have done it with a Colt."

"So, that goes back to the question of why Daniel was killed," said Destiny. "It seems to me he must have <u>done</u> something, <u>known</u> something, <u>seen</u>

something, or <u>heard</u> something. And someone found out about it. And it would have been knowledge so dangerous, he needed to have been killed to keep it secret."

"Or he was having an affair with Cindy Fielding, and her husband killed him for it," suggested Joe.

"There's your 'done something' scenario. You have evidence he was having an affair with her?"

"One witness. When we interviewed Cindy Fielding, she denied ever having an affair with Daniel. But that doesn't mean anything. I think her husband's physically abusive, but she's staying in her marriage because of the prenup she signed. She says she gets nothing if there's a divorce."

"Looking for love with someone else. Sad situation but not uncommon, I'm afraid."

"I think that may be the next path I need to go down. My gut's telling me Roselyn Bertrand is nothing more than a woman willing to prostitute herself to get ahead. I'd be surprised if she was part and parcel of all this. I need to find out who came in after she left, administered a massive dose of Benadryl to Schmidt's beer to knock him out, and then staged a suicide."

When Destiny heard that, she pulled the glass from her lips. "Benadryl. That's interesting."

"What do you mean?"

"A large dose of Benadryl is being used as a date-rape drug nowadays. Put it in some girl's drink, and she goes to sleep. More easily obtainable than Rohypnol."

"Jeez! What these cretins won't think of next. I hate those guys."

"When it comes to sex, there are no limits to how far some men will go to take advantage of a woman."

Joe paused and took in what Destiny said. "I need to have a talk with Cindy Fielding, put some pressure on her about her relationship with Daniel. She was probably lying to protect her marriage."

"Or her husband."

At that moment, Joe's phone rang. "Great." He looked at the caller, and then answered it.

"Hello, Adam."

Adam Silverman was talking so fast Joe could hardly understand him. "I was shot at. Somebody just—I was just shot at as I was driving—

"Adam, slow down. Slow down," said Joe. "Are you alright?"

"Yeah. Yeah. I'm fine."

"Did the round hit near you?"

"My car. It shattered the driver's door window."

"Where are you?"

"My place."

"Did it happen there?"

"No. Eight blocks away. I sped up and drove home. I had to get away."

"You need to call 9-1-1 and report the shooting. I have your address information at work and I'm at home now. What's your address?"

Adam gave Joe his address and it wasn't that far from where Joe lived. He told Adam he would be there in about ten minutes. He hung up the phone and rose from the couch.

"Someone took a shot at Adam Silverman?" asked Destiny.

"Yeah. He's pretty shaken up. I need to go to his apartment and get the details. It shouldn't take too long," said Joe as he walked into the kitchen to get his Glock.

"I'll be here when you get back," she said as she followed him. "And I'll have something in the oven for us."

"Thanks," he said and gave her a peck.

Joe drove to Adam's apartment on North Clybourn. A police cruiser was already there. Joe saw Adam's black BMW parked in the street, and the officer talking to Adam next to the shattered window. Joe got out of his Camaro and walked toward them holding up his ID for the officer to see.

"Detective Joe Erickson, Area 3. Adam called me. I'm investigating his brother's homicide."

"Jack Lindeman," said the officer. "Mr. Silverman said the shot occurred on Fullerton somewhere between Ashland and Greenview. He floored it and drove here to report it."

Joe looked inside the window and spotted a hole in the A-pillar where the round hit next to the windshield on the passenger side.

""You'd better call for detectives on this. I'm off duty," said Joe. "They'll need to call in a forensics team. They'll need that round that's lodged in the A-pillar."

Joe turned to Adam. "You know where the shot came from?"

Still shaken, Adam shook his head. "No. It was a total surprise. It shocked me so bad. I kinda heard a pop and the window exploded. I just reacted."

"You know of anyone who'd want to kill you?" asked Joe.

"No! No one!"

"Know anyone who might hold a grudge because of a criminal court case, maybe?"

"I'm a real estate attorney. I don't deal with criminals."

"Lawsuit over property?"

"No."

"There's something going on here I don't know about. Your brother was killed and now you get shot at? Come on. Is there something you're not telling me?"

"I don't know what this could have to do with Daniel's death. I really don't."

"All right. Let the police investigate this, and I'll get back to you later in a day or two. In the meantime, watch yourself. You're a target and we don't know why."

"Don't worry. I'll be careful."

"And when the detectives show up, you might tell them I'm investigating your brother's death, and this could be connected."

"I understand."

Joe pulled Officer Lindeman aside and emphasized the importance of getting any video from surveillance cameras in the area of the shooting since there were a lot of businesses located there. Then Joe got into his car and drove back to his apartment. The investigation would fall into the purview of other Area 3 detectives who would investigate the shooting since he was off-duty.

He gave Destiny a call to tell her he was on his way home. As he entered his apartment, the scent of something baking wafted from the kitchen. Destiny came in from the living room to meet him.

"Wow, this smells wonderful."

"I improvised based on your refrigerator ingredients so…garlic butter baked salmon with crispy roast potatoes, and asparagus in a garlic butter sauce."

"Oh, my!"

"I just put it in fifteen minutes ago, so we have some time to go."

"And it's not even vegetarian."

"Like I told you, I fall off the wagon once in a while." She handed him his half-full wine glass. "Here's your wine. What did you find out?"

"Someone took a shot at him all right, and he says he has no clue why. That complicates things. He says he can't imagine why it would have anything to do with his brother's death."

"Do you buy that?"

"Not necessarily," said Joe as he sat down on the couch. "Either he really has no clue…or he knows and he's not telling me."

"Or it could be he knows why, and it doesn't have anything to do with his brother's death."

"That's a possibility, I suppose. He wants to keep it private," said Joe, taking a sip of his wine.

"Was he pretty shaken up?"

"Oh, yeah. I'm thinking we might get lucky, and there will be some surveillance video from one of those businesses along that stretch of Fullerton."

"When his father hears about this, he's going to raise the roof."

"I know. Vincenzo's going to feel the pressure. I'm glad I'm not investigating this one."

"But it's going to impact your investigation, too."

"I know."

Joe and Destiny rehashed the situation for the next fifteen minutes, then the oven buzzer went off.

"Ah! Done!" said Destiny, jumping up and moving into the kitchen. She removed a large tray from the oven containing all the vegetables and foil-wrapped salmon.

They set the table, then sat down to eat. The food made Joe forget all about the events of his day. As he ate, he remembered something his mother told him Grandma Matilda used to say. "People who make food for you give you their heart."

Chapter Twenty

Two of Joe's fellow detectives, Michelle Cardona and her partner, Rick Murphy, got called in to investigate the attempted shooting of Adam Silverman. Joe strolled over to Cardona's desk the next morning to see if he could pick her brain about what they found.

When she saw him nearing her desk, she turned in her chair. "I figured you'd be checking in with me this morning. Silverman said he you showed up, but you left before we got there."

"I was off-duty," said Joe. "I only came because Adam called me. He knew me from the investigation of his brother's homicide."

"So he said."

Cardona went through everything they learned from Adam Silverman. It wasn't anything that Joe hadn't heard from Adam already.

"Did the Evidence Techs recover the slug from the A-pillar?"

"They did."

"You have people searching the area for any video of the shooting?"

"Yeah. So far, nothing. But it's still early. We haven't finished canvassing all the businesses yet. You think this incident is somehow connected to your case?"

"Don't know. Right now, I can't rule it out. I'd like you to share anything you find with me, no matter how insignificant it might be."

"We can do that. We'd appreciate the same."

"Deal. Thanks, Michelle."

Joe turned and walked back to his desk. It wasn't long after he sat down that Sam walked over and dropped some papers in front of him.

"What's this?" Joe asked.

"Roselyn Bertrand's credit card records for the past three months. She hasn't charged anything that's in any way suspicious. All that time and hassle for nothing!"

"When we interview her tomorrow, we'll have to ask very specific questions since we don't have any evidence that links her to Schmidt's death. She was there with him before he was killed. It could be she's telling the truth."

"Or she's incredibly sly and…"

"That's what we'll have to find out."

Having previously informed Sam about the attempted shooting of Adam Silverman, Joe told him about his conversation with Cardona and her agreeing to share whatever information they discover about the shooting.

"If you ask me, this is another leg of the same spider."

Joe nodded. "You could be right. Now, we have to prove it."

Joe's phone rang. It was Lieutenant Vincenzo, and he wanted to see Joe and Sam in his office right away. Joe had a feeling he knew what this was about, and it wasn't good. They walked to Vincenzo's office and knocked.

"Come on in you guys," said Vincenzo.

As Joe and Sam took seats in front of his desk, he said, "I just got an angry call from Jacob Silverman about the 'attempted murder' of his son last evening. I assume you know about that?"

"We do," said Joe, who went on to explain the call he received from Adam and his visit to the scene. "I spoke to Cardona this morning. She's lead on the case, and we're sharing information."

"Good. Where are you on his son's homicide?"

"We're following leads. So far, we have a neo-Nazi that Daniel had a confrontation with who was set up to take the fall for Daniel's murder. This guy's suicide was staged with the gun that killed Daniel, so we're trying to find who staged it and why, thinking that will lead us to Daniel's killer."

"We're not sure if the shot taken at Adam is connected to Daniel's murder. That remains to be seen," said Sam.

"Someone sure as hell went out of their way to cover up who killed Daniel Silverman. To set up an elaborate frame like that. Sounds like they have a lot to lose. What the hell did he know or do that got him killed?" asked Vincenzo.

"That's what we're trying to find out," replied Sam.

"Chances are it has to do with a threat to money or power. It usually does."

"That's where we're going with it," said Joe.

"Okay. Keep me posted on your investigation. I know you haven't been on this case that long, but Jacob Silverman has a lot of clout in this town, and I don't want the mayor's office getting involved and pressing us for an arrest."

"Got it," said Sam.

"All right. Get outta here."

Joe and Sam left Vincenzo's office and as they walked back to their desks, Sam said, "Well, at least he wasn't pissed."

"This time," replied Joe. "But if we don't show some results in another week, he might not be so understanding. And if he starts getting pressure from the top about it…"

"Yeah. It runs downhill."

Joe reviewed his notes and started thinking about what Vincenzo said: "It's about a threat to money or power." Joe's brainstorming method involved writing questions so he began jotting notes. What could Daniel have known or done that could have been a threat? Something to do with his internship with Fielding Enterprises or an affair with Cindy Fielding? Could he have been killed because Jay Fielding found out he was screwing his wife? Would that be worth killing for? For some men, that could be a motive for murder. But Jay Fielding is filthy rich. He could have any woman he wanted. With a prenup, wouldn't he just divorce her? Enormous ego? Did he have to destroy Daniel to soothe that ego? And Jay knew Devon Schmidt from high school, and Schmidt worked for his company. Was he devious and capable enough to set him up? Or did he employ someone else to do it?

During the afternoon, Cardona walked over to Joe's desk and said, "I've got something you need to see."

"Yeah?"

"Got some video footage of the shooting," she said. "One of the uniforms found it this morning."

Joe called to Sam, and he followed them over to Cardona's desk. "I have it downloaded to my computer," she said as she pulled up the video footage of the street. They watched, and after switching it to slow motion when Adam's car came into view, they saw a motorcycle in the other lane, pull up alongside. The quality of the video was a little fuzzy, but one could see the window shatter and Adam's car slow slightly as the motorcycle raced away.

Cardona stopped the video. "That's the moment of the shot."

"Someone on a motorcycle," said Sam. "I'll bet there was no plate on it."

Joe was staring at the image on the screen. "Keep playing it," he said to Cardona.

Cardona began the video and Joe watched as the black car swerved into the drugstore parking lot and stopped. Then he saw the car's passenger door open, and a female passenger emerge and run into the drug store. Then the car sped out of the parking lot.

"Did you see this?" asked Joe.

"No," said Cardona. "I only watched it up to the shot. I hadn't watched the whole thing yet."

Joe turned to Sam. "He didn't say anything about a passenger with him when the shot occurred." Then he turned to Cardona. "Did he say anything to you about a passenger?"

"No, he didn't."

"That's an interesting omission," said Sam.

"It sure as hell is," said Cardona.

"I know this your investigation," said Joe. "But let me talk with him because I suspect this may have something to do with our case."

"If you want," Cardona agreed.

"I'll let you know if my hunch is right. Talk to you later."

As Joe and Sam began walking back to their desks, Joe looked at Sam and said, "Let's pay Adam Silverman a visit."

Joe called Adam and told him they made a discovery in his case and needed to set up a short meeting. Adam didn't want to meet at his father's office where he was employed, so he suggested a bar down the street. Joe and Sam drove to the location and met Adam who was already occupying a booth in the back. He motioned to them when they entered. Few people were in the establishment at this time of the afternoon, so it was fairly quiet.

A half-empty glass of beer sat on the table in front of Adam. After sitting, a barmaid was there ready to take their order.

"Coffee for me," said Joe.

"Club soda," said Sam.

"So, do you have a lead on who shot at me?" Adam asked.

"We do," said Joe. "Surveillance footage from a camera across the street captured a person on a motorcycle pulling up close to your car and firing into your window."

"My god, I never even saw it."

"It's a good thing your car had heavily tinted windows. Otherwise, you'd probably be dead. From the angle, it looks like the round must have passed in front of your face."

"Did you get a license plate number?"

"No, the plate seemed to be missing from the bike," said Sam. "We can't identify it."

"We watched the entire video," said Joe. He paused to see what Adam's reaction would be. He could see him tense up.

"So, you saw me pull into the drug store parking lot?" asked Adam.

"Yeah. Who was your passenger and why did you let her out there instead of driving her to your house?"

Silence. Adam was clearly uncomfortable about answering Joe's question and took a drink from his glass of beer. "It was Cindy Fielding," he said. "I didn't want her implicated in this event. Her husband would be furious if he found out."

"How long have you two been seeing each other?" asked Joe.

Again, Adam paused. "Eight months, give or take."

"So, it was you, not Daniel, that was having an affair with her."

"Daniel? No, of course not. Daniel referred her to me. She was looking for some legal advice, and Daniel said maybe I could help her. That's how we met."

"Do you think her husband suspects anything?" asked Sam.

"I don't think so. We only meet when he's out of town, and we take great pains to be discreet. No emails or texts. And she has a burner phone for calls."

"Why did Cindy look to you? She's married to a very rich man," probed Joe.

"Jay Fielding is an abusive bully and an anti-Semite. The whole family are anti-Semites. She didn't know that when she married into it. But after repeated incidents of physical abuse, there was no longer any love there. She found herself in a dilemma: stay in a loveless marriage and enjoy what wealth brings with it or divorce him and lose everything."

The barmaid came and set down Joe's coffee and Sam's club soda. She looked at Adam and he declined.

"Cindy could marry you, couldn't she?"

"There's the other dilemma. My family would have a hard time accepting a gentile as my spouse. They're not haters by any means, but my parents have certain expectations for their children. And now, that's me. Having their only living child deviating from their cultural and religious expectations would be upsetting to them. I suppose they could eventually accept it, but it wouldn't be easy."

"So, you plan to go on having this affair indefinitely?" asked Sam.

"No. Eventually, we would have to decide on an arrangement more... acceptable. To both of us."

"The question remains, 'Who would want to kill you and why?'"

"The same people that killed Daniel?" asked Adam.

"We don't know who killed Daniel, yet," replied Joe. "We're working on it. But in what way could his death be tied to you? Any ideas?"

"I don't know."

"The only connection would seem to be the Fieldings. Your affair with Cindy Fielding and Daniel's internship with Fielding Enterprises. Can you think of anything else?" asked Sam.

"No."

"Daniel went to the same university and worked with Cindy at the same food bank. Do you think Jay Fielding could have mistaken him for you and killed him out of jealousy?" asked Joe.

"Why would he be suspicious? He's never home. And when he is, she's always there for him. She goes to the university with a lot of people. Daniel's just one of many.

"But you and Daniel have a physical similarity. One could mistake him for you at night in poor lighting."

"I suppose it's possible someone could mistake the two of us in a situation like that."

"And you said Jay's an abusive man. Could he be prone to violence toward others?"

"He's struck Cindy before, if that's what you mean."

"I'd be very careful, if I were you," said Sam. "I don't want to tell you what to do, but you might want to limit your meetings with Cindy for a while."

"Good advice," added Joe. "I'll relay what you've said to the investigator on your case. She may want to speak with you again."

"We'll need to talk with Cindy," said Sam.

"Great..." muttered Adam. "You'll keep this quiet, right?"

"Of course."

"You have any more questions for Adam?"

"Not right now."

"Thanks for your time." Joe and Sam began to get up.

"I got your tab," said Adam. "I hope this leads somewhere."

"So do we," said Sam.

When Joe and Sam returned to the office, Joe called Cindy Fielding's cellphone and asked to set up a meeting. He told her they had a few more questions for her about the case. She sounded somewhat reticent about the meeting. Joe was sure Adam called her and told her about his meeting. Reluctantly, she agreed to meet them the next morning at the Area 3 headquarters.

Chapter Twenty-One

Before Cindy Fielding arrived for her interview, Joe and Sam put their heads together and came up with questions they wanted to ask her regarding her affair with Adam, her friendship with Daniel, and the state of her marriage.

Cindy showed up right on time and was escorted to the same conference room where she was interviewed previously. She appeared to exude confidence when she greeted them, but when she sat down, her mannerisms suggested otherwise.

When Joe and Sam sat down, she opened the conversation by saying, "I know why you called me in."

"You do?" asked Joe.

"You found out about my relationship with Adam Silverman, right?"

Nodding, Joe said, "We did."

"Adam called me."

"I assumed he would."

"Why don't you tell us how this affair started?" asked Sam.

"I met Adam's brother, Daniel, in grad school. He suggested that I donate some of my time at the food bank. It's good to have community service on your resume, and he was already helping out there. And he offered to give me a lift once in a while if we worked the same hours. So, that's how I got to know Daniel."

"We know that already. How'd you meet his brother?'" said Sam.

"I'm getting to that. Daniel noticed a large bruise on my arm. It was where Jay grabbed me really hard when he'd been drinking one night. I'd established a friendship with Daniel by that point so I felt comfortable confiding in him that Jay could be physically abusive sometimes. Especially when he'd been drinking. It was an ongoing problem, and I told Daniel I was sick and tired of it and was considering a divorce. But I'd signed a prenup that would leave me with virtually nothing. That's when he suggested I talk with his brother, Adam, who was an attorney. So, he called and set up an appointment for me."

"So, that's how you met."

"Yeah. Right away, there was chemistry between us. I can't explain it. It was just there. I wasn't looking for a relationship. I just wanted to know if the prenup would hold up in court."

"And?"

"Iron-clad, unfortunately."

"The video footage of the shooting of Adam's car shows you were a passenger. Why did he let you off at the drug store?"

"So my name wouldn't be tied to the investigation. If my husband found out, he'd…"

"Shoot you?" added Joe.

Silence.

"He doesn't know. I'm sure of it."

"Then, who would've taken a shot at you?"

"I have no idea. One of Adam's disgruntled clients, maybe? Some drive-by shootings have no motive. They're random."

"That's true. But you're a married woman having an affair, and Adam's brother was recently murdered. We doubt this was random. This was attempted murder. If Adam's head hadn't been obscured by tinted glass, he'd be dead. The bullet only missed him by inches," said Joe.

"My husband isn't even in town."

"He could've hired it done," said Sam.

"Is Fielding Enterprises on the up-and-up?" asked Joe.

"How would I know that? I'm not involved with the company. I'm just a wife. Jay's arm candy. He never discusses business with me. To him, I'm an idiot."

"Why does Jay travel to Vegas so much? Does he have a gambling problem?" asked Sam.

"I don't know if he does. He travels all over the country to visit the company's centers to troubleshoot problems and keep things functioning smoothly. That's been his job for years. Maybe he takes a side trip to Vegas once in a while, I don't know."

"He ever come home in a bad mood?" asked Joe.

"Usually. He's tired. I've just learned to give him space whenever he gets back."

"Has it always been that way?"

"More so since his dad got sick. Everything's falling on his shoulders and he's under a lot more pressure now."

"Did Daniel ever mention anything about his internship with Fielding Enterprises?"

"Not a lot. He said he'd be glad when it was over. He liked Rachel, his supervisor, but said he didn't care for Robert Curtis that much."

"Did he say why?" asked Joe.

"No."

"What about your husband?"

"Daniel wouldn't have interacted with Jay. I doubt he ever saw him in the office. I think the first time he saw Jay was that evening on the yacht."

"Did you see Daniel the day he was killed?"

"We worked at the food bank that day."

"Did he say anything out of the ordinary?"

"Not really. I asked him in passing what he was doing afterward, and he said he needed to check something out."

Joe's ears perked up. "Check something out. Do you know what he meant by that?"

She gave a shrug. "No clue."

Joe felt this was important and needed to probe further. "Did you notice a change in his attitude that day?"

Shaking her head, she said, "No."

"Was he concerned about anything?"

"Not that I know of. If he was, he didn't say anything."

Frustrated, Joe paused and considered what Daniel could have meant by "checking something out." What the hell could he have been thinking?

"Did Daniel know about you and Adam?" asked Sam.

"Yeah. He knew, and he was okay with it. But we didn't discuss it. He respected our privacy."

Joe and Sam questioned her for another twenty minutes but learned nothing more. Once her interview was complete, Joe escorted her to the door.

"This won't get out, will it?" she asked.

"No," answered Joe. "This interview is confidential. It wasn't recorded, and the information we gained would only become available under sworn testimony in a court of law. I don't see that happening."

Joe followed her out the door and to her car. As she drove onto the street, he noticed a blue Toyota Camry with a slightly mismatched front fender pull out and begin following her. He called her cell phone and she picked up right away.

"Hello."

"This is Joe, again. Don't look now, but you have a tail. A blue Toyota Camry. Someone is following you. I'd advise against seeing Adam if I were you."

"Shit!"

"Don't call him, either. I'll let him know."

"Thanks, Joe."

Joe called Adam and told him that Cindy was being tailed, and he advised her not to see him or call him. Adam was concerned and angry, and he said he would refrain from contacting her for the time being.

"Time being?" repeated Joe. "Time being? You've gotta be shitting me! Someone's trying to kill you, so you'd better cut off all communications with your sweetheart until we figure out what's going on here."

"Okay. Okay, I get it," said Adam. "I get it."

"Good. Because you don't want to leave your father childless."

Joe figured he'd driven his point home. He knew how Adam felt, but at this point, he needed him to do what was necessary to protect not only himself, but Cindy as well.

That afternoon, Joe and Sam drove to the 17th to meet with Roselyn Bertrand again. Joe was convinced she had nothing to do with Devon Schmidt's death, but Sam was not so sure. And with the revelation that Schmidt had been rendered unconscious with a massive dose of Benadryl, they needed to clarify some things with her.

They arrived ten minutes early and found Bertrand already waiting for them. After a rather cold greeting, they moved into a conference room. As before, they assured her that she was not being recorded and no one would be watching.

"I don't see why I have to do this again. I answered all your questions the first time," she said as she sat down at the table.

"There have been a couple developments in the case, and we'd like to see if you could add anything based on what's been found," said Sam.

"I don't know what else I could say that I haven't already said before."

"Have you purchased any Benadryl in the last month?" asked Joe.

"Benadryl?"

"Yes."

"The allergy drug?"

"Uh-huh."

"No. Why?"

"The tox report on Devon Schmidt found he had over three times the recommended amount of Benadryl in his blood. He would have been asleep when he was killed."

"So, he didn't commit suicide?"

"No. It was a setup," said Sam.

"And you think I might have slipped him Benadryl in his wine? Well, it wasn't me. Like I said before, he was fine when I left, and he made an appointment with me in two weeks."

"So you say," replied Sam.

"Let me show you." She reached for her cell phone, clicked a couple of times, and brought up her calendar. She showed Joe and Sam the entry marked "Devon 7 pm" on Tuesday, July 6th. "See. Why would I make an appointment if I was going to set him up? Doesn't make sense, does it?"

"You could have put that in there after the fact," said Sam.

"You want more? Okay. What time did you say Devon was killed?"

"Between 10:00 pm and midnight," said Joe.

She asked for her purse. Sam handed it to her, and she pulled out her wallet. She dug out a receipt from her wallet and handed it to Joe.

"Read what it says. It's a receipt from Walgreen's where I bought a ream of printer paper and some feminine hygiene products. Note the date and time."

Joe looked at it and read it out loud. "June 22nd, 10:47 pm." He looked up and gave the receipt to Sam. "It looks like you made a purchase there during the time Devon Schmidt was killed."

"You see. I have an alibi."

"It appears you're off the hook," said Sam, and handed it back to her.

"Thank you," she said, taking back the receipt.

"I want to pursue another point of interest here, if I may," said Joe. "You said you didn't see anyone in the hall when you left, correct?" asked Joe.

"Right," confirmed Roselyn.

"Remind me. Did you take the stairs or the elevator back down to the first floor?"

"The stairs."

"And you met no one on the stairs?"

"No one."

"What about outside the building? Did you see anyone lurking about? Waiting to go inside? Anything like that?"

"No...Now, wait a minute. I did see a black car with a guy sitting in it. He covered his face with his newspaper as I crossed the street. Like this." She demonstrated how he brought the newspaper up and covered the side of his face.

"Did you get a look at him before he covered his face?" asked Joe.

"No, the car had dark tinted windows, so I couldn't see in very well. He wasn't much more than a dark image, you know?"

But you could still see him cover his face."

"Yeah. I mean, I was only six, seven feet away from his car."

"Did you notice what kind of car it was?"

"It was black. Looked fairly new. That's all I know."

Joe glanced at Sam. Alarm bells went off. They both knew that Adam Silverman drove a black BMW with dark tinted windows.

"Is that important?" she asked.

"Maybe," said Sam. "It's something we'll want to look into."

They wrapped up their interview with Roselyn and escorted her to the door. Out on the sidewalk, she asked, "Is this it? Will I have to be interviewed again?"

"Probably not," said Joe. "You've been most cooperative. We appreciate your assistance. Be careful out there."

"Don't' worry, I will." She turned and began walking down the street.

Sam said, "We need to take another look at the surveillance video and see if we can identify that black car."

"Yeah."

"You think Adam Silverman could be our shooter?"

"I doubt it. Why would he park right in front of the building if he was going to kill someone inside. He's smarter than that."

"Maybe he was just waiting for her to come out."

"How did he know she was in there, unless she was involved? I don't think she is. I'm thinking there's someone else we need to be looking for."

"Who?"

"I don't know. Let's find that video and check it out. We have to eliminate him or implicate him. One or the other."

They drove back to the office and began searching through surveillance video of Devon Schmidt's apartment building on the night he was killed. Eventually, they spotted the black car and saw Roselyn walk across the street and onto the sidewalk between the black car and another vehicle. Upon closer examination, they determined the black car was a Toyota Avalon. As they continued watching, a woman crossed the street and got into the vehicle about five minutes later. Then it drove away.

"I guess we can eliminate Adam Silverman, huh?" said Sam.

CHAPTER TWENTY-ONE

"Probably," agreed Joe. "Too bad there's no video of the other entrance."

Chapter Twenty-Two

During Joe's jog the next morning, his mind cleared, and he began considering what new path their investigation needed to take. He was convinced that Daniel's killer was also responsible for killing Devon Schmidt. But instead of spending time on Schmidt's murder, time would be better spent pursuing Daniel's case.

He thought back to what Destiny said. What did Daniel do, know, see, or hear that got him killed? He didn't buy the jealousy angle. Logically, it must have something to do with Fielding Enterprises. Something illegal was going on and Daniel stumbled upon it? And someone important found out that Daniel knew? And found out he was going to report it? Or go to the police? That would seem a more plausible reason to kill him. But what knowledge could prove so dangerous that Daniel had to be silenced? That is what they needed to find out.

In the office that morning, Joe conferred with Sam about the next phase of their investigation. Sam agreed they needed to focus their attention on Fielding Enterprises and try to learn what information Daniel found that would have prompted his murder.

"I need to interview his supervisor again. Rachel Granger," said Joe. "She said I could call her again if I had any further questions."

"What about the head of the department?" asked Sam. "Robert Curtis."

"You probably won't get anything out of him, but he has an assistant, and she hasn't been interviewed yet. Oh, hell. What was her name?" There was a pause as he wracked his brain, then it slowly came to him. "Julia...uh... Vandevere. That's it. Julia Vandevere."

Sam wrote the name down in his notebook. "I'll arrange an interview with her while you're calling Rachel Granger."

"Good idea. But set up a meeting with her outside the office, and make sure she knows what she tells you is held in strict confidence. We need to know more about Robert Curtis. In my first meeting with Granger, she said the firm is touchy about any information getting leaked. And she confirmed my suspicion he's a scumbag, but she didn't go into details."

"Gotcha. I'll try to catch her leaving work rather than calling her. You know what she looks like?"

"Never seen her. But you may be able to find her photo on the company website. If not, there's always the driver's license database."

"Yeah. Such wonderful photos. I'll track her down."

Joe returned to his desk and looked up Rachel Granger's cell number. His call went to voicemail, so he left a message and his cell number. He assumed if she was working, she would want to avoid calling him on company time.

Later that morning, Joe received an email from Sam with a photo and information about Julia Vandevere. She was a beautiful, blonde, twenty-eight-year-old who was born in The Netherlands. She came to America with her parents when she was a teenager after her father, a diplomat, was transferred to Washington, D.C. She earned her bachelor's degree and graduated summa cum laude from Indiana University with a business degree in Operations Management.

Joe thought, *No wonder Robert Curtis wanted her as his assistant.* She might have a few juicy things she would like to say about him. He wrote back to Sam, "You'd better be on your toes when you interview her. She's smarter than you are! And better looking, too!" Joe got the f-bomb with a happy face back in a return message.

That evening as Joe was entering his apartment, he answered a call from Rachel.

"I received your message. When would you like to meet?" she asked. She seemed almost eager to meet with him again.

"What's convenient for you?" Joe asked.

"I'm not doing anything tonight, if you aren't."

"Well, I do have something scheduled, but it's later. I can meet anytime between now and eight."

"That sounds good," Rachel replied. "There's an Irish pub not far from where I live on North Clark. She gave him the address and said, "Does that work?"

"Yeah, that's about fifteen minutes from me. That'll be fine. What time?"

"Say, twenty minutes from now?"

"See you then." Joe knew parking might be an issue, so he left his apartment right away and drove to the North Clark Street address. He got there about eight minutes early, and that's about how long it took him to find a place to park.

He spotted Rachel standing at the bar. She saw him, and Joe signaled the waitress to get them a booth. She took them through the Friday afternoon customers to a booth in the back. Once they were seated, she took their orders and disappeared.

"I was a little surprised to hear from you again," Rachel said.

"As our investigation continued, we had a few more questions that we needed answered," said Joe, "and you seem to be the most logical person who could fill in the blanks."

"Okay. Glad to help. What would you like to know?"

"From our previous conversation, I know what Daniel was working on for you. While he was there, did he work on anything else or for any other person?"

"Well, Robert had him working on something for him for a few days. He said it was for Jay, some program off-the-books, some personal thing for the boss. He said it involved dates, codes, and numbers, but he didn't know what any of it meant."

"You said he worked on it for a few days. Like a couple days, a week, or what?"

"If I remember correctly, it was less than a week. Maybe four days. It involved setting up some kind of database for him."

"He said it was personal, not for the business?"

"That's what he said. Something Jay wanted for himself, evidently. And he had staff available to create it. Since Daniel wasn't a paid intern, it was kosher for him to do it, so to speak."

"Did Jay do this often with staff? Have them do personal stuff on company time?"

"No, not that I know of."

"Was Daniel troubled by this in any way?"

"No, but he was naturally curious what it was about since it seemed to be secretive."

"Secretive?"

"That's the word he used. He said he could maybe have done a better job setting up what they wanted if they would have told him the purpose of the database. He told me it was something that utilized dates, codes, and numbers."

"Did he say what Robert or Jay said to him when he asked?"

"Yes. 'Need-to-know basis.'"

"Wow," said Joe. "Now that's strange."

At that moment, the waitress brought them their drinks, a pint of Guinness for Joe and a Glenlivet on the rocks for Rachel. She took a drink, then her attention went inward. As Joe took a few swallows, he noticed her attention refocus on the present.

"Daniel was a curious guy. If something was a mystery, he needed to get to the bottom of it. He wasn't the type to let something go, you know what I mean?"

"You think his curiosity could have led him to investigate the meaning of that database on his own?" asked Joe.

"Very possible. I wouldn't be surprised if he didn't build a backdoor into that database so he could get into it at some point."

Joe decided to change the subject and see what Rachel might know about Julia Vandevere. "What do you know about Julia Vandevere, Robert Curtis' assistant?"

"Oh. Well, I have found her very good to work with. Much rather deal with her than Robert. She's been his assistant for about two years. Very attractive, highly intelligent, quite efficient in the few interactions I've had with her." Her voice took on a confidential tone. "Robert leaves her alone because she's a lesbian."

"Ah."

"And she's Dutch, so if you know anything about Dutch women, you'd know most women her age are very liberated and wouldn't take any crap from someone like him."

Joe laughed. "Good to know. I'll pass that along to my partner. He's going to be interviewing her next week."

They finished their drinks and Joe thanked Rachel again for her cooperation in his investigation. As he walked to his car, he gave Destiny a call.

"What do you want to do, tonight. It's Friday. People are out and about."

"Stay home with you," she said.

"Sounds good to me."

Joe arrived at Destiny's apartment and she had a bottle of Cabernet Sauvignon rather than his usual Pinot Noir waiting for him. He noticed.

"Cabernet, huh?"

"I read this was very good. A little variety keeps things fresh wouldn't you say?"

"Are you suggesting I'm predictable?" Joe said, kissing her on the cheek.

"Let's just say I got a wild hair," she said, returning his kiss.

She reached for a glass and poured him a generous amount. After handing it to him, she filled a glass for herself. Waiting for her to place the bottle down on the counter, he raised his glass and said, "To something new."

"To something new," she repeated. And they both took a drink.

Savoring it, Joe looked at Destiny and said, "This is good."

"The article I read said it was. The writer knew what he was talking about. Let's go sit down."

They moved to the living room couch and made themselves comfortable. Joe breathed a heavy sigh after putting down his glass.

"That was a big sigh," said Destiny. "Tough week?"

Joe sat back on the couch. "It's not that we're failing to make progress. We're narrowing down our investigation to Daniel's work at Fielding Enterprises. He was called off his project to develop a personal database for

Jay Fielding. It had nothing to do with Fielding Enterprises. That's what Daniel's supervisor told me this afternoon. Daniel described it to her as a database with dates, codes, and numbers. When he asked about it, he was told it was a 'need-to-know basis.'"

"Something off-the-books. Sounds suspicious."

"It does, doesn't it?"

"Fielding Enterprises is a multi-national transportation company, right?"

"Uh-huh."

"If he is doing something or planning to do something illegal, what could it be that he needs a private database for?"

An answer popped into Joe's head immediately. "Smuggling," he said. "Either that or he's skimming money from the company. But that would eventually be caught by the auditors unless he was clever enough to hide it."

"You think he may be smuggling drugs into the country aboard his trucks?" asked Destiny.

"His trucks go all over the U.S., Canada, and Mexico. His trucks could be bringing drugs in from Mexico. But the border is getting very tough on drug smuggling. With drug-sniffing dogs and other ways of checking, it's getting harder and harder."

"But it may not be loaded in Mexico. It could be transferred onto their trucks in places close to the border, places like Texas, Arizona, and southern California."

"Then it could be driven to Chicago or any of their other centers around the country and offloaded. No wonder Jay is still making all those trips to "troubleshoot" for the centers around the country."

"The database that Daniel developed for Jay could be used for tracking the drug deliveries. Dates, codes, and numbers. It all fits."

"And if Daniel built a backdoor to get into the database and found out what it was actually being used for, it could have gotten him killed," said Joe. "Now, proving it is going to be the hard part."

"I'd say your twisted path just led you to a door to knock on."

Chapter Twenty-Three

Sam met Joe as he was dropping off his lunch at the refrigerator Monday morning. He was surprised to see Sam in the office that early as he usually showed up right on time and seldom came in early like Joe.

"You able to reach Julia Vandevere on Friday?" asked Joe.

"Yeah, and she agreed to meet with me Saturday night at a bar on North Halstead. A gay bar."

Joe disguised his amusement. "Oh, really."

"Really. Anyway, she was standing outside waiting for me, and I said it was too noisy inside to discuss anything, so we went for a walk. Pretty girl. Such a waste."

"It's only a waste if you're straight."

"I suppose that's one way to look at it. Anyway, she was nice and willing to talk about Robert Curtis off the record. She doesn't like him much. He knows she's a lesbian, so she says he's never hit on her. She described him as 'a sleaze.'"

As they began walking to their desks, Joe asked, "Find out anything else?"

"Yeah. She answers his phone sometimes and takes messages. He gets calls occasionally from someone named "Mr. Scalise." She doesn't know who he is or where he's from, but the call has a 7-0-2 area code. That's Las Vegas."

"Really. That wouldn't happen to be 'Carmine' Scalise would it?"

"Oh, shit! The mobster?"

"He lives in Vegas and has a substantial interest in one of the casinos."

"He's pretty old, isn't he?"

"Not that old. Did she give you the phone number he called from?"

"No, she just took messages and saw the number when the call came in. He never left a callback number."

"Okay. It sounds like Curtis and Jay Fielding might be into some smuggling activities based on what I learned from Rachel Granger on Friday."

Joe explained about Daniel's assistance in developing the off-the-books database for Jay at the behest of Curtis.

"You know what else she told me?" said Sam. "This is where it really starts to get interesting. Jacqueline Fielding once worked in Robert Curtis' office—before she married Thomas Fielding. That's how they met. She was working with the company when they met at a company function aboard the yacht."

Stopping dead in his tracks, Joe said, "Are you kidding me?"

"Nope."

"Interesting is an understatement."

"Sure is."

"Some surveillance is in order, but before we go any further, I think we'd better let Vincenzo know where we're going with this."

Joe knocked, poked his head in Vincenzo's door, and asked, "Got a minute?"

"Yeah. Come on in. I've been wondering when I might hear from you guys."

Joe explained what they had established and what they were presently pursuing.

"So, you think Daniel Silverman was killed because he found out what this database was being used for?"

"That's the motive we're looking at right now," said Joe.

"And the tie to this 'Mr. Scalise' in Las Vegas could be a link from Fielding Enterprises to organized crime," added Sam.

"We think Jay Fielding and Robert Curtis may be involved in some smuggling operation and using Fielding trucks to transport whatever illicit goods to their terminals," said Joe.

"My question is, why would a rich guy like Jay Fielding, who is due to inherit the Fielding Enterprises fortune, risk all that to smuggle drugs or whatever for someone like Carmine Scalise?"

"Gambling debts, blackmail…it has to be something Scalise has on him that would force him to do it," suggested Joe. "Otherwise, he'd have no reason to get in bed with Scalise."

"All right," said Vincenzo. "Go ahead and surveil your suspects. And keep me apprised of what you find. Interstate transportation…We may need to bring in the FBI on this eventually."

Joe and Sam left Vincenzo's office feeling confident knowing their lieutenant was fully informed about where their investigation was headed. Joe didn't like the idea of bringing the feds in unless they absolutely had to. He was hoping they could bring closure to this case and let the feds take care of the rest once the Chicago case was settled.

"I think I'd like to keep tabs on Robert Curtis," said Joe. "Unless you have any objections."

"It doesn't make any difference to me," said Sam. "I'll take Jay Fielding. Half the time, he's out of town, so that makes my job easy."

"While he's out of town, you might want to watch the Fielding estate and see if there are any curious comings and goings. I don't trust Jacqueline Fielding after what I heard about her being employed in Curtis' office. "Lovely person" or not, that's one coincidence I don't like."

"Do you think she could be implicated in this, too?"

"At this point, nothing would surprise me."

* * *

Robert Curtis lived in a luxury apartment in River North, an area teeming with energy and marked by historic buildings, art galleries, restaurants, and a vibrant nightlife. Joe began surveilling him by day, keeping an eye on his travel to and from his office on East Randolph. He generally drove his red Jaguar to work, which made him easy to follow. But he always hailed a taxi when he went out for lunch, something he did nearly every day.

Curtis seldom dined alone. Single, he seemed to prefer the company of women whether it was his assistant, Julia Vandevere, or some woman he would meet at a particular restaurant. Occasionally, he would dine with Jay Fielding, but this did not appear to be a regular occurrence.

Two weeks into Joe's surveillance, Joe followed him to the Palmer House at mid-morning. Curtis went inside, and two hours later, he emerged with Jacqueline Fielding and a middle-aged man Joe did not recognize. He took a photo of the three of them together. After what looked like some pleasant chatting, Curtis hailed a taxi for Mrs. Fielding, then turned and conversed with the man who was waiting for a porter to carry out his luggage. Joe shot photos until a taxi whisked the man away.

When Curtis himself had gone, Joe went into the hotel and strode up to the registration desk. The clerk behind the desk was young and wore a tag with the name Terry on it. Joe held out his ID.

"I'm Detective Joe Erickson, Chicago PD. Did you check out the man with the gray pinstripe suit and pink tie a few moments ago? Dark hair and a mustache."

"Yes."

"Could you tell me his name, please?"

"I don't think I can do that. Our guest information is private and our hotel—"

"Look, Terry. If I have to get a warrant for his name, several police officers will come in here and shut down your front desk while we check your records. Now, I don't think your hotel management will want that."

Terry's eyes widened and Joe could see her become uncomfortable, so he turned on the charm. "All I want is his name, nothing more. Could you do this small thing for me, please?" he asked in a quiet voice. "No one will know."

She looked around, took a breath, then punched a few keys on her keyboard. After a moment, she looked up, leaned over the counter, and said in a low voice, "Vincent Scalise."

"Thank you, Terry."

At that moment, Terry saw the manager come out, and Joe could see she was now shaken. He knew he needed to do something. The manager stepped over, looked at Joe and said, "Is there something I can help you with?"

Joe replied, "I was asking about getaway weekends for my wife and me, and Terry was explaining what your hotel had to offer."

"Ah," the manager said.

"We have an anniversary coming up, and based on what Terry told me, I think a stay here would be quite nice."

"Well, we'd love to have you as our guests," the manager replied.

"You need to hold on to this young lady. She's very good at her job." Joe smiled. "Thank you, Terry. I'll talk it over with my wife." He gave the manager a nod, turned, and left. *Damn, sometimes you just have to lie.*

Once outside, Joe began thinking. Vincent Scalise. Is he part of Carmine Scalise's family? And if so, what are Curtis and Jacqueline both doing meeting with him? Are Curtis and Jacqueline strictly business or is their relationship intimate as well?

Joe drove back to Area 3 headquarters and got on his computer. He ran a check on Vincent Scalise and found he was one of two sons of Carmine Scalise. His residence is in Las Vegas, and his occupation is casino owner, along with his father and brother, Antonio. Vincent is forty-one years old, divorced, and has an arrest record for assault, intimidation of a witness, jury tampering, and domestic violence, but no convictions. *Thanks to his father's connections and money, no doubt. Sounds like a real jewel. It doesn't sound like smuggling would be much of a stretch.*

Joe emailed Vincenzo and cc'd Sam on what he'd discovered about the link between the Fieldings and Vincent Scalise. As he was getting ready to leave the office, he received a call from Lisa Veroni. She was crying and wanted to see him. Joe called Sam and asked him to meet him at the West Grace Street address she shared with William Higgins. Joe pulled up ten minutes later and saw that Sam was waiting for him.

When Lisa opened the door to the apartment, they were appalled when they saw her face. Both her eyes were swollen, and her lip was split. She was holding a bag of frozen peas which she applied against her face. Stepping through the door, Joe asked, "What on earth happened to you?"

"That fuckin' boyfriend of mine is what happened to me!" she said through tears.

CHAPTER TWENTY-THREE

"Higgins?" asked Joe.

"Yeah," she said as her voice devolved into a sob.

"Here," said Sam, guiding her to the sofa. "Why don't you sit down and tell us about it? Can I get you anything? Water or—"

"No, I'm all right."

Lisa sat on the sofa while Joe and Sam sat on each side of her. She held the bag of peas to her left eye, then moved it periodically to her right eye as they spoke.

"Tell us what happened," said Sam.

"Willie got drunk, and we got into a row. He was claiming I screwed Devon," she said. "He wouldn't get off my case about it."

"Where'd he get that idea?" asked Joe.

"Devon and I had sex a coupla times when Willie was at work...and Willie found Devon's checkbook on the floor next to my nightstand. It must have fallen out of his jeans pocket. I told Willie I found it between the couch cushions after we'd been partying, and I was keeping it for him. That I must've knocked it off the nightstand when I was making the bed. I thought he believed me. I called Devon about the lost checkbook, so he'd back me up, in case Willie ever asked him about it."

"When was the last time you two had sex?" asked Joe.

"A couple days before Devon got busted up in the bar."

"I see."

"But today, he got drunk and brought it up again and accused me of screwing his best friend." Then, she reached for her handkerchief and dabbed her eyes. "He just went out of his mind. And then he said...."

"What did he say?" asked Sam.

At that point, Lisa burst into tears and said, "He said, 'Nobody fucks my woman and gets away with it. Nobody!' and then..." She tried to control herself but couldn't. Finally, she sobbed, "And then he said, 'I shoulda killed you, too!'"

Silence, as Joe and Sam looked at each other.

"He said, 'I should've killed you, too'?" asked Joe, trying to confirm what she said.

"Uh-huh." And she sobbed.

Joe looked at Sam. They knew they finally found the triggerman in Devon Schmidt's murder. Now, it was up to them to apprehend and arrest William John Higgins.

"What happened next?" asked Sam.

"I screamed, 'You killed Devon?' And then he grabbed me and started beating the shit out of me, calling me every name he could think of. I thought he was gonna kill me. I finally got away from him and ran in the bedroom and locked the door. I keep one of my guns hidden in there and told him if he tried to break in, I'd shoot him."

"What did he do?" asked Joe.

"He tried to force his way in anyway, so I fired a shot through the top of the door. That seemed to convince him I meant it. After that, I heard him leave on his motorcycle. That's when I called you."

"Do you know where Willie might be right now?" asked Sam.

"I don't know. He could be anywhere," said Lisa.

"Is he armed?"

"He probably took his Sig."

"That's it?"

"Yeah."

"You need to see a doctor?" asked Joe.

"No, I'll be all right."

"You sure?"

"I've had worse."

Joe looked at her in astonishment. "Okay. I'm calling in uniforms to protect you in case he decides to come back. In the meantime, we'll put out an APB on him. What's he ride?

"A Harley chopper. Black."

"Okay."

Joe called in an APB on William John Higgins. "He should be considered armed and dangerous and is wanted in connection with the murder of Devon Schmidt."

Joe also requested a protection detail for Lisa Veroni in case Schmidt

150

decided to come back. Joe and Sam stayed with Lisa until uniforms arrived from the 19th. Once they were on-premises, Joe and Sam drove to Higgins' employer, but no one there had seen him all day.

Late that afternoon, Joe drove home. After a long day, he felt pleased they finally caught a break in the Devon Schmidt case. After supper, he kicked back in his recliner and pulled up Netflix to continue watching a Norwegian crime drama. Just as it was about to start, he received a call from Sam.

"Hey, Sam. What's up?"

"Willie Higgins."

"Yeah?"

"He was spotted on his chopper traveling south on I-57 south of Kankakee. A state trooper gave chase. He was clocked at over a hundred ten miles an hour when he lost control and crashed his bike. He didn't survive."

"Anyone else hurt?"

"No. But I talked to the State Police. They told me he was thrown from his bike and was hit by a semi. It guess it was beyond ugly."

"Jesus!"

"So, you think we can close the book on Devon Schmidt's homicide?" asked Sam.

"We'll have to get an official statement from Lisa Veroni. But if she repeats what she told us...Yeah. It sounds like he's our offender."

"And it turns out Devon Schmidt's death had nothing to do with Daniel Silverman, after all."

"But the gun that killed him did," reminded Joe. "How did that happen?"

"You got me there."

"All this time we've been chasing our tails trying to connect dots that lead nowhere."

"Do you think Higgins could have killed Daniel, too?" asked Sam.

"It makes sense if a neo-Nazi like Higgins is the offender. But where's the connection with Higgins and Fielding?"

"I don't know. So far, there doesn't appear to be any."

"Yeah. That's the part that makes no sense. Where did he get the gun he used to kill Schmidt?" Then Joe had another thought. "Has Lisa been told

Willie's dead?"

"No."

"Okay. I'll go tell her. She deserves to know."

Chapter Twenty-Four

The next afternoon, Shari Moroso, Devon Schmidt's sister, took Lisa Veroni to Area 3 headquarters to give her statement. Lisa was psychologically fragile, wrestling with the conflicting grief over her partner's death and the anger over the violent beating he inflicted on her. Her face was less swollen, and her bruised eyes had turned a purplish red. She wore wrap-around sunglasses to partially hide the injuries. But nothing could disguise her swollen split lip.

Shari, her best friend, was also torn over her feelings of the betrayal and murder of her brother by his best friend. After Joe escorted Lisa to the conference room, Shari told Sam that Lisa was considering moving out of the residence she shared with Higgins because he was physically abusive when he drank. But Shari could have never imagined Higgins capable of killing his best friend.

Inside the conference room, Joe gave Lisa a yellow legal pad and pen, instructing her to write a detailed narrative about her encounter with Higgins the previous day, specifically noting what she believed he meant by the statement, "I should have killed you, too." Joe left the room, and over the next half-hour, Lisa wrote a lengthy account of what happened, noting that she was positive Higgins meant that he killed Devon Schmidt because he believed Schmidt was having sex with her.

When Lisa finished writing her statement, it was typed, and a printed copy was presented for her signature. A final paragraph stated, "I believe that the facts stated in this witness statement are true." Below were spaces for a signature and a date.

153

After reading through it, she looked at Joe and nodded her head in agreement. Then she signed and dated it. A copy would be included in the case file. Joe's final report and all the information generated in the investigation would be sent to Lieutenant Vincenzo and appropriate paperwork sent to supervisory personnel. With no questions or objections, the case would be closed. The file and all the evidence in the case would be boxed up, sealed, and placed in storage.

Joe escorted Lisa to the entrance where they met Sam and Shari. Sam had been keeping Shari company by asking follow-up questions while Lisa prepared her statement.

Seeing the two women together after all that had taken place, Joe looked at Shari and said, "It must be a little awkward for you knowing such a close friend's partner killed your brother."

Shari bristled at his comment, then said, "I know this may seem weird to you. But I don't blame Lisa for what happened to Devon. Willie just flipped out."

"I have one last question," said Joe, and he looked at Lisa. "Why did you decide to have sex with Devon when you knew Willie had a violent temper?"

Lisa looked at him and shrugged. "I don't know. It was just a couple of times, no big deal. I guess I did it for a lark, you know?"

Her answer rubbed Joe the wrong way. "I hope it was worth it," he replied. "Because two people are dead because of it."

Lisa's eyes went from Joe to Sam, then to Shari.

"Come on, honey," said Shari, her eyes burning into Joe before she looked at Lisa. "Let's go." As Shari pushed open the door, Lisa slipped on her sunglasses, and they both stepped into the light and were gone.

It was one of those incredulous moments. Joe looked at Sam, shaking his head. "What can I say?"

"How about good riddance?" said Sam. "We got her statement. That's all that matters."

Joe called Annie Bloom in the Civil Rights Unit to let her know about the progress made on Devon Schmidt's murder. She was pleased to hear it had been solved but asked about the Daniel Silverman case. Joe admitted they were following leads, but nothing was pointing to a suspect at the present time. He had already informed her about the gun that killed both Daniel and Schmidt and told her they would continue to keep her informed.

* * *

During the next several days, Joe and Sam continued their surveillance. Joe watched Robert Curtis while Sam kept an eye on the cars going in and out of the Fielding estate. One consistency Sam noticed was a car that drove in each morning at the same time, driven by a woman who stayed approximately half an hour. Sam ran her plate and found the car was registered to Richard and Jane Pellegrino. The car stood out from all other cars that came and went from the estate as most of the vehicles were new, high-end, expensive luxury cars. The Pellegrino vehicle was a five-year-old Ford SUV.

On Friday morning, the blue SUV did not make its usual appearance at the Fielding estate. Sam then ran a background check on Jane Pellegrino and found she was a registered nurse working for a company providing specialized in-home care. Her husband, Richard, worked in the Financial Aid Office at Northwestern University in Evanston.

After sharing his findings with Joe, they decided to pay Jane Pellegrino a visit. They arrived at the Pellegrino residence, a Tudor-style home in a nicely manicured neighborhood two blocks from campus. The Ford SUV was parked alongside a Subaru in the driveway. Joe parked in the street, and they walked up the brick driveway and rang the bell.

They heard barking from inside the house, and after a few moments, a woman in her mid-forties answered the door. "Hush, Razha!" she said, looking back at the dog. Then she looked at Joe and Sam. "Sorry."

"Jane Pellegrino?" asked Joe.

"Yes," answered the woman.

Joe held out his ID. "I'm Detective Joe Erickson, Chicago PD. My partner, Sam Renaldo. Could we have a few minutes of your time?"

"Excuse me a second." She bent over, picked up a small, long-haired dog with a mustache Sam would envy. The barking ceased and she turned back to Joe asking, "What's this about?"

"An investigation we're currently conducting. We just want to ask you a few questions, that's all."

A tall man with rimless glasses and a gray beard appeared behind her. "What's going on?" he asked.

Joe held up his ID once again. We're detectives working a case, and we'd like to ask your wife a few questions if that's all right. She's not in any kind of trouble. We would simply like to confirm a couple of things."

Jane looked at her husband, and he said, "You'd better let them in."

Without a word, she opened the door, and Joe and Sam came in. They entered a small vestibule that led to a hall with stairs to a second floor. Richard turned left through a door to a nicely appointed living room.

Pointing to the couch, he said, "Please, have a seat."

Joe and Sam sat down while Richard and Jane sat in the chairs facing them across from a large coffee table. The dog sat on Jane's lap and stared suspiciously at Joe and Sam.

Looking at the dog and then to Jane, Joe asked, "Lhasa Apso, right?"

"Right," said Jane. "How did you know?"

"Long story," Joe replied. "Well, let me get straight to the point. Your car has been seen going in and out of the Fielding estate for several days. We know you're a nurse and work for an agency that provides nursing care to patients in the home. We assume you're there to check on one of the family, most likely Thomas Fielding. Would that be correct?"

Jane looked at Richard, then back at Joe. "That's confidential information. I don't feel as though I should respond to your question."

"Well, we just find it peculiar that Mr. Fielding, who according to his attorney, had such a minor stroke, would require daily monitoring."

"Minor?" Jane blurted out. Then she caught herself and said, "I'm sorry. I shouldn't have said that."

Red flags went up, and Joe and Sam were immediately concerned by this revelation, knowing she would be the only source for additional information on Fielding's condition.

"Thomas Fielding's health is critical to our investigation, Mrs. Pellegrino.

I think you just blew a hole in confidentiality. If you know something, you need to tell us. If it makes you feel any better, we do <u>not</u> reveal our sources."

"Tell them, dear," said Richard. "They need to know."

Jane contemplated whether to tell them. She rubbed the dog's ear for a moment, then looked up and said, "I've been a Registered Nurse for twenty years, and I've never once revealed any confidential information about a patient. This'll be the first time."

"We appreciate your decision in this matter," replied Sam.

"Mr. Fielding had a massive stroke that left him completely incapacitated. It wasn't mild like his attorney told you. He's relegated to a wheelchair. His wrists are tied to the arms of the chair, and he is belted in, so he doesn't fall out. He can't talk, and only utters occasional grunts. It's a sad and tragic situation."

"So, you check on him every day, then?"

"Yes. Up until yesterday."

"Why? What happened yesterday?" asked Joe.

"I was told my services were no longer needed."

"By whom? Mrs. Fielding?"

"Vernon. Their security man."

"Do you know what the reason may have been?"

"The day before yesterday, I told Mrs. Fielding that I thought Mr. Fielding was trying to communicate with me by blinking with his eyes."

"Blinking his eyes?"

"Yes. I asked him a question he could answer yes or no to, and he distinctly blinked his eyes twice."

"What was the question?"

"Are you glad to see me, today? Then I asked him a second question, "Are you feeling well? And he distinctly blinked once. I didn't want to question him further because Vernon was in the room. He's always observing when I'm there."

"Did he see any of this?"

"No. But I told Mrs. Fielding about it and suggested he was trying to communicate with me."

"What was her reaction?"

"Concern." She paused, then her voice began to tremble as she said, "And yesterday when I arrived, Vernon told me my services were no longer needed. I was shocked."

"Did he give you a reason?"

"No. I've never been dismissed from a job. Ever." She pulled a handkerchief from her dress and blew her nose.

Richard spoke up. "My wife has impeccable credentials and references, detectives. To be dismissed for no apparent reason is infuriating. It had better not reflect badly on her employment record."

"We'll be looking into this, Mr. Pellegrino," assured Sam.

After giving Jane a few moments to compose herself, Joe asked, "What's your take on Jacqueline Fielding? I assume you had some dealings with her."

"Strictly business, but…"

"But what?"

"Cold. Indifferent. I sometimes wondered if she actually loved her husband."

"Can you describe Vernon to us?" asked Sam.

"Well, he's in his late-thirties-early forties, about six-foot-two, well-built, dark hair that he wears in a buzzcut, mustache, and goatee. Kinda scary looking, to be honest. Oh—and he has the tattoo of a raised fist on his right upper arm. I saw it when his sleeve pulled up as he helped me re-position Mr. Fielding in his wheelchair."

Joe demonstrated by holding up his hand and making a fist. "Like this?"

"Yes. Like that."

Joe acknowledged by nodding. "Thank you."

"And he has a small number eighty-eight tattooed on the back of his neck. I asked him about it once, and he said it was his number when he played football."

"I'll bet it was," said Joe. "Do you know Vernon's last name by chance?"

"No, I'm sorry."

As Joe and Sam walked to the car, Joe remarked, "Vernon's a neo-Nazi. That raised fist and the number eighty-eight are two of their symbols."

CHAPTER TWENTY-FOUR

"I know," replied Sam. "Lose one connection, pick up another, huh?"

As Joe circled the front of their car, he saw the same blue Camry with a mismatched fender that had been following Cindy Fielding. After clicking his seatbelt and starting his car, he said to Sam, "We have a tail. Same one that was following Cindy Fielding. Hold on."

Joe started the car, whipped around, and pulled in front of the Camry. Both he and Sam jumped out with guns drawn before the driver could move away.

"Hands on the steering wheel!" yelled Joe, as Sam moved around to the passenger side. The driver complied, and Joe opened the driver's door.

"Now, release your seatbelt and step out, hands on the roof."

The pudgy man in his mid-fifties got out of his car. He knew the drill, spreading his legs and saying, "I have a permit to carry."

Joe frisked him and pulled a .357 from a shoulder holster. "Let's hope you do," said Joe as he turned him around to face him. "Okay. Let's see some ID."

The man reached in his front pants pocket and pulled out his wallet. Removing his driver's license and PI license along with his concealed carry permit, he handed them to Joe.

Sam came around to the side of the car and stood next to the driver as Joe read his ID out loud.

"Theodore Matthew Doane. You're a private investigator." Looking up from the IDs, Joe looked at Doane. "Appears you could use a refresher course in surveillance, Mr. Doane. Why are you following us?"

"Job," replied Doane.

"You gotta do better than that," said Sam.

"I'm workin' on a case."

"Yeah? So are we."

"And we could arrest you for interfering with a police investigation," said Joe. "Would you like to lose your license, Theodore?"

"It's Ted. And look, this doesn't have to get ugly here," said Doane.

"I think he wants to lose his license, Joe," said Sam.

"Hey, I have to make a living, too."

"He has to make a living. What do you think, Joe?" asked Sam.

"Not by messing with us, he doesn't," Joe replied. "What do you think, Sam? Should we run him in?"

"All right. All right. It won't happen again."

"Who you working for?" asked Sam.

"You know I can't tell you that."

"Why were you following Cindy Fielding?"

"Job."

"Yeah, that pretty much narrows the field about who you're working for," said Joe. "So, tell your client if he wants you to interfere with our investigation one more time, that Joe Erickson knows who he is and that I'll rip him a new asshole. Got that?"

"Yeah. I got that."

Joe emptied the shells from Doane's .357 onto the ground, then handed it back to him along with his IDs. After getting back into their car, Sam said, "You think Jay Fielding hired him?"

"Yeah," replied Joe, "but I wouldn't be surprised if it was Jacqueline Fielding after what I've learned in the past few days."

As they pulled away from the curb, Sam asked, "Tell me—you ever ripped a woman a new asshole?"

Joe looked over at Sam. "There's a first time for everything."

Chapter Twenty-Five

On Saturday, Joe continued his surveillance of Robert Curtis. He detected no movement from his residence until evening when he and a young woman caught a taxi to one of Chicago's fine dining restaurants located on North Halsted. Joe looked up the restaurant's website and found the place's menu cost over $300.00 per person.

After about ninety minutes, Curtis, along with his date, came out of the establishment, hailed a taxi, and returned to his apartment. Joe watched until midnight, then returned home. He told Destiny he would be on surveillance this weekend.

"Sorry for the odd hours," he said when he got in.

"That's okay. Hungry?" she asked.

"As a matter of fact..."

She removed a baking dish from the refrigerator and placed it in the microwave.

"I made this earlier thinking you probably didn't have much to eat today."

"I didn't. What is it?"

"Butternut risotto with leeks and spinach."

"Sounds terrific."

"You want some wine?"

"If I drink wine, I'll probably fall asleep face down on my plate. Better not. Water will do."

Destiny got glasses from the cupboard and a filtered water pitcher from the refrigerator and poured two glasses of water.

"I was going to ask...Could you contact Loretta Affannato and see if it would be all right for me to use their yacht's fly deck for surveillance purposes. It has a good view of the Fieldings' yacht. I can get a close-up view of everything with binoculars."

"I don't see why she would object to that. You made a good impression on her."

"Good."

"You think something's up with Fieldings?"

"Jay Fielding, Jacqueline Fielding, Robert Curtis. And they all have a link to Vincent Scalise in Las Vegas."

"The Carmine Scalise family?"

"Yeah. He's Carmine's son."

"That's not good. You're thinking drug trafficking?"

"That's what I'm assuming, but there's no evidence Fielding Enterprises is transporting drugs. However…if Scalise is involved, there's a good chance something illegal's going on."

The microwave's timer went off, and Destiny removed the baking dish and set it on the table along with a serving spoon, silverware, and plates.

"Help yourself," she said.

After dinner, they adjourned to the living room. Not long after he sat down, Joe was nodding off. Destiny couldn't help but be amused by it. The third time his chin touched his chest, she said, "Come on, soldier. It's time for bed."

She pulled him up by the arm and led him into the bedroom where he flopped down on the bed. "Am I going to have to undress you, too?"

"I think I can handle that part."

* * *

Early Sunday morning, Joe was up and jogging. Some time ago, Destiny purchased another jogging outfit for him to keep in her apartment, and shortly thereafter, he added a pair of running shoes, so he didn't have to go home early to get his jogging in.

He hadn't completed a mile when he began thinking about the Fieldings and the smuggling angle. If contraband was being transported on Fielding trucks, there must be at least a few conspirators in Fielding's Chicago terminal who would unload and transfer the goods. Joe needed to get into the terminal and watch when a shipment came in. But how could he know when a shipment would arrive? The Chicago terminal for Fielding Enterprises was huge with hundreds of trucks being loaded and unloaded every day. The unloading of contraband would most likely take place at night when there would be less activity. But without a tip, there was no way to know the day and time.

Returning to Destiny's apartment, he showered and dressed. Together, they made breakfast.

Over a second cup of coffee, Destiny said, "Oh, I didn't tell you. I got some good news from my doctor. My leg has healed completely from the car accident, and he said I can resume my martial arts training."

"That's great," said Joe.

"It's going to take a while to get back into shape. I've been doing stretching and yoga trying to maintain flexibility, but now I can do weights to build my strength back and eventually resume contact activity with my instructor."

"I'm going to feel much safer walking down the street with you now," smiled Joe.

"As you should." She paused. "I haven't mentioned this because it hasn't firmed up yet. I was contacted last Friday about a possible consulting job in Virginia. Virginia Beach. They have a serial rapist, and they want to bring me in to do a profile. It's 'bad for tourism' and one of my FBI colleagues recommended me."

"When will you know?"

"By mid-week. If they do bring me in, I'll probably be gone about ten days."

"I guess I'll live."

"I figured you could tough it out. You'll have to eat my perishables."

"Wow. That's the first time a girl has asked me to do that."

Destiny rolled her eyes. "Just don't do anything dumb while I'm gone like get shot or something, okay?"

"Okay. I'll wait until you get back."

"I'm not kidding. And don't try to pull any of that David Eugene Burton round-the-clock surveillance crap, either."

"Don't worry. I learned my lesson on that. No more than twelve hours a day. Going crazy once was enough."

* * *

At 2:00 pm, Joe parted company with Destiny and drove to the tower where Robert Curtis lived. He began his surveillance of the building, judging since it was Sunday, Curtis and his lady-friend would have slept in and had a late morning brunch.

A little before 3:00 pm, a car drove up and parked at the entrance. A few minutes later, Curtis and a woman left the building, and she got into what Joe assumed was an Uber ride. Curtis kissed her, and after her ride took off, Curtis went back into the building. Half an hour later, he left driving his red Jaguar. Joe followed him at a discreet distance as he drove south on Lakeshore Drive. When Soldier Field came into view, Joe had a good idea where Curtis was headed, and a few minutes later, he took the exit leading to Burnham Harbor.

Curtis turned his Jag into the entrance to the harbor and parked in a small lot near the dock where the Fielding yacht was moored. Joe followed and chose to park in the McCormick Place lot, a short way away from where Curtis parked. He knew where Curtis was headed so there was no need to follow him closely. Joe called Destiny and asked if she had contacted Loretta Affannato about Joe's use of her fly deck. She said she had already done so, and Loretta agreed. So, Joe gave Curtis a ten-minute head start, then he began walking down to the dock where the Affannatos' yacht was moored.

He called Loretta, and she gave him her security code to open the gate. She greeted him with a smile as he boarded and asked if he needed anything. Joe brought a bottle of water and his binoculars. That was all he needed.

"I'm fine, Loretta. Just pretend I'm not here," he said.

"If you need anything, you let me know, all right?" she replied.

"I will." He climbed up to the fly deck and positioned himself so he could see the Fielding yacht. He was hoping Loretta would forget he was there. He didn't need any interruptions while watching the activity on the Fieldings' yacht.

About 7:00 pm, Loretta laid a plate and bottle of water on the deck. "You need to eat," she said in a hushed voice. "I hope you like chicken salad."

Joe couldn't help but smile. "Thanks."

Well, that kind of interruption he didn't mind. He was getting hungry, and he had drained his bottle of water. Her chicken salad sandwich really hit the spot.

Nothing noteworthy was happening on the Fielding yacht. Curtis and Jay Fielding were the only two aboard, and they spent nearly all their time inside the main deck salon. By 10:00 pm, it was dark, and Joe began thinking he was wasting his time, but he was determined to keep up his surveillance until Curtis left. The only activities he saw were Curtis coming out carrying a wine glass, walking around the deck, then going back inside.

Shortly after midnight, a blue van drove up on the access road at the edge of the harbor and parked next to the dock leading to the slip where Fieldings' yacht was moored. The passenger door opened and an athletic-looking man with a buzzcut got out and opened the side door of the van. Eight young Latina girls got out of the van, and the man led them up the dock followed by the driver. Jay Fielding disappeared inside the cabin, and a moment later, the diesel engines started. The man along with Robert Curtis stood on deck and conversed with the driver. After a moment, they ushered the girls into the main deck salon and closed the doors while the driver walked back to the van and drove away. Joe was able to write down the license plate number before it left.

A few minutes later, Curtis returned to the deck where he released the mooring lines, retracted the gangway, and went back inside. The sound from the engines grew louder as the yacht moved out of its slip and sailed toward the mouth of the harbor. Joe watched as it entered the waters of Lake Michigan. Once in clear water, the powerful diesel engines growled as they pushed the yacht forward into the night.

Damn! Joe thought. *They're not trafficking drugs. They're trafficking in young women!*

Chapter Twenty-Six

The next morning, Joe was in Vincenzo's office describing what he witnessed the night before. Vincenzo was all ears.

"So, you think they're trafficking young girls from Latin America rather than drugs?" Vincenzo asked.

"Yeah."

"You said you got a license plate number on the van. Did you find out who it's registered to?"

"A corporation registered in the Cayman Islands. You know what that means."

"Yeah." Vincenzo paused. "I don't get it. Why would some millionaire like Jay Fielding get himself involved with human trafficking? He's risking the life of Riley for an illegal operation that could get him twenty years. What the hell's with that?"

"I think he has a serious gambling problem. An addiction, maybe," said Joe. "I can't prove it, but he makes a lot of trips to Vegas, and he uses his travel to oversee the business centers out west as a cover for his Vegas trips. My guess is he owes a shit-load of money to Scalise's casino, and this is how Scalise has him working it off."

"Trouble is, we have no way to prove it," said Vincenzo.

"I'm thinking Daniel Silverman got wind of the trafficking scheme, and when he tried to confirm it, he got caught, and they silenced him. This whole time we were chasing our tails trying to connect his murder to Devon Schmidt. His high school connection to Jay Fielding and his job with Fielding Enterprises turned out to be coincidental."

167

"So, who do you think killed Daniel Silverman?"

"I don't think Fielding or Curtis would want to get their hands dirty. I'd put my money on the Fieldings' security guard," said Joe. "His name is Vernon—don't have a last name yet—but the elder Fielding's former nurse told me he has a couple of neo-Nazi tattoos. I wouldn't be surprised if he could have been the one to do it. No evidence, just my gut feeling at this point."

"It would be easy enough to kill him and dump him off the yacht in Lake Michigan late at night. But what about the gun? How did the gun get from this guy Vernon to Higgins so he could kill Schmidt?"

"All three are neo-Nazis," explained Joe, "and they could have been members of the same group. If Higgins needed a gun to kill Schmidt, and he knew Vernon from their hate group, Vernon could have unloaded the gun to Higgins to use on Schmidt."

"If Vernon did kill Daniel, why didn't he drop the gun into the lake when they dumped the body? Holding on to a murder weapon is pretty stupid."

"Unless he knew what Higgins was planning to do beforehand. That would've been pretty damned clever—helping Higgins frame Schmidt by giving him the gun used for Daniel's murder. Problem was, Vernon didn't know about Schmidt's knee injury and his dislike of Colt weapons."

"Find out who this Vernon is. See if he has a rap sheet."

"Can we set up surveillance on the yacht and get someone inside Fielding's terminal? We need eyes on when and how these girls are being transported."

"You have to give me more than eight girls getting on the yacht late at night, Joe. For all we know, they were partying."

"Lieutenant—"

"I know, I know. But I need more to justify the request. Get me more incriminating evidence, and I'll send it through."

"Okay."

Joe left Vincenzo's office, motivated to discover Vernon's identity. He thought he might need Destiny's help through her contacts at the FBI. They had resources he didn't, so he gave her a call.

"Hi," she said, surprised to hear from him so early in the morning. "What's up?"

"I hate to impose, but I need a favor. An FBI-type favor."

"Okay."

"We have a person of interest, a neo-Nazi living here whose first name is Vernon. We have no last name. He's working security for the Fieldings. Six-two, well-built, mid-to-late-thirties to early forties, dark hair, tattoos of an eighty-eight on the back of his neck, and a raised fist on his right upper arm. That's all we have. We think he might belong to one of the neo-Nazi groups in the city. Do you have a contact who could give us an ID on this guy? Or at least narrow it down?"

"Maybe. I can give a former colleague a call. Maybe she can search their databases for names of known members of neo-Nazi groups in the city. With a little luck, she can turn up some possibilities for you."

"That would be great."

"But it's going to cost you."

"I'm sure it will. It always does. Thanks."

"Talk to you later."

Joe decided to pay Robert Curtis a visit and prepared for his questioning. Then he drove to the Fielding Enterprises headquarters on East Randolph Street. He got off the elevator on the seventh floor and walked to the receptionist's desk where Astrid Nielson recognized him.

Flashing him a smile, she said, "Good morning, Detective Erickson."

"Good morning, Astrid. Is Robert Curtis in today? I have some follow-up questions regarding our investigation."

"He is. Let me see if he's available." She called Curtis on the intercom. "He can see you." She stood and escorted him to Curtis' office.

Once inside, Curtis didn't bother to stand, preferring to remain sitting at his desk. Not very welcoming, and Joe was not invited to sit.

"What can I do for you, detective?" Curtis asked as if Joe's presence annoyed him.

Joe decided to come straight to the point to watch Curtis' reaction. "You can tell me what you and Jacqueline Fielding were doing with Vincent Scalise at the Palmer House for starters," asked Joe.

"What are you talking about?"

"You and Jacqueline Fielding were seen coming out of the Palmer House with Vincent Scalise, a known felon from Las Vegas. You appeared to be, shall we say, 'chummy'?"

"Someone must be mistaken. I don't know anyone by that name."

Joe reached inside his jacket pocket and pulled out an envelope. "Are you going to make me show you photographs, Mr. Curtis? Of you, Vincent Scalise, and Mrs. Fielding?" He was hoping Curtis wouldn't call his bluff because the envelope he was holding only held photo-sized pieces of file folders he had cut in the office.

Joe waved the envelope in front of Curtis and it was like waving a red cape in front of a bull. Curtis stood up behind his desk, his face reddened with anger.

"I'm not sayin' another word. From now on, talk to my attorney, you asshole!"

"And your attorney would be?"

"Wendell DeForrest."

"I'll do that," said Joe, placing the envelope back in his pocket. "Thank you for your time, Mr. Curtis." After leaving Curtis' office, Joe felt pleased that he succeeded in rattling Curtis' cage. The next thing he wanted to do was to rattle Jacqueline Fielding's as well.

Joe drove to the Fielding estate and stopped at the iron gates that prevented entry onto the premises. Getting out of his car, he walked to the intercom and pressed the button to be identified. A man's voice responded.

"State your name and business."

"Detective Joe Erickson, Chicago Police Department. I need to ask Mrs. Fielding a few questions."

"She's not available."

"She's not on the premises or she's not seeing anyone?"

"She's not available."

"Look, this is police business. I need to speak with someone face to face, not over an intercom. Could someone come out, please?"

Silence. After a few moments, a man matching the description of Vernon came walking toward the gate. He was wearing a light blue golf shirt and navy slacks. Joe's phone was in hand and he got a few pictures of him as he got close to the gate.

Pretending to end a phone call to cover the taking of photos, Joe put his phone away and said, "Thanks for seeing me."

The scowl on Vernon's face would intimidate most people. He would have been a good fit with professional wrestling's bad guys. "So, what did you need to discuss?" he asked. Joe detected a slight accent in his speech.

"Mrs. Fielding's reluctance to see me for one thing."

Clearly annoyed, Vernon replied, "As I told you, she is not available."

"When will she be available? Is there a time I should return? At her convenience, of course."

"She told me to inform you to talk with her attorney."

"Really."

"Really."

"Let me guess. That would be Wendell DeForrest, right?"

"Right."

"Did she just get a call from Robert Curtis?"

"I can't say."

"Can't or won't?" Vernon bristled at his question, "Well, I guess I'll have to see Mr. DeForrest, huh? Please tell her this will not bode well for her in this investigation. It makes her look...guilty of something. By the way, what did you say your name was?"

"I didn't."

Vernon's piercing eyes looked at Joe with disdain before he turned and walked away.

"Thank you for your time... 'Vernon,'" said Joe.

As Joe watched, Vernon's step hesitated slightly after Joe stated his name, but he kept on walking back toward the house, fists clenching and unclenching. Joe smiled. If Destiny could not get Vernon's last name through her FBI colleague, maybe he would be able to get a hit with facial recognition on this guy.

Back in his car, Joe sent Destiny the photo of Vernon and a message saying he detected what he thought was a slight German accent hoping it would help in her search. Then an idea occurred to him. He reached for his laptop and pulled up Google Earth. Knowing it was a live feed, he entered the Fielding estate's location and took a look. Zooming in, he saw a woman in a swimsuit lounging in a chair by the swimming pool. She was speaking with who else? Vernon. Undoubtedly, he was filling her in on his visit. *I guess working on melanoma is Mrs. Fielding's definition of being unavailable.*

As he drove back to Area 3, he thought about how the young women were transported. He didn't know the location of the blue van that brought the girls to the dock. It could be garaged about anywhere and brought out whenever it was needed. Without surveillance, it would be next to impossible to trace its location. But there might be a way to track the destination of the yacht once it left the harbor.

When Joe walked back to his desk after retrieving his lunch from the refrigerator, he saw Sam getting ready to leave. He quickly filled him in on what had happened with Curtis and Vernon earlier.

"You really ruffled some feathers this morning, didn't you," said Sam.

"I thought we needed to shake things up. See if something falls out."

"Are you going to keep surveilling Curtis?"

"Yeah, but only at night since that's when these girls are being transported."

"I see no need in surveilling the Fielding estate. But I think watching Jay Fielding would be a good idea."

"Agreed. Since he's the one who pilots the yacht, he's going to be there for each of the trips out of the harbor," said Joe.

"Good. I'll start on him tonight."

"Since all three of our people have lawyered up, and since Wendell DeForrest is the attorney for each of them, I think we need to pay him a visit."

"You gonna call ahead?" asked Sam.

"As a courtesy," replied Joe. "We know when he's always available."

Joe called the Office of DeForrest, Brown, & Whittier and asked to speak with Fiona Garrick, Wendell DeForrest's assistant. When she picked up, he identified himself and asked if he and Sam could speak with "Wendell" before he took his afternoon nap. She said, "Be here promptly at 3:00 pm."

Joe and Sam arrived at the North Wabash address of William DeForrest's law firm and rode the elevator to the thirty-sixth floor. They got there ten minutes early and informed Audrey, the receptionist, they had a meeting with Mr. DeForrest at 3:00 pm. She asked them to have a seat and made a call. Five minutes later, Fiona greeted them and led them to DeForrest's office. She knocked, opened the door a crack, and said, "Detectives Erickson and Renaldo to see you."

"Send them in," came the familiar deep baritone voice from inside. DeForrest was sitting at his table, removing his shoes.

"Damned new shoes. Wish I could hire someone to break them in for me." Looking up at the two detectives, he said, "Joe, Sam. Have a seat. What can I do for you?"

Joe and Sam sat down with DeForrest at the table. Joe said, "I wanted to ask a couple people questions regarding our investigation, and they refused. They told me to speak to you."

"Who was it?"

"Robert Curtis and Jacqueline Fielding."

"Hm," replied DeForrest. "What prompted this request?"

"Robert Curtis and Jacqueline Fielding were seen in the company of Vincent Scalise, a known felon from an organized crime family, coming out of the Palmer House. They seemed quite chummy," explained Joe.

"Did you speak with each of them about it?"

"No, I only spoke with Mr. Curtis who became quite agitated when I brought it up. Mrs. Fielding refused to speak with me."

"Do you have any evidence a meeting occurred between them?"

"No. They were seen leaving the hotel at the same time."

"Well, I can understand why Mr. Curtis became agitated if you insinuated they were involved with a member of organized crime. That would be bad for business, Joe. The Fieldings go to Las Vegas and stay at one of Scalise's hotels, do a little gambling, meet Mr. Scalise, schmooze a little. You know how it is. Money befriends money. Scalise is in Chicago on business, and they see each other while having a meal at the Palmer House. Their meeting is purely happenstance."

"We don't believe in coincidences," said Sam.

"I can understand that, given your profession. It's your job to be skeptical. You encounter people who lie every day, am I right?"

"Then why wouldn't Jacqueline Curtis simply tell me that?" asked Joe. "Why lawyer up and look guilty of something?"

"Admittedly, it was not a good move on her part. She should have simply told you what happened. But knowing her, I can understand why she did what she did. You see, she's a very private person, quite protective of her husband and anything to do with the business."

"Speaking of her husband, you told me he suffered a minor stroke the last time we talked. But I later found out he had a debilitating stroke that has left him unable to talk or get out of a wheelchair. Why was I misled."

"Well...I owe you an apology for that. The reason I misrepresented his condition is because if the severity of his illness became public, the faith and trust in Fielding Enterprises could be shaken. Worst case scenario, it could cost stockholders millions of dollars. That's why we chose to keep his condition a secret until Jay is officially made President and CEO."

"So, you're saying that Vincent Scalise has nothing to do with Fielding Enterprises or any of the people in charge of the company," said Sam, seeking confirmation.

"That's what I'm saying. As far as I know, he has nothing to do with the company itself, and he's only acquainted with the Fieldings from their vacation stays in Las Vegas."

"Do you know anything about Thomas and Jacqueline Fielding's security person. His first name is Vernon."

"No, I'm afraid not. Our office has never run background checks on any security personnel. Sorry." There was a pause. "Anything else, fellas?"

Joe looked at Sam to see if he had any more questions. Sam shook his head. "I think that answers all of our questions for now. Thank you for seeing us, Wendell."

"Always have time for the CPD," said DeForrest, rising. "You'll forgive me if I don't put on my shoes to see you out."

After leaving DeForrest's office, Sam said, "Either he doesn't know anything or he's lying."

"It's hard telling. His clients could be keeping him in the dark about things, especially if they're illegal. And if he knows anything about their relationship with Vincent Scalise, then he's in on the take."

"You think someone like Wendell DeForrest is dirty?"

"I'd like to think not. But like they say, there are only three lawyer jokes. The rest are all true."

Sam snorted a laugh and drove them back to the office. When Joe got out of the car, he told Sam he had to pick up something before his surveillance tonight and he would see him first thing in the morning.

Chapter Twenty-Seven

That evening while he was surveilling from the Affannatos' flybridge, Joe saw no activity aboard Fieldings' yacht. He told Loretta that he could be there until the early hours of the morning and not to wait up for him to leave.

After midnight when he figured no one would be coming aboard the Fielding yacht, he changed into a black t-shirt and black swim trunks. He tied a small bag around his neck, made his way down to the stern's platform, and slipped into the water. Using a breaststroke because it caused little splashing and thus no noise, he swam toward the Fielding yacht.

Once he reached the slip where the yacht was moored, he pulled himself up onto the stern platform. Wringing out his t-shirt so he wouldn't leave an obvious trail of water, he kept in a low crouch as he climbed the steps to the main deck and ascended to the fly deck. Once on the fly deck, he crawled to the helm station and got on his hands and knees.

Joe removed the bag from around his neck and took out a sealed plastic bag containing a GPS device in a waterproof case along with a small flashlight. Sliding under the helm station, he looked for anything metal where he could attach the magnetic back of the waterproof case. The yacht was constructed of a sophisticated fiberglass composite, but there was a steel reinforcement strip under the helm, and he stuck the GPS device to it. It would feed the yacht's location information to his cell phone.

Joe slipped the flashlight back into the plastic bag, sealed it, and placed it into the bag he carried around his neck. He finished descending from the fly deck and froze as he heard voices. He glanced in that direction and saw Jay

176

Fielding and a blonde woman he recognized as Astrid Nielson, the company's receptionist. She must have been the blonde he saw on the yacht previously. Quickly, he ducked down, moved to the other side of the main deck, and slid down into the water. Taking a deep breath, he swam underwater until he reached the boat in the next slip. As he swam under it, he felt as though his lungs were going to burst. Coming up out of the water gasping for air, he waited until his breathing was back to normal. Then he swam to the end of the bow and looked toward the Fielding yacht. No one was in sight, so he swam back to the Affannatos' yacht where he changed back into his dry clothes.

Checking his phone, he pulled up the new GPS app, and it showed the location of the Fielding yacht. Success! Right where it was moored. Using his binoculars, he hoped to get a look at Astrid and Jay, but he could not see anyone aboard. Apparently, they had gone to one of the rooms in the lower main cabin. At 2:00 am, Joe stuffed his wet clothes into his knapsack and left the Affannatos' yacht. As he walked to his car, he was feeling good about his accomplishment tonight, despite the close call. Hopefully, Jay was concentrating on Astrid and didn't notice the drips of water Joe left on his way to the fly deck. Once at home, he would catch a few hours of sleep before going into the office. Swimming would substitute for jogging in the morning.

* * *

Joe slept until 6:00 am and got ready for work as usual. He wasn't going to let anyone know what he did the night before since his actions broke the law. Criminal trespass for starters, not to mention tampering and illegal electronic surveillance. Destiny would read him the riot act if she found out what he did, and he didn't want to think about the disciplinary actions he could face at work if his actions became known. But in his view, the law sometimes needed to be bent for the greater good, and he figured this time, the possible benefits outweighed the risk.

Carrying his lunch as he approached his Camaro, Joe happened to look down and saw fingerprints reflected in the shiny black paint near the bottom of the door and rocker panel. That was odd. Setting his lunch on the roof, he squatted to examine the fingerprints, not understanding how they could have gotten there. Suspicious, Joe got down on hands and knees, looked under the chassis, and saw it: a bomb attached to the undercarriage, strategically placed under the driver's seat. Seeing the cellphone attached, he jumped back knowing the bomb would be detonated remotely. He ducked away as fast as he could and was two cars away when the bomb exploded.

The force of the explosion was immense, and a fireball engulfed everything around him, sucking all the oxygen out of the air. Parts of his car rained down from the sky and landed on other cars in the lot. Once he felt safe from flying debris, he stumbled back to the door of his apartment building which had sustained several broken windows.

The explosion rendered his Camaro and a car on each side of it unrecognizable hulks. Looking around the street for a person or a parked car with someone inside, he failed to see anyone. *Son-of-a-bitch!* he thought. Someone wanted him dead. And what pissed him off even more, his Camaro was blown to bits!

He called 9-1-1 and reported the incident. Within minutes, uniformed officers were on the scene. The evidence technicians arrived, and what was left of the cars parked next to Joe's Camaro got removed to give technicians room to gather evidence about the bomb. Uniforms on the scene worked to keep the curious and news people at a safe distance. An officer was stationed at the entrance door to the apartment building to keep tenants from entering the parking lot.

Sam came, as did Vincenzo, since Joe was the target. He explained how it was simply by chance that he noticed the fingerprints on the door and rocker panel before getting into his car.

"It's a good thing my car is black because if it was red or some other color, those prints would never have shown up. You'd be investigating my death right now."

"Who do you think's behind it?" asked Vincenzo.

"Vincent Scalise. He's the one with the connections to do this."

CHAPTER TWENTY-SEVEN

"We're getting too close, and he doesn't like it," said Sam.

"Yeah. You'd better watch yourself, Sam. You could be a target, too."

"Did you lean on anyone in particular in the last coupla days," asked Vincenzo.

"Robert Curtis, Jacqueline Fielding, the Fieldings' security guy, Wendell DeForrest, their attorney. And a private investigator before that."

"Jesus. You've been busy," remarked Vincenzo. "Any one of them could have contacted Scalise about you."

"I'd put my money on Curtis since I questioned him about seeing him with Scalise at the Palmer House."

At that moment, a car pulled up and Destiny got out of the back seat. She saw Joe, Sam, and Vincenzo conferring and walked up to them. Joe caught her approaching out of the corner of his eye.

"Joe?" Destiny asked. "Are you okay?"

"Yeah. How did you find out about this?" Joe asked.

"I had the local news on TV, and they cut in with a developing story. I looked and saw your apartment building, and then they showed you. And I thought, 'Omigod!' So, I came over."

"Someone blew up my car," said Joe.

"And nearly got him with it," said Vincenzo.

"For god's sakes!" said Destiny, taking a step back.

"I would avoid getting a replacement until this case has been resolved," suggested Vincenzo. "Start using a police vehicle and change it out every few days like you did on the Burton case."

"Better yet, have an Uber ride take you to and from work. That way, they can't target your car," said Destiny.

"Good idea," said Sam. "At least for the time being."

"I guess I don't have any other choice, do I?"

"You put a lot of work into that car, didn't you?" asked Vincenzo.

"Supercharger, new suspension, upgraded brakes and tires. Yeah. It was better than anything you can buy." Looking at Destiny he asked, "What do I need to do to get hooked up to Uber?"

"I'll help you," she said. "It's easy."

They watched as the evidence techs scoured the parking lot looking for bomb fragments. Joe told them he got a look at the bomb and said it appeared to be constructed with several sticks of dynamite and a cellphone wrapped together with electricians tape. Joe walked over and spoke to one of the evidence techs scouring the parking lot for bomb fragments.

"Detective Joe Erickson. That's my car over there," said Joe, pointing to the remains of his Camaro.

"Lucius James. You mean, that was your car."

"Yeah. It was. Any idea how long you'll be here?"

"Hours, man. Hours."

"Thanks."

"You're a pretty lucky guy. If that bomb had gone off with you inside, the ME'd be picking up pieces of you right now."

"Joe looked to see if Destiny heard that. Unfortunately, she did, and the horrified look on her face disturbed him. He hadn't seen her this upset before, and he didn't like it.

He walked back to her. "Hey, I'm okay," he said, trying to reassure her.

"I know," she said.

Vincenzo walked up to them and said to Joe, "Why don't you take the day off. Take the time to get yourself squared away, write your report, and get your Uber rides set up. We'll deal with everything."

"Thanks, Lieutenant."

"This may not be the time," said Destiny. "I think I got an ID on Vernon, the Fieldings' security man."

"Go ahead," said Joe. "We need to know who he is."

"His name is Vernon Leo Becker. He's a member of the United Socialist Alliance, a neo-Nazi group operating here in Chicago as well as all over the state. He's been suspected in some anti-Semitic and white supremacist violence, but he's never been arrested and charged with anything.

"How did you find this out?" asked Vincenzo.

"I called in a favor from a former colleague."

"You have a photo, besides the one I sent you?" asked Joe.

"I do," replied Destiny, pulling up her email. Finding his photo in one of her messages, she showed it to Joe as he looked at the photo he snapped of Vernon while standing at the Fielding gate.

"Looks like him to me," said Joe.

"I'd say Vernon Becker is your security guy."

"What do you know about him?" asked Vincenzo.

"He's forty-two. Born in Munich. Served in Bavaria's Protective Police. He emigrated to the US after marrying an American woman twelve years ago. After getting his Green Card, he began working as a private security guard. His wife died of lymphoma five years ago."

"Why hire a neo-Nazi as a security guard?"

"Birds of a feather?"

"As in Jacqueline Fielding?" asked Sam.

"More like Jay Fielding," said Destiny.

"Cindy Fielding told me her husband's family came from a long line of anti-Semites. Neo-Nazis aren't that much of a leap," said Joe.

"Robert Curtis. Where's he play into this?" asked Vincenzo.

"I think he's into it for himself, for the money. If he held those views, he never would have hired a Jewish intern. He heard Daniel was brilliant and used him to achieve his own ends," explained Joe. "But I don't understand the link they have with Scalise."

"Organized crime is getting its fingers into more and more legit businesses," said Vincenzo. "And if they can muscle their way into one of the biggest transportation companies in the country, it would be a real coup."

"A perfect opportunity to run a cover for their human trafficking business," said Sam.

"All right. You two come in tomorrow morning and discuss where we need to go with this," said Vincenzo. "Nice seeing you, Destiny. Thanks for the help." Vincenzo left and returned to Area 3. Sam followed a short time later.

Destiny waited until the police finished asking questions. Then she and Joe went into his apartment. Destiny helped Joe download the Uber app to his phone and explained how it worked. He tried it out and made a call. Five minutes later, their ride came and took them back to Destiny's apartment.

As they prepared lunch, Destiny said, "I'm not so sure I want to take that job in Virginia now with everything that just went on here. Someone just tried to assassinate you."

"Look," said Joe. "You need to work, and I can take care of myself. There's nothing you can do to protect me by staying here."

"I know but leaving doesn't feel right. Not now."

"You said it's for what? Two weeks?"

"Ten days."

"If it makes you feel any better, I'll talk to you every night and keep you apprised. This investigation could go on for weeks with no progress."

"I know that."

"So, don't throw away an opportunity just because of what happened today."

"Joe, I—"

"When do you have to let them know?"

"Tomorrow."

"I'm not going to tell you what to do. Think it over. You'll make the right decision."

"I hope so."

That night when Destiny was asleep, Joe got up and went into the bathroom with his phone. He pulled up the GPS app, and to his dismay, he found the Fielding yacht had traveled forty-three miles out into Lake Michigan where it stopped at 42.25 North latitude by 86.98 degrees West longitude. That put the position outside the boundaries of Illinois and six miles into the boundaries of Michigan. Wonderful! That complicates things. But the kicker is: he can't tell anyone about it.

He slipped back into bed. As he pulled up the covers, Destiny opened her eyes and asked, "Another bad dream, babe?"

"You could say that."

Chapter Twenty-Eight

When Joe got up to jog, Destiny said in a firm voice, "Make sure you choose a different route today. If someone tried to kill you once, they could try again."

"I will," he said as he pushed his Glock into its holster under his nylon jacket. It was an extra two pounds he could do without but was necessary given the present circumstances.

For the first time, Joe felt uncomfortable jogging. He chose a new direction that took him past different buildings, and along the way he made unpredictable moves such as suddenly doubling back and making quick jumps across the street in the middle of the block. He took special care, looking for people behaving strangely and for suspicious movements of cars that could be stalking him. And he treated the people he saw with suspicion, ready to react should they make an aggressive move. Joe always liked to relax when he ran, to let his mind go and think about his cases, but he couldn't today since he was constantly on defense. He hated it.

At breakfast, Destiny said, "Now that I've slept on it, I've decided to take your advice and tell the Virginia Beach Police Department I'm going to work with them."

"You made the right decision," added Joe. "They need someone like you to help them catch their rapist."

"I know..."

"Besides, if you were here, could you prevent someone from trying a second time?"

She was silent for a moment as she contemplated his question. "Well...no.

Probably not."

"See. It won't make any difference whether you're here or there. And it's only for ten days or so, right?"

"Right."

"There's only one thing."

"What's that?

"I'll miss you. But I'll live."

"You'd better."

Joe's Uber driver dropped him off at Area 3 around 7:15 am, and when Sam got in, they walked to Vincenzo's office as planned.

Joe gave a knock and Vincenzo barked, "What?"

"It's Joe and Sam."

"Come in and shut the door."

Joe and Sam took seats in front of Vincenzo's desk.

"How much more have you found out about this case?" he asked.

"We interviewed the nurse who was taking care of Thomas Fielding after his stroke," said Sam. "She was canned after she reported she thought he was attempting to communicate with her using eye blinks."

"Fired for that?"

"By their security guard."

"Thomas Fielding had a debilitating stroke and is in a wheelchair, not a minor stroke like his attorney told us. I confronted him about it, and he came clean about his condition. Said word about the seriousness of his stroke could negatively impact the company's investors."

"Okay, what else you got?"

Fieldings' yacht. I saw eight Latino girls go aboard after midnight, and the yacht left the harbor and sailed into Lake Michigan. Fieldings' yacht left after midnight again on the evening my car was blown up, but I don't have evidence of any women brought aboard."

"How do you know that?"

"Someone I interviewed saw it leave. Next time, I think I need to be there so I can take photos."

"That would be the kind of evidence we need to get a surveillance detail on the van and the yacht," said Vincenzo.

"Lieutenant, what if the yacht meets another boat out in Lake Michigan, but it crosses the line into Michigan's territorial waters? What do we do, then?"

"If we suspect human trafficking, we call in the Coast Guard. Jurisdictional boundaries mean nothing to them."

"We need to have someone on the inside of Fielding's terminal who can alert us to when a shipment of girls arrives," said Sam. "Can we get someone undercover as a terminal worker?"

"I'll look into it. I'll check with Narco and see if they already have someone inside."

It would be nice if we could get a tracking device on board that yacht. Any possibility of that?" asked Joe.

"You get photos of girls being brought aboard that yacht, and then we'll discuss a tracking device."

"Good, because that could pinpoint the pickup area and the other boat that's taking the girls. We need both parties."

"Agreed."

"Until we have someone on the inside of the terminal, I'm doing night and day. Is it all right if Sam and I trade off working shifts surveilling the yacht?"

"Not a problem. I'll let you know later today if Narco has someone inside the terminal. Anything else?"

Joe looked at Sam who gave him a small shake of his head. Looking back at Vincenzo, he said, "I guess not."

"Okay. Get outta here."

In the hall, Joe said to Sam, "I'm going to introduce you to Loretta Affannato."

"Who's she?"

"I've been observing the Fielding yacht from the flybridge of her yacht. I don't think she'll mind if you and I trade off shifts."

"Is she cute?"

"As seventy-year-olds go, yeah. She's kinda cute."

"Oh."

"She's one of Destiny's mother's friends, so be on your best behavior."

"When am I not?"

Joe didn't dignify that with an answer, but he knew Sam had a lot of charm when he chose to use it. And given the fact he would be a guest on Loretta's yacht, he knew Sam would make a good impression.

"I'll take you to the Affannatos' yacht and introduce you to Loretta," said Joe. "The sooner we can begin trading off surveilling the Fielding yacht, the better. I don't know how long it could take to get someone inside the terminal."

"I have a Nikon with a telephoto lens," said Sam. "We can use it to record photos of the girls coming aboard. You know how to use a camera, right?"

Joe gave him a look and said, "Yeah. I own one, too. How long is your lens?"

"Three hundred millimeters."

"That should do it."

"Just, don't drop it in the lake, okay? That lens cost me a pretty penny."

"I'll try my best to hang on to it," assured Joe with a touch of sarcasm. He knew Sam was touchy about his stuff, but he didn't need another one of his little reminders about how valuable his stuff was. Joe would have used his own camera, but he didn't have the high-quality lenses Sam owned.

Joe called Loretta Affannato and asked her if it was alright if he brought someone by for her to meet that afternoon. She happily agreed and suggested Joe bring his friend to the harbor for lunch. Normally, Joe would want to wait to go to the harbor in the evening so he would not be spotted by the people they had under surveillance. But he felt it would be safe to be there in the afternoon with the hustle and bustle of activity on the dock.

When Joe and Sam showed up, Joe showed Sam the code to use to open the security gate. Sam was impressed by the size and opulence of the Affannatos' yacht. Loretta greeted them at the gangway, and she invited them aboard.

"So, who's this handsome fellow?" asked Loretta in a sultry voice.

Joe had never seen Sam blush, but there was a first time for everything. "This is Detective Sam Renaldo, my partner," said Joe.

"Well, if you're a friend of Joe's, you're all right with me," she said as she offered her hand.

"Nice to meet you," said Sam, shaking her hand.

"Welcome aboard."

They followed her onto the stern platform and up steps to the main deck. Once in the main cabin salon, the aroma of her cooking tickled their senses. Joe saw two large pots simmering on the stove.

"Oh, my," remarked Joe. "What have you cooked?"

"My Bolognese ragu," Loretta replied. "It's one of our favorites."

"It smells wonderful," said Sam.

"Thank you. And I made a pot of homemade farfalle."

After dining was over and they were all drinking coffee, Joe explained their surveillance goals and asked Loretta if she would agree to let him and Sam alternate evenings on her fly deck.

"So, you think the Fieldings are up to no good and you need photos to document their unlawful activities?"

"That about sums it up," confirmed Joe. "But we don't know what night they're going to try something, so we need to keep watch each night."

"Well, I don't have a problem with you being up on the fly deck. I don't go up there much, especially at night." She looked at Joe. "You've been so quiet I don't even know when you're there."

"Thanks, Loretta," said Joe. "You won't notice when Sam's up there either. Would you mind if I show him the fly deck?"

"No, no. You go ahead."

Joe and Sam climbed up to the fly deck. They sat at the helm, and Joe pointed out Fieldings' yacht and the road where he saw the van park, and where two men let the girls out and escort them aboard.

"You won't be able to sit at the helm station when you watch them because they'll be able to see you." Joe pointed to an area to the left. "I sit there. You should be able to lean the camera on the ledge right here."

Sam got down into the position and mimed holding his camera onto the ledge and taking a photo. Looking back at Joe, he said, "Yeah. This'll work."

"So, how am I going to get the camera from you? Passing it on to each other at work every day will be awkward," said Joe.

"Is this place secure?" asked Sam.

"Well, yeah. I'm sure it is."

"Okay. I have a waterproof case I can leave everything in. It should fit under this seat. I'll leave it here tonight after I leave. You'll know where it is when you come on tomorrow night."

"Right," said Joe. "And if it rains?"

"The lens has a hood so the filter shouldn't get wet unless the wind is blowing. In that case, you won't get a picture, anyway."

"Okay."

"And don't mess with the settings. I'll have the camera set to the best possible exposures."

"Got it."

They climbed down the ladder and spoke to Loretta before leaving. She asked which one of them would be "on duty" this evening. Sam spoke up and said it would be him. She smiled and said, "Oh, that'll be nice." It appeared Sam succeeded in making a very good impression. Joe couldn't help but tease Sam a little on their way back to the car.

"Hey," said Sam, "I can't help it she finds me attractive. You'd be surprised how many women I've had to fight off with a stick."

Eye roll. "Wow," said Joe. "I had no idea you were such a magnet for women."

"Yeah, it's a burden I've been a little reluctant to share."

* * *

After work, Joe took an Uber ride to Destiny's apartment. When he entered, he found her busy spinning something in a blender. There was cilantro, lime, cashews, garlic, and a few other ingredients on the counter.

"What are you making?" asked Joe.

"I'm making a lime-cilantro-cashew cream dressing to go with the roasted sweet potato salad I made earlier."

"Ooh. Sounds yummy. What's the occasion?"

"I'm leaving for Virginia tomorrow. I thought I'd make us something special tonight."

"That's very thoughtful of you," said Joe, stepping behind her and giving her a kiss on the neck.

"I'd like you to stay here while I'm gone."

"So, you want me to move in?"

"In a manner of speaking. Will you do that?"

"I can do that. What time does your flight leave?"

"Eleven o'clock. Are you on surveillance tonight?"

"No. Sam is on tonight. Vincenzo wants us to trade off—every other night—so I called Loretta and introduced her to Sam today. She made lunch for us. I should say, she fed us like we were long-lost sons."

"Great. So, you're mine all night?"

"If you like."

"Well, of course, I like." She shut off the blender and poured the ingredients into a cruet. "I got us a nice sea bass fillet."

"Us?" asked Joe.

"A big piece for you and a little piece for me. I have it wrapped in foil and ready to go in the oven whenever you feel hungry. And there's a bottle of Sauvignon Blanc chilling in the refrigerator."

"Nice."

"Why don't you open it and pour us each a glass."

Joe poured two glasses of the chilled wine. Destiny set the cruet aside and placed the blender's container in the dishwasher. Together, she and Joe cleared the counter of the ingredients and put them away.

She turned on the oven to baking temperature. "Come on. Let's go sit down," she said, and they adjourned to the living room.

"Vincenzo wants photos of girls being off-loaded from a van and then brought onto the yacht before the yacht leaves the harbor. With that evidence, he can set up an operation to arrest Fielding and the others for human trafficking the next time," Joe explained.

"So, in other words," Destiny said, "You're going to sacrifice a group of girls to obtain evidence of human trafficking?"

"I know," said Joe. "But there's no other way to do it without tipping off the principals."

"Well, I think it's terrible for the girls they're trafficking," Destiny protested.

"But once we arrest these people and intercept their accomplices who are waiting for them in the middle of Lake Michigan, authorities should be able to trace where the girls have been taken."

"You hope. And how do you know where their accomplices will be in the middle of Lake Michigan?" Destiny asked.

"You don't want to know that." He took a sip of his wine.

"What did you do?"

Looking at his glass, Joe remarked, "Um. This is good."

"Don't be changing the subject. Did you do something…?"

"Like I said, you don't want to know."

"Sheesh! I can't believe you sometimes."

"I shouldn't have mentioned it." He took another sip.

With a sigh, Destiny said, "No one will hear about your vague, suspected activity from me."

"I appreciate that," he smiled, leaned over, and kissed her. "How long does the sea bass take to bake?"

"Twenty-minutes. Why? Getting hungry?"

"Not yet."

Destiny laughed. "Drink your wine." She paused a few moments and said, "I have a big announcement when I get back from Virginia."

"You do?"

"Uh-huh."

"So, you're going to keep me in suspense the whole time you're gone."

"I am."

Joe thought for a couple seconds, then it struck him. "Omigod! You're not pregnant, are you?"

"Bite your tongue."

Chapter Twenty-Nine

As Joe was showering the next morning and thinking about the investigation, he had one of those "a-ha" moments. He investigated the backgrounds of everyone in the case but one: Jacqueline Fielding. Why did he skip over her? All he knew about her was the cursory information Wendell DeForrest told him and some basic background information Sam dug up.

After getting dressed, he ate breakfast with Destiny, kissed her good-bye, and picked up his Uber ride to work, even though it was Saturday, and he had the day off. He logged onto his computer and began a background search on Jacqueline Fielding.

Jacqueline Rossi Fielding was born forty-four years ago in Los Angeles, California. Her father, Gino Rossi, was an entertainment attorney and her mother was a former actress who had appeared in minor roles in several television series. She retired from the business when she married Jacqueline's father. Jacqueline has one sibling, Francesca, who is two years younger. Nothing looked out of the ordinary until Joe found the family changed residences and moved to Las Vegas where her father went into private practice.

Jacqueline graduated with a bachelor's degree in communications from the University of Nevada at Las Vegas. Two years later, she married Gary Richardson, also a graduate of UNLV, and they moved to Mesa, Arizona, where they began a real estate business. By their reported incomes, their business prospered. But Gary Richardson had been arrested twice during this time, once for DUI, and once for domestic abuse. Ten years ago, he was killed in a one-car accident near Chandler, Arizona. Shortly thereafter, Jacqueline sold the real estate business and moved back to Las Vegas. She moved to Chicago and began work on a master's degree at the University of Illinois at Chicago. Upon graduation, she secured employment with Fielding Enterprises, and five years ago, she married Thomas Fielding.

Joe found the Las Vegas connection suspicious, so he decided to conduct a background check on Jacqueline's sister, Francesca. She graduated from UNLV with a bachelor's degree in business administration. And then, BINGO! Married to Vincent Scalise. *Holy shit! There's the mob's foot in the door. Vincent Scalise is Thomas Fielding's brother-in-law.*

Joe wondered if Thomas Fielding even knew that his wife's sister was married to a mobster. And was Jacqueline's marriage to Thomas for love or was it simply a way for organized crime to infiltrate one of the largest trucking operations in the country? Vincenzo would love to hear about this.

Sam came in late since he was on surveillance the previous night, and before he could sit down, Joe said, "Hey, Sam. You're not going to believe what I just uncovered."

"Good morning to you, too. Aren't you going to ask how my first night went?"

"Okay, how did it go?"

"Nothing."

Joe laughed. "Well, my news is a hellava lot better. Because I just found out that Jacqueline Fielding's sister is married to Vincent Scalise."

"No shit?"

"No shit."

"I guess I shoulda dug deeper when I was doing her background check."

"Let's go see if Vincenzo's in."

Vincenzo was, and he was pleased Joe had found the mob connection. And he added, "How much do you want to bet that Jacqueline's father was an attorney for Scalise's casino, too. One of Carmine's old buddies."

Joe decided to bring up Destiny's concern about the girls. "Do we still need photographic evidence on the human trafficking aspect? I'm not too keen on sacrificing a dozen girls just to get photos," asked Joe.

"Unfortunately, yeah. We do. I don't like it either."

"Can we at least get a court order for a tracking device for the yacht? So we know where the girls are being taken. It would help if we knew where they were meeting their accomplices."

"I'll look into it," said Vincenzo. "It's going to be tricky getting one on board."

"I know how to do it."

"Okay. I'll leave that up to you." Then Vincenzo sat forward in his chair and said, "Oh, I need to tell you—Narco has someone inside at the Fielding's terminal. That person has been informed what to look for and will call when one of those deliveries arrives."

"Great," said Sam.

"Good work, you guys. Keep it up. Now, get outta here."

Joe and Sam left Vincenzo's office, and as they walked down the hall, Sam asked, "What did the insurance company say about your car getting blown up?"

"I had special agreed-upon value coverage on it. They're gonna pay in full. But I'm not replacing it until we close this case. I don't want the bomber targeting me again."

"Good point."

That evening Joe watched the Fielding yacht, and there was no activity all evening. At 3:00 am, he called it quits and walked up the dock to the parking lot where his unmarked car was parked. One good thing about driving in Chicago at three in the morning, you can make good time on Lakeshore Drive. It was good to get to Destiny's apartment and sleep for a few hours.

The next evening didn't bring any results for Sam, either. No activity was seen aboard the Fielding yacht, and Sam left at 3:00 am.

The following day, Joe got some good news. Vincenzo told him the court order came through for a tracking device. Joe told him he knew how to surreptitiously install one. He reinstalled the app on his phone to show today as the installation date in case the information would be called into evidence.

That evening was Joe's turn at surveillance, and at 11:10 pm, he received a call on his cell phone from a woman identifying herself as Stephanie from the Fielding's terminal. She said she witnessed a semi-trailer truck arrive and unload about a dozen Latina girls. They got transferred to a blue van that left the terminal just minutes ago. Before Joe could even say thanks, she ended the call.

Preparing for what he needed to do, he checked the camera's memory card, switched on the camera, double-checked its battery life and the camera's settings, removed the lens cover, and looked through the viewfinder. He used the edge of the fly deck to steady the camera and focused on the area where he saw the van stop previously. He was ready.

As Joe watched, Jay Fielding and Robert Curtis walked down the dock and entered the slip where the yacht was moored. Joe shot photos of them stepping aboard. A couple of minutes later, he heard the sound of the twin diesel engines rumble to life and begin idling, warming up for the trip to meet accomplices out in Lake Michigan.

Ten minutes later, the blue van pulled up on the access road alongside the dock. When it stopped, Joe began snapping photos. Becker got out and slid open the side door. About a dozen girls stepped out of the van and followed Becker to the security gate where he punched in the code to open the gate. Then he and the driver ushered the girls to the gangway leading to the main deck. Once they disappeared into the salon, Becker spoke to Curtis as he released the mooring lines and the driver returned to the van and drove away. After Curtis activated the automated gangway, he and Becker entered the salon. The diesel engines revved up and pushed the eighty-foot yacht out of the harbor and onward toward the waters of Lake Michigan. Joe got photos of everything.

For the next hour, Joe watched the GPS app on his phone as the Fielding yacht sailed at 35 knots toward the rendezvous point at 42.25 North latitude by 86.98 degrees West longitude. Seventy minutes later, it was back, re-entering Burnham Harbor. Joe shot more photos of it backing into its slip and tying up, and more photos of Jay Fielding and Robert Curtis leaving. The 127 photos Joe shot should prove what the high muckety-mucks needed to see—evidence of human trafficking and who is doing it.

Joe opened the camera case and carefully placed the camera and lens into their foam cutouts. He left the yacht and walked up the dock to the parking lot. When he got to Destiny's apartment, he downloaded the photos to his laptop and emailed them to Vincenzo and Sam. He was asleep as soon as his head hit the pillow.

The next morning was Saturday, and he got up at his usual time after only a couple of hours of sleep. As he jogged, he felt pumped about what he accomplished the previous night. Running on adrenalin, he got ready and drove his unmarked to the Area 3 headquarters. When Sam got in, he handed him his photo case. Sam had already seen the photos Joe sent him last evening.

"Nice work last night, partner," said Sam, giving him a tap on the shoulder.

"Thanks," said Joe. Out of the corner of his eye, he noticed Vincenzo walking toward them. They both turned toward him, unaware he was working this Saturday.

"I saw the pictures you sent," said Vincenzo. "Who were those guys?"

"Vernon Becker, Fielding's security guard. He brought the girls from the van to the boat along with the van driver. Then Becker, Curtis, and Jay Fielding sailed with them out of the harbor," said Joe.

"Now, if we just knew where they went."

"We do. I got the GPS tracker installed. They were gone for a little over an hour," said Joe. "They must have met another boat because they stopped here." Joe showed Vincenzo his phone, and the map of Lake Michigan showed the point, just over the border into Michigan waters.

"We'll have to let the Coast Guard know to pick up that vessel at those coordinates when we make the bust. Can you save that information?" asked Vincenzo.

"Yeah. I can do that," said Joe.

"Good. I think we have enough to nail these guys. What about Daniel Silverman? I'm getting some heat from my superiors on this. His father is pressing people for an arrest."

"We think Daniel found out about the smuggling operation and was silenced for it. We don't know who pulled the trigger. My guess, it was Becker, but we have no proof."

195

"I think we may have to rely on Fielding or Curtis rolling over to get a deal after we make the bust. Fielding and Curtis have to know who killed him," said Sam.

"All right. What we'll do is keep up the surveillance. Once the next group of girls is aboard, we'll take them down. The van, the yacht, and their conspirators. Send me the coordinates for the meeting place on Lake Michigan, and we'll start a dialogue with the Coast Guard. They can take them into custody. This is going to take some planning and coordination with Marine Operations, too."

Vincenzo walked back to his office with a bounce in his step, something Joe had not seen in some time. Apparently, the lieutenant was feeling enthused about making arrests in this case. And who wouldn't be? This was one of the most convoluted cases Joe had worked. He remembered what Destiny told him weeks ago: "You've taken the twisting path because, despite its obstacles and distractions, it will ultimately lead you in the right direction." She was right. The investigation of Daniel Silverman's murder led to the discovery of the trafficking of young women by organized crime.

Chapter Thirty

For the next week, the only activity aboard the Fielding yacht was on Sunday evening when Jay Fielding brought Astrid Nielson aboard. *Looks like she's gotten pretty cozy with the boss.* He shot photos of them with his phone thinking they might prove valuable at some point. Joe left at 3:00 am, the lights on the yacht having gone dark shortly after midnight.

When Joe was on surveillance Thursday evening, he received a call from Stephanie inside the Fielding Enterprises terminal saying she witnessed about a dozen young girls being transferred from a semi-trailer into a blue van just minutes ago. Joe made a call to his contact at Area 3 saying the takedown was on. At the same time, Jay Fielding and Robert Curtis arrived at the slip and boarded the yacht. Fielding started the engines.

About twenty minutes later, the blue van pulled up on the service road at the dock leading to the slip. As before, Becker got out and slid open the side door. One by one, a dozen young Latina girls got out. They looked unsure and confused as they stood next to the van.

Joe grabbed his megaphone and scrambled down from the flybridge and onto the slip. He quickly ran hunched over to the security gate and opened it, allowing himself access to the dock. Carefully, he crept closer to where the Fielding yacht was moored. He could see Becker and the driver ushering the girls to the gangway and up onto the aft platform. Fielding guided them up the steps and into the main deck salon while Curtis released the mooring lines and activated the automated gangway.

Joe pulled out his police radio and said, "Now." Police cars pulled in on each end of the blue van as officers began swarming the dock. Joe jumped up and said into his megaphone, "Freeze! Chicago PD!" Curtis and Becker dashed into the salon and the diesel engines roared as the yacht lurched forward out of the slip and on toward the entrance of the harbor.

Joe ran down two docks and raced to the end just as the Fielding yacht was about to go past. He dropped his phone and kicked off his shoes on the end of the dock, jumped into the water, and swam as fast as he could, catching the aft platform at the stern and pulling himself up onto the passing yacht.

As he crawled up the steps and looked up onto the main deck, he saw Becker emerge from the salon with a handgun. Joe pulled his Glock and raised up saying, "Police! Drop it!" Becker raised his gun to shoot, and Joe fired. Becker's knee exploded, sending him to the floor, screaming in agony. Joe pulled himself onto the main deck and ran to Becker, kicking his gun away. He cuffed him, then stuck Becker's gun in the back of his waistband.

The salon door was not locked, and Joe went inside. He didn't see Curtis or the girls, so he assumed they were in one of the lower deck rooms. As he made his way forward, he saw Jay Fielding sitting at the helm station.

"Shut her down, Jay," said Joe as he stood six feet behind him. "You're busted."

Jay stood up and whirled around with a gun in his hand. Joe leaped on him, pushing him back against the controls. The yacht lurched forward, accelerating as Joe and Jay Fielding fought for control of the gun. Jay was not a fighter, but he was no weakling, either. Finally, Joe got in some hard punches to Jay's face that rendered him dazed. Just as Joe removed the gun from Jay's hand, Joe was suddenly thrown forward into helm controls. The yacht had hit the end of the harbor with a vicious crunching sound, its fiberglass hull cracking under the force. Joe reached over, pulled the throttles back, and switched off the engines.

A moment later, Robert Curtis emerged from the lower deck lobby, blood dripping from a cut on his forehead. Joe pointed his Glock at Curtis. "Hold it right there, Curtis. You're under arrest." Curtis froze, his eyes registering surprise. Joe shoved him up against the wall and patted him down. He wasn't carrying. Joe pushed Curtis out onto the main deck and told one of the uniforms who just came aboard to cuff him and read him his rights.

Joe returned to Jay Fielding who was sitting semi-conscious on the floor near the helm station. Joe pulled him up, placed him under arrest, and helped the wobbly-kneed pilot out to the main deck as more police swarmed over the yacht. He asked another uniform to cuff Fielding and read him his rights. Then Joe returned to the salon, went down into the yacht's lower deck lobby, and began checking rooms. He opened the door to the VIP cabin and found the girls, most of whom looked to be teenagers ranging in age from fifteen to eighteen. He looked over the frightened girls and asked if anyone spoke English. One of the girls answered, "I do." He told her to inform the girls they were safe now and asked them to stay in the cabin until authorities showed up. But when he noticed water on the floor, he decided to escort them up to the lounge area of the salon.

Joe went out to the main deck and kneeled next to Becker whose knee was bleeding badly. "You need a tourniquet. Hold still."

Joe read him his rights as he reached up, unbuckled Becker's belt, and pulled it off him. Then he wrapped it around his thigh above his knee and pulled it tight. Afterward, Joe leaned over and looked into Becker's face.

"Did you kill Daniel Silverman?"

Becker gave Joe a defiant look, so Joe placed his hand above Becker's wounded knee and leaned on it. Becker let out a guttural scream. The pain was too much. "Stop! Stop! All right!" Joe removed his hand. "I didn't kill him," grimaced Becker. "Maybe I cut the swastika in the Jew-boy's back... but I didn't kill him."

"Then who did?"

Becker didn't answer so Joe started to apply pressure to his knee again. "Okay. Okay," winced Becker. "It...It was Jacqueline."

Joe released his leg, surprised by his answer.

"Jacqueline?"

"Uh-huh," breathed Becker.

"Why?" asked Joe.

"Be-cause...Because she runs this whole thing...I caught him spying and it made her angry. She's ruthless. Even keeps her husband drugged...so he seems helpless."

This revelation took Joe by surprise. Having never met her, he didn't know quite what to expect from Mrs. Thomas Fielding. He got the attention of a uniformed officer and said, "This man needs medical attention." The officer got on his radio called for an ambulance.

"Why did you shoot my knee?" groaned Becker.

"I'm a lousy shot. I was aiming at your head." That wasn't true, of course. Joe wanted Becker alive, and a leg shot would leave him incapacitated and able to talk.

Looking back at Becker, Joe said, "You can help yourself here, Vernon. Tell me, where did Willie Higgins get the murder weapon?"

"From me. He said he wanted to off Devon Schmidt for betraying him... asked me if I knew where he could get a piece...I told him if he did it right... I could make it look like he killed himself. I knew if he used that gun... Schmidt would get blamed for killing the Jew-boy."

"Pretty clever, Vernon. And by the way, his name was 'Daniel Silverman', not Jew-boy."

Joe got to his feet and told a nearby officer to watch him. Then he made a beeline for the dock to get his cell phone and shoes. On the way, he met Sam.

"We need to go to the Fielding estate and arrest Jacqueline Fielding. Becker just told me she's the one who killed Daniel Silverman."

"Her?" asked Sam.

"And something else. Becker said she's been keeping Thomas Fielding drugged. He may not be as incapacitated as everyone's been led to believe."

Joe picked up his cell phone and slipped on his shoes. Then he and Sam drove their unmarked cars toward the Fielding estate and met two cruisers Joe had called in for backup. When Joe got to the iron gates, he didn't stop. Much to Sam's amazement, Joe crashed through the gates. Sam and the two cruisers followed Joe on toward the house.

When they came to a stop, Sam hollered, "What the hell were you thinking back there, crashing through those gates?"

"Exigent circumstances," replied Joe. "Thomas Fielding's life might be in danger." With emergency lights flashing, the four vehicles parked near the front door.

Officers Stone and Bailey got out of their cruisers and joined Joe and Sam. Stone went around back with Sam while Joe and Bailey took the front. Joe rang the bell and waited for a response. There was none. He rang again and still nothing. Then he told Bailey to get the ram. Moments later, he returned with it.

"Do it," said Joe.

"You got it."

Bailey swung the ram and the big mahogany door splintered but didn't open. He swung it again, and the door crashed open. Bailey dropped the ram, and both men entered the large foyer with weapons drawn.

Joe called out, "MRS. FIELDING? POLICE!" There was no answer. Joe motioned to Bailey to begin checking rooms. When the downstairs rooms had been cleared, they opened the back patio doors and let in Sam and Officer Stone.

Joe motioned to Sam, and they went upstairs and began clearing rooms one by one. By the time Joe came to the master bedroom, he pushed open the door and saw Jacqueline standing behind Thomas Fielding's wheelchair holding a gun to his head. Joe held his gun on Jacqueline as he entered the room.

"Stop right there," said Jacqueline.

"It's over Jacqueline. Jay, Curtis, and Becker are all under arrest. We know you killed Daniel Silverman. We also know you've been running this trafficking operation. We know everything."

"Then you know I have nothing to lose," said Jacqueline.

Sam appeared behind Joe, saw what was happening, and left. He informed both officers downstairs of the situation and raced outside.

"Why'd you kill Daniel?"

"He couldn't mind his own business. Becker caught him spying by the yacht and called me—asked me what I wanted to do. I came down there and interrogated him. Asked him what he thought he was doing. He knew everything, and he was going to expose the whole operation. That couldn't happen, so I took Becker's gun and popped him."

"Just like that."

"Just like that. And Becker made it look like a hate crime. I think he enjoyed doing it to tell you the truth."

Joe continued speaking to Jacqueline, buying time and trying to talk her down. "I know your sister's married to Vincent Scalise. Is that why you got involved with Thomas Fielding? To use the trucking operation for Vincent's scheme?"

"Not at first."

"No?"

"But when Jay gambled away a quarter-million dollars, Vince owned him. He couldn't go to his father for the money, and he couldn't skim that much from the company. So, to pay it off, he had to do Vince's bidding."

"And that's when you got involved."

"I had to. Thomas had a stroke. A minor one. But when Thomas found out what was going on, he threatened to go to the FBI. He needed to be out of the picture, so Vince suggested we drug him and paralyze his vocal cords so he couldn't talk. Amazing what Botox can do. He appeared to be the victim of a serious stroke to his nurse and anyone else who saw him."

"Clever."

"I thought so."

"Why didn't you just kill him?"

"Because as long as Tom was alive, Vince would have leverage over Jay. If Tom was dead, Jay would take over the company and shut down this whole operation."

"You didn't kill Thomas then; you're not going to kill him now."

"You're right. I'm not."

Jacqueline moved the gun away from Thomas's head and toward Joe.

"Don't!" warned Joe, his finger on the trigger.

"It's going to be you or me."

Just as she was bringing the gun up toward Joe, Sam took three quick steps from the open door of the balcony and grabbed her gun as he tackled her to the floor. Joe ran forward and wrestled the gun from her hand. Jacqueline, screaming in anger, was pushed onto her belly as Sam pulled her hands behind her back and cuffed her. Then Sam pulled her up to her feet, placed her under arrest, and began reading her rights as he escorted her out the door.

Joe placed the gun on the bed and walked back to Thomas. He leaned down to him, looked in his face, and said, "We're going to get you to a hospital and have those drugs flushed from your system, Mr. Fielding. You'll be back to normal in no time."

Thomas managed a small nod as tears welled up in his eyes. Joe got behind his wheelchair and began pushing him out of the room. He called to Officer Bailey, and the two men managed to move Thomas' wheelchair down the stairs to the first floor where paramedics could check him over before transporting him to a hospital.

Officer Bailey stayed with Thomas while Joe met Sam at the door. Giving Sam a pat on the back, Joe said, "Well done, partner."

"Thanks, partner." Then Sam pulled Joe aside and said, "I hate to tell you this, but you smell bad."

"You don't care for my new 'harbor noir'?"

"No. I wouldn't advise wearing it around Destiny."

"Well, she's out of town, so I'm safe. But I think I'm going to give her a call and let her know what went down. Joe walked to the car, sat on the damaged hood. He gave a quick call to Margaret Kummeyer, a reporter for the *Tribune,* and gave her a tip. Then, he called Destiny. She picked up and he explained what happened. She told him she would be back in Chicago on Friday. He had to cut the call short when Lieutenant Vincenzo pulled up.

Joe walked over as he was getting out of his car. Vincenzo looked at his disheveled appearance and sniffed. "You smell bad," he said. "And you look worse."

"I went for a swim in the harbor."

"I heard what you did. What happened here?"

Joe explained what Becker told him and how they apprehended Jacqueline Fielding.

"Becker's admission led us here. She admitted to killing Daniel Silverman. She was going for suicide by cop when Sam tackled her to the floor."

"Good for him. We have the semi and we've arrested the driver who transported the girls to the terminal. It had a specially constructed compartment used to smuggle the girls. He drove straight through from the Fielding terminal in Texas, so we've notified the FBI. As I was driving over here, I got a call—the Coast Guard intercepted a large fishing boat at the coordinates you provided. The captain and crew are being detained, and the Coast Guard is towing the boat in as we speak. Since it was found in Michigan waters, the FBI's been notified."

"What about Vincent Scalise?"

"It depends on who's willing to sing. But I'm betting Jay Fielding will roll over on him in exchange for a plea deal. We've got him and Curtis in custody, and Becker's been taken to the hospital for treatment of his gunshot wound."

Vincenzo stopped talking and looked over his shoulder as he saw the arrival of the EMTs. "Someone hurt?" he asked.

"Thomas Fielding. He's been pumped full of drugs for months by his wife so it would appear he suffered a debilitating stroke. That way she could call all the shots."

"What a snake."

"What about the girls?" asked Joe.

"Immigration's been called. It's in their hands."

Vincenzo and Joe walked toward the house. As they passed the unmarked car Joe was using, Vincenzo noticed the damage to the front end.

"Where'd the damage come from?"

"I had to crash through the gates leading to the house. Exigent circumstances, Lieutenant."

Vincenzo sighed. "Make sure you put it in your report. Now get your ass back to the yacht so the IRT team can investigate the shooting. You shouldn't have left the scene."

"Exigent circumstances."

"Yeah, yeah. Get back there or you'll be in trouble."

Vincenzo moved to the interior of the house, and as Joe turned to go to his car, he came face to face with Margaret Kummeyer.

"Jesus," said Joe. "You're here already."

"I guess you could say I was in the neighborhood. So, what can you tell me, Detective Erickson?"

"Thomas Fielding is being taken to a hospital for of an unspecified ailment."

"Oh, come on. You have to do better than that. Look at the front door."

"And his wife has been detained for questioning related to the arrests made on their yacht in Burnham Harbor this evening. Does the word 'mastermind' mean anything to you?"

"Ahhh," said Margaret, taking in the information like a bear who just found honey. "Anything else."

"Mrs. Fielding's sister is married to Vincent Scalise of the Las Vegas crime family. But you could have found that on through an internet search."

"This is getting interesting."

"Very interesting. See you around, Margaret. I have to get back to the harbor."

"See you around. And Joe...you smell bad."

"I love it when you talk dirty to me, Margaret."

She snorted a laugh as she began writing on her notepad.

Joe slid into his car, and as he started it, Sam opened the passenger door and jumped in. "There's a black BMW motorcycle in the garage. Might match the one on the surveillance footage we got for Adam Silverman's shooting."

"Good. Cardona will want to know. Nice going tonight, Sam."

"See you later." Sam climbed out of the car, and Joe returned to Burnham Harbor where he met with the IRT team, an investigative arm of Chicago PD. He provided a detailed narrative of what happened up to the time of his shooting of Vernon Becker. Such investigations are part of departmental protocols anytime there are officer-involved shootings. Joe knew his shooting was justified. He would still need to provide a formal statement to the Civilian Office of Police Accountability within twenty-four hours. They would determine if the shooting was justified. Joe would be represented by counsel provided by FOP to ensure his rights were protected. A lot of red tape involved with an officer-involved shooting.

At 2:00 am, Joe pulled into his parking space at his apartment, a place he had not been for some time. He didn't want to undress and leave his smelly clothes in Destiny's apartment, so he decided to go to his own place. But as he got out of the car, something didn't feel right. He sensed he was being followed as he returned from the Burnham Harbor even though he thought it was unlikely since he was driving an unmarked car from work.

He looked around and saw a pickup truck slowly pass by. It didn't seem like anything out of the ordinary, so he went inside his apartment building. But then he stopped. Instead of going upstairs to his apartment, he went out the back entrance and circled around so he could watch the parking lot. Ten minutes later, a man appeared across the street. He was carrying a small package. After looking around, he quickly crossed the street, headed for Joe's unmarked car, and dropped down next to it.

Joe moved like a cat into the parking lot, and as he rounded the car parked next to his, he saw the man lying on his back, his torso under Joe's car. Joe drew his Glock and turned on his flashlight.

"Police! Freeze!" said Joe. "You move, and I'll shoot your ass." The man did not move. "Now, show me your hands." The man moved his arms down to his sides. Then Joe walked up and kicked him hard in the groin. "That's for blowing up my Camaro!"

Joe called 9-1-1, identified himself, gave his address, and reported that he apprehended a car bomber. Within four minutes, a police cruiser arrived on the scene. Joe held up his ID as the officer came forward.

"I caught this guy in the act of tampering with my car. Someone already tried to blow me up once. And I think this guy was trying to finish the job."

"All right," said the officer, whose nameplate read "O'Hara." He leaned down to the suspect and said, "Can you hear me?"

The suspect replied, "Yeah."

"I want you to slowly scoot out from under the car."

The thin man placed his hands flat on the ground and began pulling himself out from under the car. When Joe saw his face, he didn't recognize him. While Officer O'Hara pulled up the black-clad offender and patted him down, Joe aimed his flashlight under the car. Several sticks of dynamite with wires and a cell phone wrapped with electrical tape sat on the asphalt.

Joe called Area 3 and told them he found a bomb under his car, and that he apprehended the bomber. Detectives from Area 3 arrived and called in the bomb squad. They came and secured the bomb, placing it in their EOD vehicle. The bomber was arrested, taken to 19th District, and held pending charges.

Vincenzo got there, having driven in from the Fielding estate. He walked up to Joe and said, "You're bound and determined to keep me up all damned night, aren't you?"

"Looks like it," replied Joe. "But I caught him in the act. I haven't been back here since my Camaro was blown up. He must have been following me after what went down tonight. He knew what I was driving."

"We'll interrogate him tomorrow. Don't worry. We'll find out who he's working for. Now, go on in and get cleaned up. Try to get some sleep. Did the bomb squad check your apartment before they left?"

"Yeah. It's clear."

"Okay. Go on inside. We'll take it from here."

"Thanks, Lieutenant."

Joe went inside, took a shower, and tried to sleep. He couldn't.

Chapter Thirty-One

The next day, Joe watched the interrogation of the bombing suspect at the 19th. The suspect's name was Byron James Norris, an explosives expert with a construction company, and a former Explosive Ordinance Disposal Specialist in the US Army who served two tours of duty in Afghanistan. He was honorably discharged ten years ago.

Norris was forty years old, had no criminal record, was twice divorced, and was the father of two children. He sat in the interrogation room alone, fidgeting with his hands and tapping his feet. Clearly, he was not comfortable being there.

Sam and Detective Gary Nelson walked in to conduct the interrogation. Of all the people you did not want to interrogate you, Dirty Gary would be at the top of the list. He made a great bad guy to Sam's good guy.

Intimidated by Nelson, Norris agreed to talk, knowing that it was his first offense and cooperating would help land him a lighter sentence. He admitted he was paid $20,000 to blow up Joe Erickson—half up front and half when the job was done. When asked who paid him, he said he didn't know. The money came through a third party, a fellow army buddy named Jack Renfro who lived in Springfield. Renfro looked him up while visiting Chicago and asked him if he wanted to make an easy twenty grand. Being short on money, given he was paying child support for two kids, he decided to do the job. He swore he had never done anything like this before.

A search was done on Jack Renfro, aka John Calvin Renfro, who owned a roofing company in Springfield. Renfro had no arrest record, but a check of his company found it was cited for some minor violations over the years. His

Facebook page showed photos of him in Las Vegas with several celebrities entertaining in casinos. And one photo showed him standing with a pretty girl sandwiched between him and...Vincent Scalise.

Sam and Gary Nelson traveled to Springfield, and Jack Renfro was arrested and brought back to Chicago. While he was being interrogated, he lawyered up. He was charged with two counts of solicitation of a murder for hire. When brought before a judge, his request for bail was denied.

After consulting with his attorney, Renfro decided to cooperate, and a plea deal was struck. He stated he was approached by Vincent Scalise about finding someone to kill a particular Chicago detective. He offered Renfro $50,000 to do the job. The detective's name was Joe Erickson. That was when Renfro offered the job to his old army buddy, Byron Norris, for $20,000.

Vincent Scalise, who was already under indictment by the FBI on a charge of human trafficking, was now in deeper trouble as a charge of solicitation of a murder for hire was added. His father, Carmine Scalise, was so furious with his son's unsanctioned activities, he removed him as part-owner of their casino.

Joe met with COPA and made a formal statement regarding the shooting of Vernon Becker. He had an attorney provided by his Fraternal Order of Police. His statement went smoothly, and given the shooting was in self-defense, he felt COPA would rule the shooting was justified.

* * *

When Destiny returned from Virginia, she asked Joe to come to her apartment and explain everything that happened in detail. She read about the human trafficking arrests and scandal with Fielding Enterprises in the news as the story had been picked up by all the largest newspapers as well as CNN and the major media outlets. He had already called to tell her about the takedown at the Fielding Estate. She was relieved to hear Joe caught the bomber in the act.

"So, the bomber rolled over on his buddy, and his buddy rolled over on Vincent Scalise. Is that it?" she asked.

"In a nutshell," he replied. "So, Scalise got a solicitation of a murder for hire added to his list of charges. The Feds are prosecuting him since it's an FBI case now. "His father's money and influence aren't going to get him out of this."

"What about Thomas Fielding? Will he be all right?"

"Apparently. The last I heard, he was in satisfactory condition in the hospital, and they expect him to regain his speech at some point, whenever the Botox wears off. Hopefully, he can return to heading the company once he's well enough."

"Some family," said Destiny.

"Yeah. I'd like to be a fly on the wall when father meets son."

"You remember before I left when I said I'd have an announcement when I got home?" she said with a glint in her eye.

"Yeahhhh," said Joe, letting the word drag out.

"Don't worry. I'm not pregnant and I'm not leaving Chicago."

"Okay."

"But I do have something I want to show you."

"And you're not going to tell me?"

"No, I'm going to show you. Come on, I'll take you there?"

They got into Destiny's Mercedes, and she drove to the heart of the Lincoln Square neighborhood, pulling to a stop in front of a lovely two-story stucco home on North Leavitt Street. She looked at Joe and said, "So, what do you think?"

Joe didn't know quite what to say. "Mm. Nice house. I see the 'For Sale' sign. Are you thinking of buying it?"

"I'm thinking…We should buy it. Together."

Joe looked at Destiny. "You sure about this? I mean, I don't have the kind of money to put down on a house like this. Only what my dad left me and… My god…This place has gotta cost—"

"Don't worry about that," she said. "What you don't have, I do. And the monthly payments should be less than what the two of us are paying in rent."

He looked at it, the landscaping, the stucco, the trim, everything beautifully maintained.

CHAPTER THIRTY-ONE

"You want to go inside and look at it?"

"Sure."

They walked up the steps onto the front porch. Destiny, who finagled the key to the lockbox from the real estate agent, unlocked the door, and they went inside. Looking through the house, Joe could see it had been meticulously cared for by its previous owners and updated with all the modern amenities and appliances while retaining its early twentieth-century charm. Then Destiny opened a door to show Joe something he always wished for: a two-car garage.

"What do you think?" she asked, watching for his reaction with anticipation.

"Oh, wow! A place for my tools. I could build a car in here."

Destiny smiled. "Yeah, you could."

He turned to her and said, "You really want to do this?"

"I'd be much happier if we lived together. I hate every minute we're apart."

"I know. I feel the same way."

"And you're so vulnerable living in an apartment with your car in an outside parking lot. I don't want to see you getting blown up or some sniper waiting to pick you off."

"It's never happened before. It was—"

"I looked at this house when it came on the market a couple days before I left for Virginia, and I talked to the realtor and put some money down to hold it until I got back.

"Do you like it?"

"Well, yeah. What's not to like?"

"Let's talk with the realtor tomorrow morning," said Destiny.

Joe agreed and said he was grateful she was looking out for his welfare. The more he thought about it, the more he liked the idea.

"Then I'll call my mother. She'll want to know about our decision."

"She won't try to buy it for us, will she?"

"Oh, no," Destiny reassured him. "She knows I wouldn't allow her to do that."

"Do you think she'll be pleased?"

"All she wants is for me to be happy. Besides, she thinks you're awesome. She told me if she was thirty years younger, she'd steal you away from me."

"She wouldn't stand a chance," said Joe. He put his arms around Destiny, looked her in the eyes, and smiled, "Not a chance in the world."

Acknowledgements

Joyce Johanson, Jerry Fess, Jennifer Moore, Justin Kiska, Leonard Grossman, Detective Timothy O'Brien, Chicago PD, Mike Inman, Harriette Sackler, Shawn Reilly Simmons, Verena Rose

About the Author

Lynn-Steven Johanson is an award-winning playwright whose plays have been produced on four continents. Born and raised in Northwest Iowa, Lynn holds a Master of Fine Arts degree from the University of Nebraska-Lincoln. His two previous Joe Erickson mysteries, *Rose's Thorn* and *Havana Brown*, are published by Level Best Books. He lives in Illinois with his wife, and they have three adult children.

AUTHOR WEBSITE:
  www.LSJohanson.com

Also by Lynn-Steven Johanson

Rose's Thorn

Havana Brown